BOOKS BY ROSS WELFORD

The 1,000 Year Old Boy

What Not to Do If You Turn Invisible

Time Traveling with a Hamster

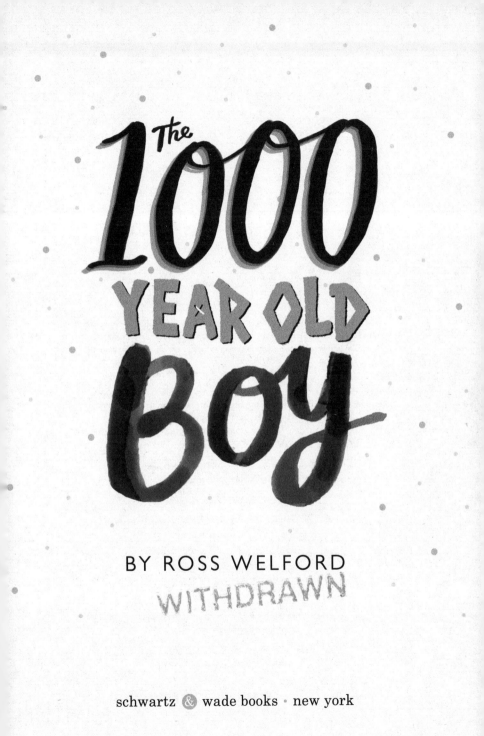

The 1000 YEAR OLD BOY

BY ROSS WELFORD

schwartz & wade books · new york

Text copyright © 2019 by Ross Welford
Jacket art © 2019 by Jack Noel

All rights reserved. Published in the United States by Schwartz & Wade Books, an imprint of Random House Children's Books, a division of Penguin Random House LLC, New York. Originally published in paperback in the UK by HarperCollins Children's Books, London, in 2018.

Schwartz & Wade Books and the colophon are trademarks of Penguin Random House LLC.

Visit us on the Web! rhcbooks.com

Educators and librarians, for a variety of teaching tools, visit us at RHTeachersLibrarians.com

Library of Congress Cataloging-in-Publication Data is available upon request.
ISBN 978-0-525-70745-5 (trade)
ISBN 978-0-525-70746-2 (lib. bdg.)
ISBN 978-0-525-70747-9 (ebook)

The text of this book is set in 12-point Whitman.
Book design by Stephanie Moss

Printed in the United States of America
10 9 8 7 6 5 4 3 2 1
First U.S. Edition

Part One

Alfie

Would you like to live forever? I am afraid I cannot recommend it. I am used to it now, and I do understand how special it is. Only I want to stop. I want to grow up like you.

This is my story. My name is Alve Einarsson. I am a thousand years old. More, actually.

Are we friends? In that case, just call me Alfie. Alfie Monk.

CHAPTER ONE

SOUTH SHIELDS, A.D. 1014

We sat on the low cliff, Mam and I, overlooking the river mouth, and watched the smoke from our village over on the other side pluming into the sky and mixing with the clouds.

Everyone calls the river the Tyne. Back then, we pronounced it "Teen," but it was just our word for river.

As we sat, and Mam wept and cursed with fury, we heard screams from across the water. The smell of smoke from the burning wooden fort on the clifftop drifted toward us. People—our neighbors mostly—huddled on the opposite bank, but Dag the ferryman was not going to go back for them. Not now: he would be killed too. He had run away from us, stammering apologies, as soon as his raft had touched the shore.

Above the people cowering on the bank, the men who had come in boats appeared. They paused—arrogantly, fearlessly—then walked over to their prey, swords and axes at the ready. I saw some people entering the water to try to escape. They would not get far: a smaller boat waited mid-river to intercept them.

I lowered my head and buried it in Mam's shawl, but she pulled it away and wiped her eyes. Her voice trembled with rage.

"*Sey*, Alve. *Sey!*" That is how we spoke then. "Old Norse" it is called now, or a dialect of it. We didn't call it anything. She meant, "Look! Look at what they are doing to us, those men who have come from the north in their boats."

But I could not. Getting up, I walked in a kind of daze for some distance, but I could still hear the murder, still smell the smoke. I felt wretched for being alive. Behind me, Mam pulled the little wooden cart that was loaded with whatever stuff we'd managed to fit onto Dag's river ferry.

My cat, Biffa, walked beside us, darting into the grass on the side of the path in pursuit of a mouse or a grasshopper. Normally this made me smile, but I felt as empty as if I had been cut open.

A mile or two on, Mam and I found a cave in a deep, sheltered bay. The sun was strong enough to use the old fire-glass that had belonged to Da: a curved, polished crystal that focused the sunlight into a thin beam that would start a fire. I was scared the raiders would come after us, but Mam said they would not, and she was right. We had escaped.

Three days later, we saw their boats heading out to sea again and I made the biggest mistake of my life. A mistake that I waited a thousand years to put right.

CHAPTER TWO

If you want to ask me "Why did you do it?" go ahead: I do not mind. I have asked myself that many, many times. I still do not know the whole answer.

All I can say is that I was young, and very, *very* scared. I wanted to do something—anything—that would make me feel stronger, better able to help Mam, better able to protect us both.

And so I became a Neverdead, like Mam.

It began long ago, and when I say "long ago," I mean ages, literally. This is what happened.

My father had owned five of the small glass balls that were called *livperler.*

Life-pearls.

They were the most valuable things we possessed. Mam said that they might be the most valuable things in the world, ever.

People had killed to obtain them; Da had died trying to keep them. And so we told no one that we had them.

Now there were three left. One for Mam, and two for me when I was older.

I knew all that. Mam had told me enough times. "Not until you are grown, Alve. You must be patient."

But I could not wait.

On the third evening in the cave, while Mam was out looking for fresh water, I opened the little clay pot and took out the *livperler*. Although they were old, the glass marbles shone in the half twilight from outside, the thick liquid within seeming to glow amber when I held one near the fire.

Biffa sat up on a little rocky shelf on the opposite side of the fire, her yellow eyes shining like the glass balls. Did she know? She mewled: the little cat-growl that made us think she was talking to us. Biffa often seemed to know things.

Crouching on my haunches, I took the knife, the little steel one that had belonged to Da, with the blade that hinged into the wooden handle, and held it to the flame. I glanced at the mouth of the cave to check I was alone, and swallowed hard.

When I drew the hot blade twice across my upper arm, the blood seeped out. Two short slashes, like the scars Mam had. Like Da had had. I do not know if doing it twice made any difference; probably not. It was just the way.

It did not hurt until I used my thumbs to pull the wounds apart. I bit down on the life-pearl and the glass cracked. The yellowish syrup oozed out like the blood from my cuts. I gathered it on my fingertips and rubbed it into the wounds. Then I did it again, and again, until there was none left. It stung, like a fresh nettle in the spring.

What happened next was an accident. I have played it over and over in my mind, like people play videotapes today. Could I have done anything differently?

I do not know.

I think Biffa was just curious. She cannot have *known*—but as I said, she was a very knowing cat. Suddenly she gave another little growl and leaped at me, right across the low flames of the fire. The knife was still in my hand, and without thinking, I raised it: a defensive reflex. It nicked her front paw slightly, but she did not mewl again. When she landed, I spun round and, in that action, my tunic dislodged another life-pearl from the low rock shelf where I had placed them. I was unbalanced, and my bare foot came down on it, hard, and it cracked open.

I stared at it, horrified, for a few seconds.

It was bad enough that I had disobeyed Mam's orders. But I had now wasted another precious life-pearl.

The thick amber liquid began to drip out of the rock. Thinking only that it should not be wasted, I grasped Biffa by the long skin of her neck and rubbed the liquid into her cut paw.

(It was *not* mischief, as I said to Mam again and again over the years. I was just trying not to waste it.)

Then I wrapped up my arm with a long strip of clean cloth and tied another one round Biffa's leg. She did not even seem to mind. She licked her whiskers, yawned, and curled up again. I could see Mam's shape against the blue twilight sky as she came back to the cave with a bucket of water, and I was overwhelmed with shame.

I sometimes think I still am.

By then, I had seen eleven winters.

I was to stay eleven years old for more than a thousand years.

CHAPTER THREE

All of that happened ages ago.

I have tried telling my story before, but I soon learned that people do not want to know. I have to leave out crucial details like the life-pearls, and so people think I am teasing them (at best) or that I am dangerously mad (at worst).

So I stay silent.

I sometimes wonder if people's reactions would be different if I *looked* old. That is, if I were wrinkled and stooped and bald, with a quavery voice and huge, veiny ears and badly fitting clothes. Then again, people would not bother with the "teasing" bit, would they? They would immediately assume that age had sent me mad.

"Bless 'im, old Alf," they would say. *"He was going on about the Vikings again today."*

"Was 'e? Aww. It was Charles Dickens yesterday. Reckoned he'd met him!"

"Really? Poor old soul. Still, he's harmless, in't he?"

As it is, I do not look old at all: I look about eleven.

At the point I stopped aging, the Vikings had more or less completed their occupation of northeastern England. It was the Scots that Mam and I were fleeing. It was to be another fifty or more years before the south of the country was invaded: in 1066, by the Normans (who were basically Vikings who had learned French, if you ask me, but nobody does. Nor-man, north-man—you can see the link).

And in case you are interested, I *did* meet Charles Dickens, but not until many, many years later.

See? You do not believe me, do you? I cannot really blame you, seeing as I am the last remaining Neverdead on earth. And now that Mam has gone, living forever is no life at all.

The trouble is, if you do not believe me, what chance do I have of convincing Aidan Linklater and Roxy Minto? I will need their help if I am to lift the curse of my endless life.

And if *they* do not believe me, then I am, as you say these days, doomed.

AIDAN

I should probably start by telling you why I'm annoyed. Get it out of the way. Then we can get on to how I came to meet Alfie and my life changed forever.

CHAPTER FOUR

WHITLEY BAY, PRESENT DAY

For a start, we've moved house. That's bad enough. But get this:

1. It's a smaller house. *Much* smaller, with hardly any back garden—just a scruffy yard that's way too small to kick a ball in. Mum has reminded me (more than once) that I'm lucky to live in a house with any outside space at all, and when she says that, I feel guilty, and sorry that I even mentioned it, because I know why we've moved. Thing is, my friend Mo, who lives in a flat, used to come round to our old house because he had no garden, but now there's no point, is there?

2. If people come to stay, I will now have to share a room with Libby, who's a pain at the best of times. She's seven and likes My Little Pony.

3. Inigo Delombra, who's in my year at school, now lives in my old house. I think he even has my old *room*. He

smirks at me every time I see him, as if to say, *"You sad loser."*

At least I haven't had to change schools, but, with the way things are going with Spatch and Mo, I might as well have.

Another thing: Mum and Dad are arguing all the time. They've always argued—"bickering" they call it—but lately it's become louder, and they think I don't notice. It's money—always money. I don't know the details. All I know is that they made a "bad investment," and Mum says it was Dad's fault. Mum now works in a call center and hates it. I found Libby listening at the top of the stairs the other night.

She said, "Are they going to get divorced, Aidan?"

I had to say, "No, of course not." Her chin wobbled but she didn't cry. Not in front of me, anyway, which is just as well because it would probably have set me off too.

So with *that* information out of the way . . .

Be honest. If some kid that you'd just met told you he was a thousand years old, what would your reaction be?

You'd laugh, maybe, and say, "Yeah, right!"

Or you might ignore him—you know: don't provoke the crazy, and all that.

You could, I suppose, come back with a zinger, like "And I'm the Queen of Sheba."

OK, so I'm not big on zingers, but you get the idea.

So when Alfie said to me, "Aidan, I am more than one thousand years old," obviously I didn't believe him.

And then I had to because, although it was unbelievable, it was the truth.

But for it to make sense, I'm going to have to rewind a bit.

CHAPTER FIVE

We moved in—me, Mum, Dad, Libby—at the start of the Easter holidays, and everything was unpacked in three days. My Xbox was smashed in the move. I asked Mum if I could get another one, and she just gave this sad-sounding little laugh, which I guess meant no. She said we had "other priorities," and that made me feel bad for asking.

I had the rest of the holidays stretching out before me.

"Call up your friends, go down to the beach," said Mum every five minutes.

Problem with that was Spatch was away in Naples with his Italian grandparents, where he goes every Easter; worse, he'd invited Mo to go with him. And not me.

I pretended I wasn't hurt when they told me, but I was. When I talked to Mum about it, she was all like, "Oh well—we couldn't have afforded the airfare anyway, so no harm done," but that's not the point, is it? Spatch was a bit embarrassed, I think. He said it was because there wasn't room at his grandparents' farmhouse, but

I've seen pictures and it's huge, and besides, I'd have been happy to sleep on the floor. I nearly said that, but I'm glad I didn't.

To make things worse, Aunty Alice and Uncle Jasper came to visit. Aunty Alice is OK, but Jasper? *Sheesh.*

I know Dad wasn't happy because I heard him moaning to Mum: "Can't they stay in a hotel, for heaven's sake? It's not like we've got loads of space."

"She's my sister, Ben."

Dad just tutted and rolled his eyes.

So, day four of the holidays. Aunty Alice and Jasper had arrived that morning, and I had moved into Libby's room, on an airbed. She was at Brownie camp for the next couple of days, so at least I wasn't *actually* sharing with her yet, but still. . . .

We all sat in the kitchen among the boxes left by the moving company. Dad's not working at the moment, so he was at home and he made tea and asked about Jasper's boat (it's a "safe topic," apparently). Mum fussed over Aunty Alice's blouse. Aunty Alice is much older than Mum and Jasper is much younger than Aunty Alice, although—thanks to his beard—he looks older than both of them, if that makes sense.

After Aunty Alice had said how much I'd grown, just about the only thing directed at me was Jasper saying:

"And what about you, son? Are you getting enough fresh air? You look like a ghost!" and then he grinned, showing his long white teeth, as if he didn't really mean it, but I could tell that he did.

Aunty Alice said, "Aw, Jasper, he looks lovely!" and Mum said to him with the faintest edge to her voice:

"He's fine, Jasper. Aren't you, Aidan?"

I nodded vigorously, as if by nodding I could show my uncle that I was—to borrow one of his phrases—"as fit as a flea."

He went *hmmph* and added, "Sea air. A bit of the old *ventum maris*. That's what you need, son," then took a noisy slurp of his tea (black, no sugar).

He talks like that a lot, does Jasper. So far as I can tell, he has no regional accent, and no foreign accent, either. At times, he sounds slightly American, and at others more Australian, like when his voice goes up at the end of a sentence as if he's asking a question? It's hard to figure out. He was born in Romania and has narrow dark eyes—almost black—behind tinted glasses, and he's lived in lots of countries.

I asked him once where he was from. "Just call me a nomad," he said, baring his teeth. Between you and me, I'm terrified of him.

With my milk finished and having heard the words "Prime Minister" come from under Jasper's beard, I figured it was time to make myself scarce. Once anyone mentions the government, the conversation—so far as I'm involved in it—is not going to improve.

"I'm going outside," I said, and I got a grunt of what might have been approval from Jasper.

CHAPTER SIX

It was good to get out of the house. I did that big breathe-in-through-your-nose thing and exhaled with a loud *"Haaah!"*

Our house is on the very edge of the old bit of the estate. There are about ten tiny houses in a row, and then the new houses start next door. Over our back fence is just woodland. The woods don't even have a name, so far as I know. They're just "the woods" or "that bit of woodland beyond the golf course."

It would be really cool if there was a gate in the back fence that I could just open and be in the woods, but there isn't, so it's just this wooden wall, basically, at the end of the empty, rectangular yard.

On one side is an alleyway piled up with junk and smelling of cats' pee. There's an old mattress, and a rusty washing machine, and a trash bag spilling out old clothes. Dad says it's the council's job to clear it up, but they're obviously not interested. On the other side of Junk Alley live two ladies with short gray hair, Sue and Pru, who Mum has already met and declared "very nice," adding, "One of them is a doctor." (I always thought doctors were quite well paid, so I don't know why they're living round here.)

Their yard has been turned into a neat, paved garden, and they have about five rescue cats. (Dad snorted when Mum told us. "Never trust anyone with more than two cats," he said, which I thought was a bit mean. I kind of like cats.)

On the other side of us is another garden, a real one with grass, separated from our yard by a rickety fence.

So on the morning it all started I was standing there with my back to the fence, staring at the old houses made of dirty bricks. Half of the houses look as though they're not even occupied, and a couple have got broken windows. No wonder our house is cheap to rent. Mum and Dad say it's only temporary.

"Hello, Aidan!"

I looked round, startled, but I couldn't see anyone. Then the voice laughed: a short bark of high-pitched glee. A girl. I did a full 360, trying to figure out where it was coming from.

"Over here!"

"Where?" I said. And then, "Ow!" as something hard hit me on the cheek. A few seconds later, something whizzed past my nose.

"Hey! Stop that," I said, and the terrier-bark laugh started again. Then I saw it: the yellow tube of a ballpoint pen withdrawing through a large hole in the back fence. Someone was using it as a peashooter to fire paper pellets at me, and she was a good shot.

I went over to the knothole and stooped to peer through it, and almost immediately felt a hard kick on my backside. Spinning round, I saw the *tiniest* girl grinning wickedly and cackling. I recognized her from school, although I didn't know her name. We didn't share any classes.

"Wh-where did you come from?" It really was as though she'd materialized from nowhere before my eyes.

"I'm Roxy Minto. I live next door. You're Aidan!"

"Erm . . . I know. How did you know my name?"

She gave a little snort to show that she thought it was a stupid question. "How do you think? Your mum spoke to my mum. I saw your movers carrying stuff in. You've got a red bicycle and a white wooden desk in your bedroom. Turn around."

"Why?"

"Just turn around." She said it with such confidence that I found myself obeying, even though I half expected another kick in the pants.

"How do you know the bike and desk are mine?" I said over my shoulder, but there was no reply. I turned back . . . and Roxy had gone. Vanished.

"Roxy?" Then a plank in the fence that separates our gardens swung up, hinged on a horizontal strut. She poked her head through, giggling. "This way!"

It was a squeeze but I made it. (Roxy's so tiny that she passed through and barely touched the sides.) And there I was in her overgrown garden, with ratty shrubs and flowers and weeds, and an old plastic slide.

Roxy strode through the uncut lawn to a massive bush that

spilled over the fence and ran tendrils up a hazel tree. She pushed a branch aside and disappeared into it. Seconds later, I heard her voice on the other side of the back fence.

"Are you coming or are you too scared?"

I pushed aside the branch. The big bush concealed a hole in the fence that led to a path separating the back fences from the woods. Up against the fence, and completely hidden from the garden side by the bush, was a shed: one of the pre-made ones that you see on building sites.

Roxy stood in the doorway. "Welcome to my garage!" she declared in her squeaky voice, and I could tell she was proud. She reached inside for a switch and a neon sign hanging from the roof flickered to life. It said GARAGE in pink letters, but the first three didn't work, so it just said AGE, but—I have to admit—it was still pretty good.

Inside was a battered desk, a wonky swivel chair, two wooden stools, and a tiny fridge in the shape of a beer can. There was carpet on the floor, a lampshade on the light, and even curtains at the windows. A *very* battered old sofa had yellow foam escaping from tears in the vinyl cushions. I laughed.

"What's so funny? Don't you like it?"

Secretly I thought it was completely awesome, but I wasn't going to say that, was I?

"It's OK," I said. "Wh-where did you get all this stuff?"

I could tell she was disappointed with my reaction, and I immediately felt a bit bad. "Dumpster diving, mainly," she said. "People chuck so much away in them, so, you know—reuse, recycle, blah-di-blah. The neon sign's the *pièce de résistance!*" She did an exaggerated French accent and waved her hand theatrically.

"You'd never know there was so much in here!" I said, to make up for my earlier comment.

"Not much to look at, but plenty on the inside, you mean? That's what they say about me!" She hopped onto a stool and reached across to open the fridge. "Fancy a beer?"

"I . . . er . . ."

"Kidding. Hey, you know 'gullible' isn't in the dictionary?" And she tossed me a box of juice with a straw. "Have a seat. Take the weight off your feet. *Mi casa es su casa!*"

We sat for a bit, sipping our juices. I had known Roxy for about six minutes, and already I was certain that I hadn't met anyone quite like her before.

When I said she was tiny, I wasn't exaggerating. She was so small that, if I were guessing her age, I'd say about six, but her behavior suggested someone much older, more like sixteen. Her skin was a rich brown, with dark freckles across her nose, and her Afro was cut roughly and short. Her clothes gave nothing away: shorts, flip-flops, dirty white T-shirt, denim jacket. Standard kid-in-summer gear. Only, she had to be at least eleven because she was at Percy Academy.

It was her grin that I noticed the most, though. You know how some people, when their faces are resting, look naturally grumpy? It's not like they're in a bad mood or anything—it's just that, when they have nothing particular to smile about, they don't? Dad's face is like that. People are always saying to him, "Cheer up, mate—it might never happen!"

Anyway, so far as I could tell, Roxy was the *exact* opposite. Her mouth seemed to be fixed in a permanent smile, as if she was laughing to herself about some private joke.

She caught me looking. "What you starin' at? Haven't you never seen a toff?" Suddenly her accent was that of a Londoner, and my surprise must have shown on my face. She laughed. "It's a line from *Oliver!*"

I must have looked blank.

"*Oliver!* You know—the musical? *Oliver Twist* by Charles Dickens. When Oliver meets the Artful Dodger, that's what Dodger says. We're doing it in my drama club. I'm gonna be Dodger. I've got the costume and everything!" She pointed to a long velvet coat and a man's hat on a peg.

That I could believe. "How old are you, Roxy?"

Her voice changed again, this time to a posh old lady's: "How dare you ask a lady her age, young man!" She was clearly quite the actress, this new neighbor of mine. "Same as you. Four weeks older, actually."

"You know my birthday?"

She jumped down from the stool and opened the shed door.

"There's a lot I know about you, Aidan Henry Linklater. And your sister, Liberty, born on February the fifth. Put the juice box in the re-cycling there and follow me. There's something I need to show you."

I followed her into the woods, down a barely visible path. If only I had known what was to happen, I might have avoided a whole lot of trouble.

But I also would never have met Alfie Monk.

CHAPTER SEVEN

Roxy stomped ahead of me through the woods, pushing aside branches and beating nettles with a stick. We lost sight of her "garage" after only thirty yards or so.

"You know where you're going?" I said, trying to sound casual—as though I wouldn't really care if she said no. I don't think she heard.

The woods were shady but not quiet. So far, the spring had been much warmer and drier than usual, and the leaves and twigs crunched loudly under our feet; when we stopped, I could hear a bee, and Roxy breathing. If I cocked my head, I could just make out the traffic on the highway shushing past—a comforting sound: a reminder that, even though it felt like we were in the middle of nowhere, we actually weren't.

Then Roxy stopped and crouched down. "There. Can you see it?"

"See what?"

"*There,* man! You *must* see that?"

Lower down the steeply sloping forest floor, between the silvery-

gray trees and about as far away as I'd be able to throw a

I saw it: a mossy, slate-covered roof.

I glanced over at her to check if she was joking. I mean

what? Roxy clocked my doubtful expression.

"It's better when you get nearer. Come on," and sh

through the trees. She was no longer bashing the nettle

stick, and she advanced quietly, glancing back to check

following. Then she stopped.

We had a better view of the roof. It seemed to be lev

which was odd, till I realized it was just because we were

hill: it led down to a stone-built house surrounded by t

bushes—as if someone had planted the area especially

discourage intruders.

"Careful here," whispered Roxy, and she pointed ins

at a coil of rusty barbed wire; the branches had grown

Farther along, the bushes thinned out very slightly and

a sign, one of those ones you can buy in hardware shops

BEWARE: THE DOG ALWAYS ATTACKS

"Erm . . . Roxy?" I said.

She flapped her tiny hand dismissively. "There's no

worry. Come on!"

I followed, feeling like an obedient puppy.

We came to a gap in the bushy barbed-wire fences

have been easy to squeeze through it had I been Roxy's size. All I could do was lie absolutely flat on my belly and try to shimmy forward, following her flip-flops.

Her feet and lower legs were scratched all over and stung by nettles, but she didn't seem to care.

Then the gorse bush cleared and we were in long grass: long enough to hide us if we lay flat. That's when I saw the house properly.

The sloping ground extended another couple of yards and then dropped away sharply to become a brick wall about the height of a person. There was a neat, paved yard with a round fire pit made of stone. A smoldering log gave off a thin wisp of smoke that rose up straight in the still air, and a few chickens pecked around on the ground. Next to the fire pit was a round metal pot, blackened with age and smoke.

The house itself was made of stone bricks, mottled and misshapen with age, and topped with a roof of the mossy slates I had seen from a distance. We were looking at the back of the house; the door was one of those ones that's split in half. The top half was open but I couldn't see inside. The paint on the door and window frames was a bit flaky; in fact, everything about the house looked old and dry and worn.

"So, Roxy . . . ," I began.

"Shhh!"

I lowered my voice. "So, Roxy. It's someone's house."

"Yes!" she whispered back excitedly.

"And this is a big deal?"

"Well . . . yeah!"

"Why exactly? People have houses, you know. They live in them."

"You don't know who lives in this one."

Roxy paused and took a breath, building the suspense. Then she stopped, both of our eyes drawn to a movement inside the doorway.

A woman appeared, framed in the open half of the door, and scanned the bushes and grass where we lay hidden. Instinctively we both shrank back.

I only got a quick look at her before she went back into the house. How old was she? I couldn't tell. Long skirt, headscarf, sunglasses.

"That was her," said Roxy.

"That was who?" I know this sounds like I was being deliberately uninterested to tease Roxy, but I just could not work out why she was so excited about some woman in a house. Big deal.

"The witch."

And, at that point, I forgot all about being quiet, and said— louder than I should have, probably—"Oh, *Roxy*!"

I was genuinely quite annoyed. Disappointed as well.

Annoyed with Roxy because I was lying in the grass, a bit scared, and covered in forest gunk and nettle stings, spying on someone's house, probably breaking some law or other, and all for nothing. And disappointed because, well . . .

I'd thought Roxy might be a bit different. Someone fun to hang out with. Especially with Spatch and Mo in Italy.

And then she mentioned witches, for heaven's sake. If I want witches, or unicorns, or animals in clothes, I just need five minutes with my little sister.

"Shhh! She *is*, I'm telling you. She's, like, two hundred years old and she lives in a cottage in the woods. She even has a black cat—look!"

Right on cue, a cat—not entirely black, but anyway—strolled along the top of the wall right in front of us. It flashed us a look with its striking yellow eyes, then leaped gracefully down into the yard, mewling loudly, causing a chicken to flap out of its way.

"Have you tasted it? The house?" I said.

"What do you mean?"

"Is it made of gingerbread?"

The glare that Roxy gave me could have melted an ice pop, but I didn't care. This was just a silly fantasy.

"I'm going back," I said, and I started to get up.

"Get down!" hissed Roxy. "She'll see you."

"What? And turn me into a toad? I'll take the risk, thanks."

What happened next may have been my fault. I'm not really sure.

CHAPTER EIGHT

As I got to my hands and knees, Roxy grabbed my collar and pulled me back down really hard, and, for someone so small, she had plenty of strength.

"Stop it!" I whispered, and struggled from her grasp, and as I did so, I pushed her. She rolled down the bank, scrabbling for my hand or for grass, or for anything to stop her tumbling into the yard, which was where she was headed.

For a split second, her eyes locked on mine, pure terror etched onto her face, and then she was over the edge of the slope and out of sight.

There was a loud thump as she hit the ground, but no shout, no scream. I had drawn breath to shout her name, and to check she was OK, but the shout stilled in my throat as I saw the back door of the cottage burst open and the witch come running out.

"Ay, ay, ay!" she cried. And then something else, something I couldn't make out, because it was in a language I'd never heard before.

It wasn't French. I know what French sounds like (third from top in my class, *en fait*). And it wasn't Italian, because I've heard Spatch talking with his dad at home.

It was like nothing I had ever heard before: a throaty, musical language. The witch—or "witch," I suppose—hurried to where Roxy had fallen right below me. Then, in her language, she called out again, as if shouting for someone.

That's when I saw him.

He stood in the doorway: a pale, skinny blond boy. A pair of sunglasses hung on a loop round his neck and he put them on before scuttling out into the sunshine of the yard to where Roxy lay.

Was she dead? I was terrified, but I didn't think it was likely, even though it was quite a long drop. Then I heard her moan. *Thank God for that.*

Should I stand up? Reveal myself? I was caught in a terrified panic of simply not knowing what to do, when the boy picked up Roxy and carried her little body easily into the house, a dripping trail of blood coming from her head.

Both halves of the door clattered shut, and I realized I hadn't breathed since Roxy had fallen.

CHAPTER NINE

alfie

This is what I know about the life-pearls:

1. They contain a thick liquid which, when mixed with your own blood, immediately stops you from getting any older.
2. If you repeat the process with another life-pearl, the aging starts again.

That is it. That is pretty much all I know, and all Mam knows too.

As for my father, I am afraid I can hardly remember him, although Mam has told me all about him. One thousand years is a long time to hear stories again and again, but I never get bored of them.

(Sometimes I can almost touch a memory of him. A fuzzy mental picture of a tall blond man; the smell of a ship's rope dipped in tar; a feeling of fear in a storm; but they are indistinct recollections. They seem thin, as though constantly trying to bring them to mind has somehow worn them out.)

Da's name was Einar. He was a soldier-turned-trader from the island of Gotland in what is now called the Baltic, but in her stories Mam still called it the *uster-shern*—the Eastern Sea.

Where did they come from, these "life-pearls"? No one knew, not for sure. There was a saga—an ancient poem—that Mam would tell by the light of the fire's embers, of an alchemist's manservant escaping from a massive tsunami in the Middle East. He carried a bag of the life-pearls across the desert, to the mountains of Carpathia in Eastern Europe. How much of it was true, though, was anybody's guess.

Mixing the liquid in a life-pearl with your own blood stopped you from getting older. It did not make you immortal, however: you could still be killed in battle, or by disease, or—as Da found out—by accident.

Mam said he had obtained the life-pearls when he had heroically fought some vagabonds who were raiding a tiny village. I loved this story.

"Like a true and noble warrior," said Mam, "he spared the life of one of the bandits in exchange for the life-pearls.

"Straightaway he used one of them himself. He made two cuts in his arm and poured in the liquid from one of the glass balls. Four life-pearls remained. The valiant Einar knew, though, that they were so valuable that anyone who owned them was at risk: people would kill to have eternal life. So he told no one until he met . . ."

"You!" I would fill in, and Mam always smiled.

"That's right. By then, he was already a hundred and forty years old. He was living in the land of the Danes, and speaking their language. We had been married for only six months when I learned I was pregnant with you, Alve."

("We married for love," she never tired of telling me. "That was unusual then." A thousand years ago, love was very low down on the list of reasons to get married—a long way below things like family alliances, wealth, and security.)

Mam was poor, Da was not, and people were jealous of Mam's good fortune in marrying the rich and handsome Einar of Gotland. And when people are jealous, they start to talk, and the talk turned to Einar's age, and how strange it was that the village elders remembered him from their own youth.

Could he be one of the fabled Neverdeads?

And if he *was* a Neverdead, might he possess the *livperler*—the life-pearls?

Already the Neverdeads were so rare that many people thought it was just a tall tale told by those who had traveled and met people from distant lands. For example, there were stories of a vast land to the south where there were four-legged creatures with tremendous long necks that could reach the topmost leaves of trees; where there were fat horses that lived in rivers;

where there were tiny, hairy people, with long tails, who swung through the branches of the forest.

No one quite knew how much of this to believe. Perhaps stories of the Neverdeads were just more travelers' tales?

But when the rumors about his long life reached my father's ears, he was taking no chances. With his wife and child, he made plans for a new life in the land of the Britons, where he hoped they would be safe. As it turned out, he was right . . . in part.

He saved me and Mam. But he did not save himself.

CHAPTER TEN

Einar of Gotland was unrecognizable as he stood on the wooden jetty of Ribe on the west coast of Denmark with Hilda, his wife, and a small child—me. That was exactly what he wanted.

He had shaved his beard, cut his hair, and dressed in the clothes of a middle-ranking tradesman. Not too rich to attract attention, nor so poor that people would question his ability to pay for a passage on the ship to Bernicia in the land of the Britons.

No one knew him in Ribe, but he was taking no chances. We stayed a little way out of town. Da was on edge, said Mam. He thought he was being followed. Hilda was now a Neverdead as well, the bloody process carried out on the night of their marriage. Together they would live forever in the new land with their son.

If they made it.

Einar had bought passage on a cargo ship that would sail straight across the North Sea, stopping first north of the old

Roman Wall to offload cargo and take on another shipment, and then carrying on down the coast to the mouth of the Tyne.

The captain had said four days, maybe five, depending on the wind—and the wind was not cooperating. Cargo ships relied on sail, rather than the oars that the longships used, so if the wind was coming from the west—as it usually did—a journey to the new lands was hard sailing.

After a week, the wind changed, and in less than a day the battered old *knarr*, with its filthy, patched sails and old, tarry ropes, was gliding out of Ribe harbor.

Da boarded separately from Mam and me. We were to pretend for the whole journey that we were unconnected. Da gave the pearls to Mam, to keep them even safer, in case anyone recognized him. "Until we land," Mam had said to me, with her most serious face as she put it when retelling the story, "you must never speak to your da."

She said I was clearly puzzled but did as I was told. I was always a good, obedient boy, she said.

We had very little luggage: a bag each, made of hemp, and, for me, a wicker basket containing a young cat that I had called Biffa. It was not a name, nor even a word. I think I just liked the sound of it.

On the boat there was no privacy. If anyone needed to pee, or more, they had to do it in the sea as the boat shuddered along over the cloud-colored waves. The crew were not fussy: they just dropped their trousers and put their bottoms over the side of the boat.

And that is how we lost Da, said Mam. No one saw him go. The wind had come up, and the skipper had pulled in the sail, and the long *knarr* was rising and falling on the swell. As the boat bucked and reared on the white-capped waves, Da got up and clambered to the rear, which was where everyone went. It was a *little* bit private, as there was a stack of barrels secured with rope that would give you some cover and you could hang on to the rope straps.

And that was it, the last anyone saw of him.

Mam was the first to notice. Everyone had been huddled over, trying to stay dry, when she said, "Where's Einar?"

When it became clear what had happened, the skipper turned the boat into the storm and tacked to and fro, going back way farther than we had come that day, in case Da had been carried on the current. There was no sign of him. Even if he had yelled when he went over, he probably would not have been heard over the noise of the waves and the wind and the creaking old boat.

What a way to go. It still makes me sad, even though I can hardly remember him, and this was centuries ago, but it still comes back to me, even after all the sad and bad things that I have seen.

"The hardest thing," said Mam, "was being unable to grieve. I had to pretend to be as sad as someone who had only just met him—and that you were crying because you were small, and any death upset you, not because your father had gone missing."

"But why?" I used to ask.

"Because that was the plan, to avoid those who might be after the pearls. And I stuck with it. I did not know—I still do not know—if he was pushed overboard. There was another passenger on the boat: a mean-looking devil with a huge black beard, and he and your da had argued earlier that day. I know Einar did not trust him. When you cried with the cold, he told me to 'Shut that bairn up!' and when you howled for the man who had gone overboard—your da, though no one knew it—he threatened to throw you over to join him."

If I close my eyes, I can remember that face, inches from mine, growling *"Holl munnen!"* to a grieving child. "Shut your mouth!" The memory can still make me cold.

And so, six days later, freezing cold, soaking wet, and smelling strongly of sheep's cheese, sealskins, and ship's tar, Mam and I sailed up the Teen and got out of the boat on the long wooden pier by the fishing huts.

She had set off from Denmark as a young wife, and arrived in Teenmooth a widow, with a young, fatherless boy.

Little. Old. Me.

Then, more than a thousand years later, a tiny little girl fell into our yard and banged her head. That was when everything changed.

CHAPTER ELEVEN

The morning it all happened, Mam said to me, "Do you know what day it is today, Alve?" She still called me by my birth name when we were alone, which was practically always.

I knew, but I pretended not to so that she would have the pleasure of reminding me.

"Thirty years in Oak Cottage. Thirty years since we moved back into this house," and she smiled her gappy smile, and hugged me with her strong arms. "I do not want to move again. Not after the last time," she said for maybe the hundredth time.

In response, I forced a smile, and nodded, and did not remind her that the world was changing faster than ever.

Mam worried. We both did. Moving house, staying anonymous—living in general—was becoming harder and harder.

It had never been exactly easy. Mam and I, however, had always been quite mobile and we had found that there was always someone willing to rent us a small house, or even just a room; we kept our possessions to a minimum, or stored them elsewhere, especially our books.

But these days? These days, everybody wants to know everything about you. Rental agreements, bank accounts, licenses for this, permits for that, forms to fill in, identification documents . . .

Mam seldom listened to the news on the wireless. It was, she would say, "too confusing." I think she meant "too scary." We had shut ourselves away for so long that Mam no longer understood the wider world of motor cars, jet airplanes, computers, cell phones.

But sometimes, when Mam was upstairs in bed, I would listen to the news. I would try to understand, and I would long to live in that world: the real world, with all of its wonders.

Mam tutted. "She is here again, Alve." She wiped her hands and peered out the scullery window. "That is the second time this week. And there is someone with her. Over there on the left. Can you see?"

The "little nosy girl" was what Mam called her. I now know her as Roxy Minto. Mam had initially seen her spying on us nearly a year earlier. At first Mam thought the worst—that it would be a repeat of the last time we had lived here, when the boys had made our lives a misery, and all the questions had started, and we had had to move away.

It turned out not to be that. All the little girl wanted to do was to watch. We would hear her, trying her best to be quiet in the bushes.

Until now she had always been alone. She would approach, and lie in the long grass in front of the gorse bush, and watch us go about our business. Then autumn came, and the leaves dropped, and she stopped coming because—I think—she would not be hidden so well.

It was annoying to be spied on, but better than the fear that we might be attacked, or accused of who knows what.

Witchcraft?

I know that no one is accused of witchcraft in the twenty-first century, but we have feared it for so long that our solitude became our life, and being anonymous our only goal.

And so we let her be. Then the spring came back, and the leaves, and so did the little girl in the bushes.

Mam went to the half door that led into the backyard and squinted out. Once more she said, "I am not moving again, Alve. Not after the last time."

The last time. I cannot forget the last time. Because the last time involved Jack, and Jack was the last friend I ever had.

CHAPTER TWELVE
AIDAN

I don't know how long I stood there, staring at the back door of the cottage in the woods where they had taken Roxy inside, but eventually I ran.

I meant to get help: tell Dad, or whoever, what had happened, and it would all be OK, but in my panic, I got lost.

I know, the woods aren't even that big, but there were no paths, and I kept crisscrossing my way through, passing the big gorse bush at least twice, and then trying to head uphill because I knew that that, at any rate, would be *sort of* the right direction.

It must have been nearly an hour later when I emerged, sweating and filthy and panting and scared, at the top of the slope, a little way along from Roxy's "garage." I began running back to our house, and there she was.

I stared, openmouthed, at Roxy, looking so chilled, sitting in the doorway of the shed beneath the still-flickering AGE sign. Shouldn't she, I wondered, be a bit more traumatized after her encounter with the witch of the woods? She certainly didn't look it.

"Your dad was here," said Roxy. "Well, there. Looking over the fence. He's nice. He's called Ben."

"Yeah, Roxy. I know. He's my dad." I was thrown by all this. I wanted to know what had happened to her.

"I'm OK," she said. "If that's why you look so weird."

"Do I?"

She inspected me, head on one side, really considering the question.

"Yep. You're covered in mud, your hair's full of leaves, and your face is red and sweaty. That's weird to me."

"But what about you? What happened?"

"Well—" she began, but was interrupted.

"There you are," said Dad, peering over the back fence, which came up to his chin. "Gee! What happened to you? You look like you've been dragged through a hedge backward!"

This was *far* closer to the truth than I actually wanted to admit.

And why was that? Why, at that very instant, did I not say something like this:

"Wow, Dad—you'll never believe what's just happened! Me and Roxy (Roxy, meet Dad; Dad, this is Roxy) have just found this amazing house in the woods. Did you know it was there? It's, like, *really* well hidden. And this lady lives there that Roxy reckons is a witch, which obviously she isn't, although she looks like one! And anyway, Roxy fell into their backyard and banged her head, but it looks like she's OK now. Cool, huh, Dad?"

But I didn't. And I think I know why.

Apart from the fact that we'd been trespassing—all those signs and barbed wire had ensured that I wasn't even a tiny bit relaxed about our whole adventure—it was Roxy's casual behavior that was freaking me out. I had noticed a thick surgical dressing stuck behind her ear by her hairline.

It all made me think that there was something else going on here. Something that could be spoiled if I said too much.

I also felt bad about not rescuing her. About standing still like a mannequin while Roxy, bleeding, was carried into a strange house. I don't think Dad would have been impressed by that.

And so I lied—and I am the world's worst liar. When Dad said his "dragged through a hedge backward" thing, I just laughed like it was the funniest thing I'd ever heard.

"Yeah! I know! Just exploring, you know, Dad! Got a bit lost and that, but hey—no bones broken, eh? Ha-ha!"

Dad gave me a funny look. "Well, get in here quickly, son. I want your help with the baseboards." He turned to go back in the house.

Wonderful, I thought. *More decorating.* The house hadn't been in great condition when we moved in.

We watched him go before Roxy said to me, "You're a lousy liar, Aidan. If there were prizes for bad acting, you'd win them all. In fact—"

"Yeah, yeah—all right. Thanks a lot. It did the job. I want to know what happened to you."

Inside the shed, Roxy sat behind the ratty little desk. Her fingers were together like a tent in front of her mouth, and her elbows were on the table. I swear she was trying to be all cool and intimidating, but she was too small and scruffy to carry it off. Instead she looked like a kid impersonating a stern headmistress.

"It's stranger than we thought," she said.

"It's stranger than *you* thought," I corrected her. "To me, it's some lady and her kid living a quiet life in a secluded house until you fall into their backyard."

"She had a cauldron, a black cat, and a broomstick," said Roxy, counting them off on her fingers, and nodding her head as if that proved everything.

"No, Roxy. She had a cooking pot, a black-and-white cat, and a . . . I dunno . . . a *broom,* like we've all got at home."

"But you didn't see inside the house."

"Well, no. But I was hoping you were going to tell me. By the way—how's your head?"

Roxy touched the back of her ear gently and frowned. "OK, really. Doesn't hurt anymore. She put some lotion on it."

"You mean a potion," I scoffed.

She narrowed her eyes at me. "If you're just going to mock me, then you can get out of my garage." She pointed at the door.

I sighed. "I'm sorry. It's just . . . well, you do know that witches don't exist? That magic and stuff aren't real? It's all just stories. You do know that?" I was being sincere, and I was careful to avoid any tone of voice that might have sounded teasing.

Roxy visibly relaxed. "I do know that. Or at least, I did."

She reached under the desk and pulled out a laptop computer and flipped it open. Roxy hit a few keys and a film started. As it did, my mouth fell open until my jaw hit my knees. Well, almost. You know what I mean.

CHAPTER THIRTEEN

At first, I had no idea what I was watching. It was just noise—rustling, crunching—and blurred gray-green stuff as the camera moved through . . . what?

Leaves. Undergrowth. Bushes. And there was a voice, clear as anything. *My* voice, saying: *"Something flattish, with green bits?"*

Then Roxy's voice: *"You've got it. It's a roof!"*

"Stop the video!" I said to Roxy, and she leaned forward to hit the space bar.

"You were *filming* all of this?"

She said nothing but grinned and nodded.

"But . . . *how?* You didn't have a camera."

With her left hand, she pulled at the side of her denim jacket and thrust it at me. Peering closely, I could see a tiny glass dome set into the brass button. She flipped open her jacket to reveal a black cable leading to an inside pocket and a little silvery box.

"That's a camera?"

"Yep. Surveillance camera, 720p HD res, audio and video."

I nodded wisely, as if I knew what the heck she was talking about, and added an "Oh wow!" for good measure. It seemed to work, because she became more enthusiastic.

"Yeah, and, even better, this records at 16:4 Mbps rather than MPEG4, so that you can . . ." She trailed off, looking carefully at me.

I adjusted my face to the one you use in class when you haven't been following what the teacher says, but you don't want him to know. (Mr. Reid, our math teacher, knows this face well on me.)

"You don't know what I'm talking about, do you?"

I shook my head and then said, "Did you get this dumpster diving as well?"

She nodded distractedly and pressed Play again.

It was strange watching back everything that had happened only a few hours ago. Roxy fast-forwarded the bit where we were just hacking through the woods until we came to the part just before she fell into the witch's yard.

(See? I'm doing it myself now. *She's not a witch!*)

The picture at this stage was just a bit of ground, as Roxy was lying down in the long grass.

"*Get down! She'll see you.*" That was Roxy.

"*What? And turn me into a toad? I'll take the risk, thanks.*"

There was a scuffling noise, then a gasp as Roxy tumbled down the slope, and a loud, hard thump as she hit the ground.

"Ow!" I said. It sounded like a painful fall.

The picture swooped and blurred and then just stopped, showing mostly sky as Roxy lay on her back, out cold.

"That must've hurt!" I said.

"Like hell," said Roxy. "But not till I regained consciousness."

On the film, there were footsteps, and then a replay of what I had heard, in my cowardly horror, from the bank.

That strange language. The woman first.

"Al-vuh. Al-vuh! Kuma!"

That's what it sounded like, anyway. And then a load of garbled stuff that I couldn't make out. I gasped as a close-up of the woman's face filled the laptop screen. She was leaning over and peering at Roxy, and the tiny camera caught it all.

Roxy paused the film. "And there she is!" She said it like she was announcing a celebrity appearing on a red carpet.

We stared at the screen and the woman's face.

How old was she? I admit that I'm not so brilliant at guessing adults' ages. After thirty, I reckon, they all look pretty much the same until they're sixty or so. That's when they start to get wrinkly and white-haired like Gran and Grandad Linklater.

So this woman could have been anywhere in that range. She had lines on her forehead and at the side of her eyes, but that might have been because she had a worried expression on her face. Her hair was in a cloth scarf, but some blond bits were sticking out. Her cheeks were shiny and light red, like Pink Lady apples.

Roxy pressed Play again, and the woman's face moved back a

bit, and side to side, as if assessing Roxy's injury. She might once have been pretty, but when she opened her mouth, her teeth were discolored and worn, with gaps in both rows.

Then she removed her sunglasses and I saw her eyes, a watery blue color with pink, damp rims and pale lashes.

"Have you ever seen anyone look as tired as that?" I murmured to Roxy. "She looks like she could sleep forever."

The picture went back to sky and there was more conversation in their language, and something I could make out as *"In-ann bolld."* She said it twice.

"This is where they pick me up," said Roxy. The image moved and there was a wall, and more sky, and then it went darker as they moved inside. The picture went still again, and I could see what looked like the ceiling and a light hanging down.

"Hello? Hello?" A different voice now: the boy's. *"Can you hear me? Hello? Are you all right?"* There was a light slapping noise, which I took to be someone gently tapping Roxy's cheek to wake her up, then the woman's voice came back in, followed by a sharp intake of breath, a gasp, and a little moan.

The boy said something to the woman, and then there was a cough and another moan of pain.

"That's me," said Roxy. "I'm coming round, and I try to get up."

Sure enough, the picture moved, as if Roxy was trying to sit upright, but then went back to the ceiling as the woman said, *"No, pet. Lie back down. You've banged y'heed bad. Just rest there a bit, pet. Divvent move. Shhh."*

It was a gentle, soothing voice, with a strong northeastern lilt, and something else as well: another accent. She sounded like Kristina Nilsen at my old school, who was Norwegian but had a local, northeastern Geordie accent as well.

Anyway, this was not the cackling voice of a witch, but I didn't say that to Roxy.

She fast-forwarded a bit more.

"It's just me lying down, and them talking in their language."

On the screen, there was a glimpse of a china bowl. Roxy said, "She had something in there that she bathed my head with, where it got cut. Smelled gross and it stung like anything."

Then the woman's voice said, *"D'you reckon you can sit up, petal? Come on, up you get. Easy does it. How ye feelin'?"*

Suddenly there they were, standing in front of Roxy as she sat up and the tiny camera took everything in.

The woman's shapeless sweater appeared to be hand-knitted. Her long hands were rough-looking and clasped in front of her in an appearance of concern.

The top of her head was cut off by the camera, but there was a soft look on her face. She said something to the boy: *"Go-ther svine, Alve. Go-ther svine."*

The boy was obviously her son: they looked very alike, from the pale eyes to the dirty-blond hair and the long fingers. His teeth, too, were yellowed and gappy. His clothes were old-fashioned: proper trousers (not jeans), button-up shirt. Aunty Alice would have said he looked "right smart," but to me he looked like he'd borrowed his dad's clothes. The sunglasses hanging round his neck completed the unusual look.

Behind them was a room that was darkish and cluttered, with old-fashioned easy chairs, and a table piled with papers, and a mantelpiece covered with vases and knickknacks, and piles of paper on the floor, and . . .

"Sheesh—look at the state of the place!" I said.

Roxy laughed. "Listen to you, Mr. Houseproud!" she teased. "But I know what you mean. And it smelled . . ." She hesitated.

"Bad?"

She wrinkled her nose as if that would help her to recall the smell. "Not *bad*, exactly. Just . . . *old*. Like an old person's house with old stuff in it. A bit dusty, maybe? It was clean, though."

I nodded. Gran and Grandad's house smells a bit like that, and they're not even all that old. We looked back at the screen.

"How are you feelin', pet? Are you dizzy at all? Try standin' up— gently, now."

"She sounds normal," I said. "Nice, even."

"I know," Roxy said. "You wait, though."

"Can you move all yer bits? Nothin' broken? That was quite a bump y'had."

The picture moved while Roxy, presumably, twisted her arms and legs about to check, then her voice said, *"No, nothing broken, thanks. I'd better be going."*

And then the boy piped up, off-screen: *"Are you sure? You do not have to go straightaway. It might not be safe, you know, if you have been concussed."*

There followed an exchange in their language, but I still couldn't make anything of it, though I did hear the word "Al-vuh" again. It was hard to tell because I couldn't see their faces, but it sounded like the woman was being a bit firm with the boy.

"Pause it," I said to Roxy, and she did. "What was all that about?"

Roxy shrugged. "How would I know?"

We rewound and played it again. "If I had to guess," I said, "it would be that *she* was telling *him* not to invite you to stay. It's in her tone."

We played it a third time, and Roxy agreed. "I didn't want to stay anyway. I was terrified."

On-screen the camera turned so that we saw the rest of the room. Parts of it were piled so high with stuff that the towers of paper and books looked as though they might topple over. On one wall was a bookshelf that probably contained as many books as our school library, crammed in higgledy-piggledy. The camera was moving too fast for me to see any titles, but they looked like old books, not brightly colored paperbacks. There was a glimpse of a cat's black-and-white tail passing the camera's eye.

Roxy's voice: *"I . . . I really have to go. Thanks. Thank you."*

The woman stepped in front of her, and her face had become much less friendly.

"But, pet, you haven't told me what you were doing. I mean, why

were you on our property in the first place? It's clearly marked as private, and there are fences which you and your friend must have broken through."

"My . . . my . . ."

"Your friend. Oh aye, we saw him, didn't we, Alve?"

The boy nodded with a pained expression on his face. It was clear he didn't like this new line of interrogation.

"W-we just got lost."

The woman leaned in close. "Did y'now? Well, divvent get lost again, or I'll have the Peelers onto ye." Then she smiled: a cold smile that said I'm not being mean, but don't underestimate me.

I had no idea what this "having the Peelers" meant, and looked across to Roxy, who gave a half shrug. It didn't sound good, whatever it was.

As Roxy's voice on the film stammered apologies, the picture showed her progress out of the room, into an equally dark and cluttered hallway, and toward a large wooden door with a small window in the front. Her hands scrabbled for the handle, and then she turned and only the boy was standing before her.

"I'm sorry," Roxy repeated, and the strangest thing happened.

The boy gave a shy smile, which was only just visible at the top of the screen, because of Roxy's lack of height. Then he said, "Me too." He glanced behind him, then added, quieter, "Perhaps I shall see you again?" His tone was sad, and hopeful. On the film his mother's footsteps came closer.

The wooden door was open and he said, "That way." At the edge of the picture, he raised his hand in a shy wave, and the (mostly) black cat scuttled away in the corner of the frame.

Then the picture started jerking up and down as the sound changed to Roxy's running feet slapping the road as she got away as quickly as she could.

And now she was sitting in front of me, looking smug.

"Told you," she said. "The strange language, the lotion, the old books, the threat? She is *totally* a witch."

CHAPTER FOURTEEN

However much I pleaded and scoffed, nothing would convince Roxy Minto that she had not had an encounter with a witch.

If you're convinced of something, I guess it's easy to become stubborn about it if the alternative is admitting that you were wrong and a bit childish.

"Well, *obviously* she's not going to wear a black hat and have warts. That would just give the game away, wouldn't it?" she declared.

"Oh, so the fact she doesn't *look* much like a witch proves she's a witch, does it?" I said in exasperation. "So what if she *had* had a black, pointy hat? What would that prove? That she *wasn't* a witch?"

She ignored this logic. "*And* she's got a cauldron and a black cat!"

"Black and white, Roxy," I said wearily.

"So what?"

Everything I said was batted back to me with wide-eyed innocence. Our voices were getting louder and it was becoming an argument, which I didn't want because Roxy was daring and fun.

"I can prove it, you know," she said, and then her phone rang: a jolly, tinkly-tonkly tune on the piano that somehow suited Roxy perfectly. She glanced at the screen but didn't pick it up. I looked at her quizzically.

"It's my mum. Gotta go."

I'd barely noticed that Roxy had been alone all this time. I mean, wherever I am, usually there's a parent kicking around somewhere in the background: bringing out juice, checking you're wearing a warm top or not running with scissors—just being parentish. But Roxy had been parentless all day.

Her phone rang out and went to voicemail.

"Where is your mum?" I asked.

Roxy jerked her head in the direction of the house. "Inside."

"And she's phoning you?"

She let out a deep sigh as she jumped down from her chair and stood up. "Long story. Another time, eh?"

It was as if Roxy had been pricked with a pin and her sigh was all the air escaping, along with her fun and liveliness and everything else. I would swear that even her sticky-up hair lay flatter on her head. She locked the door to the garage and put the key under a stone. She said nothing: she knew I was watching, so I knew I was trusted.

She turned and a flicker of light returned to her eyes when she said, "Midnight."

"Tonight?"

"No. In ten years' time. Of course tonight." She turned to slip through the gap in the fence. "It's the witching hour," she said, and then she was gone, leaving me staring into the thick woods, trying to piece together what had been going on.

Roxy had said, "I can prove it, you know."

What did she mean by that? Was it, "I can prove it: she did a magic spell," which of course would be yet more nonsense?

But there was something in the way she said it, a light of *certainty* in her eyes, which I couldn't stop thinking about.

You see, I was on the point of dismissing Roxy as a harmless crazy: we'd have been friendly but not "friends," the boy and the woman in the forest cottage would have been left in peace, and Roxy would have grown out of her belief in the "witch in the woods."

But then the disaster happened, and Roxy and I became the last people to see the witch alive.

CHAPTER FIFTEEN

Alfie

I watched the girl go back up the lane. I wanted to go with her, make sure she got home safely, but I do not think Mam would have approved. Besides, she did not live far: on the other side of the woods. She had a funny little shed with an illuminated sign hanging by the door. I knew that much.

Biffa jumped into my arms as I stood there. It meant that when the girl turned back to look, she did not see my hand give a little wave because it was sort of hidden by Biffa. I am not sure. Maybe she did see.

R. Minto.

It was sewn into her jacket on a label. I saw it when I carried her in. She also had something with wires going into the pocket. Probably one of those cellular telephones or something.

I watched her all the way to the bend in the lane in case she turned back again, but she did not. Biffa hopped out of my arms then and gave a little growl, which made me smile.

"Do you like her, Biffa?" I said in our old language. "Me too."

I sniffed the air in the lane. The weather had been hot for spring, but it would cool down later: I could smell it. The sky was cloudless, so when the sun dipped, the evening would get cold and Mam would want the fire to be lit to keep the chill from the old stone house.

I should have gone right away to the woodshed to get some old logs, but I was still thinking of R. Minto and her friend in the bushes, and how Mam had been suspicious of them. Then Biffa came back with a big beetle she had caught and dumped it on its back by my feet, where it lay, waggling its legs.

"No, Biff!" I laughed. "Leave the beetles alone!" I crouched down to flick the insect back the right way up, and it scuttled gratefully into the undergrowth.

I completely forgot about fetching the old logs, which turned out to be the biggest mistake of the last thousand years.

CHAPTER SIXTEEN

AIDAN

It was before midnight when the fire sirens started.

I got up to look out the bedroom window—Libby's bedroom, where I had been moved to make room for Aunty Alice and Jasper. My stomach lurched with fear when I saw the glow of the fire coming from the woods, fierce enough to light up the sky, although it was still quite a distance away.

I knew instantly what was burning.

"Dad! Dad!" I called.

"Strewth!" I heard. "That's a hell of a conflagration." I swung round and Jasper was standing behind me in his pajama bottoms, leaning on a stack of boxes that hadn't been unpacked yet.

A smell of smoke was seeping through the open window, so I shut it.

"There's a house there, you know," I said. "In the woods."

"Really? Well, I hope they're all right. Ghastly things, fires, eh?" Jasper scratched his thick beard and his fingers traveled from his cheek to his throat to his chest and it was hairy all the way down.

The beard never actually stopped, but just merged with the rest of the hair on his body.

I heard the doorbell ring downstairs. *I bet that's Roxy,* I thought.

Dad opened the front door not to Roxy but to a fireman, and while I ran down the stairs he spoke to Dad. Through the door, I could see a fire engine in the street, its blue lights flashing.

"Sorry to wake you, sir, but we have to run a hose down the side of your house. If that fire spreads, it poses a risk to the buildings, so we have to soak the trees," he said.

The firefighter wasn't expecting a refusal, I could tell that much, because the others were already unspooling the hose from the fire engine and opening up the fire hydrant right outside our house.

"No need for alarm, son," the fireman said to me. "Just a precaution."

"What about the house? The witch . . . the house in the woods? Are they all right?"

"Dunno anything about that, son. Now 'scuse me." He turned his attention to the others, who were by now running up the junk-filled alley, shifting stuff to make room.

He was lying. I knew it at once, and I felt scared.

I stood on the front path, watching the firemen. That's when I saw Roxy, in short pajamas, shivering in her doorway, fingering the dressing behind her ear. Our eyes met and we both knew what the other was thinking. I beckoned for her to come over. I wanted to talk to her about what was happening, about the possibility that the witch's house was on fire, that people might be hurt or worse. . . .

She shook her head and pointed upstairs, mouthing the word *"Mum."*

Then my mum came up behind me.

"Come on, Aidan. We mustn't get in the way. If you want to see what's going on, look from upstairs."

There were loads of neighbors in slippers out in the street, watching the commotion, and I didn't see what difference I was making, but I couldn't be bothered to argue.

Back at the bedroom window, I saw another fire truck arrive, one with a huge ladder, which they extended higher than the houses. The fireman who climbed up it then directed those on the ground where to point the hose, and a huge arc of water sprayed out over the trees till they were soaked and dripping.

The orange glow of fire, meanwhile, grew bigger and spread, getting closer. Showers of sparks would fly up into the purple sky when a tree came crashing down, then a few minutes later that part of the wood went up in flames as the sparks caught hold of the dry leaves on the ground.

Dad came into my room. "Pack some clothes, son. Use your sports bag. The firefighters say we may have to evacuate."

I stared, not understanding what he'd said.

"Evacuate. Leave the house. For safety. Chop-chop."

"But . . . we're safe here, aren't we?" I protested.

"Not if the fire gets much closer. Look." He pointed out of my window, where another tree, much closer than the others, had small tongues of flame licking up its trunk. I could make out the branches catching fire, before the hose was directed on it and the flames went out.

I pulled on some jeans over my pajamas and found a thick sweater and put that on too.

Grace Darling Close is a circular dead end, and the road had filled with vehicles and people. Sue and Pru, the ladies from next door, both wore identical blue dressing gowns. Sue was holding a huge and cross-looking ginger tom that was hissing at every passing fireman. "*Ach*—don't vorry: he iss just being friendly," I heard her say in her German accent, which I thought was stretching the truth.

As well as the three fire engines, I counted two police cars and an ambulance. As I watched, another car pulled up, and two women got out, one of them holding a movie camera and a portable light. She immediately started filming pretty much everything: the trucks, the huddles of neighbors. I wandered about in my slippers, just looking at this strange gathering.

Sue and Pru were talking to the reporter. "Our cats are very *atch-itated,* aren't zey, Prudence?" said Sue, and Pru nodded in agreement. "Thomas here has already emptied his bowels *vere he shouldn't,* haven't you, Thomas, you *vick-ed* old sing?" Thomas yawned.

And then I heard a voice rising above the general hubbub.

"Put me down! Put me *down,* darn you. I'm fine—will you let me *go!*" Along with everyone else, I turned in the direction of the voice. It was coming from Roxy's house, where two firemen were carrying what looked like a large chair down the front steps, draped in blankets with a head in a hairnet poking through the top of them.

"Here! Put me here! No, *here,* you imbecile! Are you *deaf?*" A hand appeared from under the blankets and actually hit one of the firemen on his yellow helmet, in time with her words: "Stop!" *Hit.* "Stop!" *Hit.* "Stop!" *Hit.*

They got to the end of the path and put the chair down, and only then did I realize that it was a wheelchair.

"Wha' on earth is wrong with you all?" she said, gathering her blankets around her.

Out of slapping range, the fireman she had been hitting managed a wry smile. "You're welcome, madam. Only too happy to be of service and save you from a fiery grave."

"Fiery grave, my foot! I was perfec'ly fine! What on earth . . . GET THAT DAMN THING OUT OF ME FACE! HOW DARE YOU!" Her attention had switched to the camerawoman, who, spotting the commotion, had scuttled over and started filming the lady screaming at the firemen.

"I'm sorry," said the camerawoman. "I was just wondering if you could say a few words for television news."

"Yes, I can," said the lady. "Is that thing on? Right: here are a few words for television news," and she let off a stream of swear words like F . . . and B . . . and another B . . . plus some that I didn't even know, and it was such a vicious string, and so loud, that even the fireman she had hit started to laugh.

The camerawoman said, "Er . . . thanks," and slunk off.

Then Roxy was next to me.

"Met my mum, have you?" she said, indicating the lady in the wheelchair.

"H-hello?" I stammered. "How do you do?"

She didn't even look at me.

"Go 'way!"

CHAPTER SEVENTEEN

We didn't evacuate in the end. Slowly the chaos in the street died down. One by one, the cars left. The ladder on the fire engine was retracted.

The smell of woodsmoke hung about and the air smelled like the leftovers of a huge bonfire.

As the sky in the east started to lighten, the Chief Fire Officer (who had two stripes on his helmet—the only thing I remember from a trip to the fire station in nursery school) was making his way around the groups of neighbors who had not yet gone inside.

Roxy had wheeled her mum back inside. I hadn't spoken with her any more (and hadn't really wanted to).

Dad was drinking from a mug of tea and had made one for the fireman who had been up the ladder. I don't think they noticed me sitting on the step behind them.

". . . Can happen so easily, mate," the fireman was saying, and he slurped his tea thirstily. "One spark, dry conditions, bit of a breeze, y'know?"

"Was anyone hurt?" said Dad, as if he could read my mind. The fireman took another sip and looked thoughtful.

"I'm not really supposed to say until it's official, but, well . . ." He paused, and Dad didn't prompt him. "It's not gonna help him now, is it?"

Him? Did he just say "him"? My heart plummeted.

"Or her, I suppose," he continued. "Anyways . . . one body that we know of. We don't even know who lived there. We couldn't get the trucks down the lane, and the hoses weren't long enough. They never stood a chance."

They? Was that "they" as in "he or she" or "they" as in . . . I was confused and tired, and didn't know what to think.

Dad tutted and shook his head. "Dreadful way to go."

"They're all bad if you're not ready. But this? Probably quicker than most. You suffocate long before you burn." He smiled as if this was encouraging, but I was still unbelievably sad. I rested my forehead on my knees and felt myself wanting to cry. I think I made a slight sobbing noise in my throat, because it made Dad and the fireman look down. The fireman spoke and his gentle Geordie accent was reassuring.

"Hiya, son. Time you got some sleep, eh? It's bin a hell of a night!"

I stood up and gave a stiff nod, and I felt a tear run down each cheek. I wiped them on my sleeve.

"It's . . . it's the smoke. It's got in my eyes," I said, though I don't know why.

"Aye. It does that. We all get it," he said, and patted my shoulder. "Have a shower, son. You'll feel better and you won't smell it."

CHAPTER EIGHTEEN

I woke up at ten o'clock and spent a few minutes staring out of Libby's bedroom window. The sky was a clear light blue with no clouds, and there were a few lone wisps of smoke rising from beyond the trees. I opened the window and there was still a faint smell of burning wood.

Downstairs the local TV channel was showing pictures of firefighters and people in white overalls standing by the burnt-out shell of a building. And by "burnt-out" I mean it was just a few blackened walls and a doorway, and half of an upper floor supporting a bit of roof. I could make out the remains of a table and some other furniture, and the camera showed close-ups of some burnt books, a stone sink, a bookshelf, and a picture hanging wonkily on the wall.

". . . blaze was well established by the time firefighters arrived on the scene. The secluded house, parts of which are believed to date back to the eighteenth century, was completely destroyed in the inferno, which one firefighter described as one of the worst house fires she had ever seen."

Chief Fire Officer Harry Oxley: "We have recovered one body from the scene which has been removed for forensic examination. I cannot say more than that at the moment."

Reporter: "Can you say what started the fire?"

CFO Oxley: "At this moment in time, we are pursuing all avenues of inquiry, but there is nothing at present that indicates foul play."

Reporter: "The fire spread to other parts of the woods, and locals from the nearby Delaval Estate were warned they might have to evacuate. . . ."

At this point, the picture cut to our street, and there I was, gazing up at the fireman on the ladder. Normally I'd have gone, "Dad! Dad! I'm on TV!" but I didn't. I just watched in glum fascination as the reporter finished her piece.

". . . finally brought under control shortly before dawn. The area has been cordoned off while fire and police investigators try to establish both the cause of the fire and the identity of the unfortunate victim. This is Janey Calvert in Whitley Bay for *North Today*."

When I heard *BANG BANG BANG* on the window, I jumped so hard I spilled milk on the sofa. It was Roxy.

"Still in your pajamas?" she said, her high voice muffled by the glass. "See you in the garage in ten minutes. It's important."

CHAPTER NINETEEN

The trees were still dripping from their soaking the previous night, and the ground underfoot was soft pale mud, with fresh footprints. Roxy, I figured, must already be inside, and I pushed the door, which swung open, but no one was there.

Just then, Roxy squeezed herself through the gap in the fence, her tiny foot first, her tousled head last.

"Hiya," she said, immediately noticing the door was open. "How did you get in?"

"It was open," I said, then raised my finger to my lips to say "Shhh" and pointed to the footprints in the mud, which, it seemed, were *not* hers. Now that I looked, I could see that the trail led inside the garage. Instinctively, I think, Roxy lowered her voice.

"Someone's been in here. One of the firemen, you reckon?" she said.

I pointed at the small footprints. "It'd have to be one with very dainty feet."

She gave her little bark of laughter. "Very good, Sherlock! But what about my laptop?"

I shrugged, and she pushed past me to the other side of the desk where she kept the computer. Then she just screamed.

And I mean *screamed*.

For all her small frame, it was a big shriek, followed by little gasps, "Ah-ah-ah," then, "Aidan!"

"What?" I was just standing there, unable to do anything because I had no idea what had caused her to shriek.

Roxy's eyes were fixed on something under the desk, something I couldn't see.

"Th-there's a . . . a person."

OK, so what we should have done was calmly leave the shed-cum-garage, locking the door behind us, and call the police.

That would have been *sensible*. That's what *you* should do if you're ever in the position of finding a person hiding under your desk in an old hut.

Instead I stepped forward and seized the desk with both hands, tipping it toward me on two legs till it crashed over, revealing a smallish figure curled up in a ball like a scared hedgehog and visibly trembling.

"What the . . ."

"Who the . . ."

Slowly, like a leaf uncurling in spring, the figure lifted its head, straightened its back, and looked up at us.

"*You!*" Roxy and I said in unison.

The boy from the cottage blinked hard at the light coming through the doorway and slowly stood up and said, "Memam . . . memam . . . memam . . ."

Just that. Babbling and blinking, looking first at me and then at Roxy.

She, of course, understood first.

"Your mam?"

He nodded. "Me mam." He swallowed hard and carried on blinking in the light.

CHAPTER TWENTY

Alfie

The last friend I ever had was Jack McGonagal. It was Jack who changed everything.

You probably do not remember 1934. Me, I liked it. We had no refrigerator or telephone, but nor did most people. Televisions and computers had hardly even been invented and it would be another sixty or more years before everyone used email and the Internet, and everybody knew everything about everybody else. Which was not entirely a good thing if you were trying to hide a secret.

By then, Mam and I had been living in Oak Cottage for nearly eighty years. Mam had bought it in 1856 for three hundred pounds cash. You could do that then. It was all legal, and Mam and I had enough money.

It was certainly remote, and perfect for us. There were no housing complexes nearby then. We grew stuff on a little patch of ground that had been cleared when the cottage was built.

We had a goat called Amy and some chickens. (We did not give names to the chickens, because we sometimes ate them.)

Biffa loved it. The house had been empty for a while when we moved in, and there were a lot of mice. Biffa caught them all within a few weeks.

We read a lot, and—once it had been invented—we listened to the radio, which we called the wireless.

Once or twice a week, Mam would cycle into Whitley Bay on our rickety old bicycle, and sometimes I would go instead to fetch groceries. I made sure I went outside of school hours so no one would think I was playing hooky.

There was a grocery shop in Eastbourne Gardens run by a couple, Mr. and Mrs. McGonagal. He was tall and thin with huge red ears and sharp eyes, and she was short and dumpy. They had a boy my age called Jack who helped behind the counter.

Jack and I eventually got to the point where we would say "hello," and he once helped me put the chain back on my bike. I let him have a ride on it to pay him back, and he said, "Where do you live?"

"Hexham," I lied. I knew the routine. "I'm just visiting my aunt."

That was the story that worked, if anyone asked—which they seldom did because we did not talk to many people. Hexham is a town about forty miles away: near enough not to be unusual, but far enough not to be familiar.

"Where do you go to school, then?" asked Jack. This was on a school-day afternoon, at about four p.m.

"In Hexham," I said. "Only our schools are closed this week. It's a local holiday."

"Wow," said Jack. "Lucky!"

And that was it: no further questions. I liked Jack. I gave him a ride on the back of my bike down to the Links, and we threw stones at a tin can. He could walk on his hands, and when he tried to teach me we laughed and laughed. It was fun.

It had been quite a long time since I'd had a friend, and Jack seemed a bit lonely too. So when it began to get dark and I would have had to cycle home with no lights (and risk being stopped by a policeman who would take me home and ask awkward questions), I said to Jack, "I am coming back here on Saturday; shall we meet?"

And so we did. There was a brass band playing on the bandstand, and we ate chips (which I bought), looking at the big white dome of the Spanish City pleasure gardens, and Jack told me about how his dad had once shot a moose in Canada, and . . .

Why am I telling you this?

Because you have to understand how hurt I was when my new friend Jack—funny, skinny Jack with his knobbly knees and his baggy shorts—betrayed me, although it was not even his fault. Well, not entirely.

CHAPTER TWENTY-ONE

You see, Jack grew older and I did not. It was always the way with friends, and it was always hard. I never got used to it.

After a year or two of knowing him, Jack started to wear long trousers instead of the shorts all boys wore then. A year or two after that, he grew a wispy mustache, and his voice became deeper.

So far as he knew, I came to visit my "aunt" most weekends. I had several periods when I said I was recovering from a mystery illness, which required longer stays to benefit from the sea air, and there were always the summer holidays.

Jack would even come to our house in the woods. Mam liked him but she was wary. She was not keen on anybody getting too close.

"It will end badly, Alve," she would warn. I did not want to believe her. Jack would be different, I was sure of it.

If Jack thought it odd that I did not grow taller, or grow hair on my legs, he said nothing. Not so his mother, though.

"Ee, Alfie Monk, your mother not feedin' you or summin'?" Mrs. McGonagal said to me one day in the shop. "Look at ye! There's more growth on a moldy cheese."

"Ma!" said Jack, but he was laughing too. I don't think he intended to be mean, but when he laughed, I shriveled inside because I'd seen it all before. The suspicion, the mistrust, the gradual—or sometimes sudden—withdrawal of friendship from the strange boy who does not get older.

Not long after, I heard them talking about me. I had come into the shop; the tinkling bell that normally announced a customer's arrival was broken, so nobody knew I was there.

I heard Jack in the back room of the shop. He was repeating his mother's joke from before in his new, deeper voice.

". . . more growth on a moldy cheese, I tell you!"

"Come on, Jack. Don't mock the afflicted. He's prob'ly got a growth condition or somethin'." The voice belonged to a young woman: Jean Palmer, whom Jack had started courting. I had met her once or twice. She was pretty.

"Alfie's different. It's not right," said Jack. "He's not changed in five years. *Five years!* And have you heard how he talks? Reckons he's from Hexham. Well, I know Hexham, and they don't talk like *that* out there."

By now, I had moved from my position by the counter and was sort of crouched down behind a stack of cardboard boxes. I did not want them to come out and see that I had been listening.

"Aye, he does talk funny, I'll give y'that," Jean Palmer said. "But I like him."

"He's not right, Jean. And his aunty's not right, either. Never looks you in the eye when she's talking to you. Living out in the woods like that—with a *goat*, of all things. Old Lizzie Richardson told Ma she used to know her years ago, in North Shields, when she had a son of her own, and *he* was called Alfie as well. That's odd, isn't it?"

"Lizzie Richardson? She's over ninety."

"That's what I'm saying, Jean. And if Mrs. Richardson knew her back in Shields, that puts that Mrs. Monk at nearly seventy if she's a day."

"Well, she's lookin' good is all I can say."

At that point, another customer came in and shouted, "Hello?" and hardly noticed as I scuttled out. I cycled home, despondent.

This was how it happened, again and again, although this time was quicker than I was used to.

You see, it is simply not possible to get no older and expect nobody to notice. People talk; people gossip. You can often get away with it for much longer than you might expect, but eventually people behave just like, well . . . people.

They make up reasons to explain the inexplicable, and Mam and I helped them, creating a little confusion. Was I Mam's son, for example, or was I her nephew? Mam would often encourage people to think that her own mother lived in the same house.

And old people with long memories, like Lizzie Richardson, eventually die and take their suspicions with them, and those that are left conclude that they were the ramblings of an aging mind because the truth is just too unbelievable.

But you cannot fool everyone. Not forever.

CHAPTER TWENTY-TWO

By 1939, Jack was sixteen: a tall young man with a lopsided grin. I had bought him a packet of cigarettes for his sixteenth birthday because that was what you did back then. He offered me one, but I had tried tobacco before, years ago. I knew I did not like it, so I said no and he gave me a sneering look.

One day in the summer I went round to the shop in Eastbourne Gardens. It was a few weeks after I had overheard him talking in the back room. Mrs. McGonagal shook her head.

"He's not in, son. He's very busy these days. He's helpin' in the shop a lot, so he cannit come out."

Well, which was it? I thought. *Is he not in, or is he in and unable to come out?* I knew she was lying.

"Shall . . . shall I come back tomorrow?"

"No, son. I think it's best if you don't. Like I say, he's busy in the shop."

"W-will you tell him I was here?"

"Aye." Her attention had already switched to the next

customer. "Mrs. Abercrombie. How's your little Queenie? Ee, have you heard the news about Mr. Hitler? There's going to be an announcement later."

Then I heard it: a girl's laugh, a giggle, from the back room. The door to the back was closed, but not shut tight, and the noise came through easily. So did the smell of cigarettes.

I knew then, just as you know now, that they were laughing at me. That Jack was there with Jean, and I understood.

He did not want to hang around with a boy who looked like he was eleven. A boy who would not be allowed into dances, a boy who did not smoke, a boy who was not interested in girls, a boy who was just, well . . . a boy. A strange boy: that was me. Is me.

I swallowed hard and took a deep breath. It had happened before, but I was still angry.

I was outside when Jack and Jean came out of the shop door and went in opposite directions.

I watched him walk off up the street, my cheeks burning with shame. Centuries of staying in the shadows, of not causing a fuss, were cast aside and I ran to catch up. "Hey!" I shouted. "Hey, Jack!" He turned.

"Oh. Hello, Alfie." I could see he was blushing.

What should I say now? I had not worked this out. For a moment, we stood facing each other: me still a boy, he a young man. He took a languid drag on his cigarette and looked down at me. He was much taller. There was no point in pretending.

"I heard what you said. To Jean. The other week. About me not being right."

"Ah. Hmm." He chewed his bottom lip and looked away before exhaling a plume of smoke.

"I thought you were my friend."

"I am, Alfie. I am, only . . ." His eyes flicked to the side. He was embarrassed but I did not care. "Look, shall we sit down?"

There was a low wall and we sat. He unbuttoned his jacket and hitched up the knees of his trousers before sitting. It was all so . . . *grown-up.*

"The thing is, Alfie . . ." And he paused. I do not think he quite knew what "the thing" was. I spoke in the pause.

"I embarrass you—is that it?"

He hesitated before saying, "No, Alfie!" but the truth was in the hesitation, and it told me everything I needed to know. I could feel my throat tightening with emotion.

"I do not *have* to be like this, you know!" I said, my voice getting louder. "I can reverse it!"

"You can reverse it? Reverse *what?*"

I had said more than I had intended, so I kept quiet, but I was panting.

"Listen, Alfie," Jack said, getting to his feet. "You're a good boy. You were a good friend. But . . . well, people change." He ground the cigarette under his shoe.

And that was it. He turned and walked up Eastbourne Gardens, and once again I tried to swallow the lump high in my chest.

CHAPTER TWENTY-THREE

I did not tell Mam: it would only upset her. That evening I milked Amy, and turned the cheeses in the little cheese pantry as usual. All the while, I had the same lump in my throat that I could not swallow.

Mam and I listened to the wireless. Mr. Chamberlain, the Prime Minister, announced that we were at war with Germany again, and we both agreed that it only seemed like yesterday that the last war had finished.

Finally I cried. Sitting there in front of the fire, I felt a fat tear roll down my cheek, and the sob broke over my heart like a wave over a shipwreck.

Mam thought I was crying because of the war, but I was not. I longed—for the umpteenth time—to grow up, to be like Jack, like all the boys I had ever known who had grown up.

Could Mam read my mind? It certainly felt like it sometimes. She got up and came over to me, sitting on the side of the chair and rubbing my back. I traced the two little scars on her upper arm with my fingers as I had done countless times before, while she sang a mournful, low tune. The words were in the ancient language we shared, and Mam's wavering voice deepened my sadness so that I wept like a small child with my head on her lap.

I thought then that I would not see Jack McGonagal again, and that *this* war would probably end the world.

I was wrong on both counts.

CHAPTER TWENTY-FOUR

We had known many wars, Mam and I, but this one was different. In all of the other wars, the fighting was nowhere near us. It took place in battles, fought by soldiers or navies, and we were not involved. The closest I had ever been was all those years ago when the tribe from beyond the Roman Wall had sailed up the Tyne and we had fled.

We had once had to travel past the fields where a huge battle had taken place weeks before, where the smell of war and unburied soldiers still lingered in the air.

But with this one, it was the bombs that made the difference. Now the enemy came to us, and it was all one battle, all the time. Again and again, in 1940 and 1941, the German planes would fly over us. Usually it was at night; sometimes it was in the day.

The bombs were aimed at factories in Newcastle, or at the shipyards in Wallsend and North Shields. But their aim was poor. Mam came back from the shops one day and sat down heavily in the chair in the back room.

"Nearly a hundred souls, they reckon, Alve. Sheltering from the bombs, they were. The shelter took a direct hit. And Mr. McGonagal from the shop was in there."

Poor Jack. His dad.

(When they had counted every body, there were 107 dead from one bomb, which had hit the lemonade factory in North Shields with the air-raid shelter beneath it.)

Before the war started, I had been worried that gossip would begin about Mam and me. It only needed one person to start talking. As the wartime months turned to years, however, we found—as we had found before—that it was comparatively easy to go unnoticed.

If you keep your head down and cause no trouble, officials will ignore you. They have more important things to worry about, especially during a war. A woman and her "nephew" living a quiet life could safely be ignored.

So, for a year or more, we stayed put. There were forms to fill out for obtaining foods that were rationed. Mam was good at that: she had birth certificates and official deeds that would convince almost anyone.

Thanks to our chickens, we ate a lot of eggs, because meat was in short supply. We would also eat chicken now and then, when a bird stopped laying and we killed it. That was usually my job. It was what I was doing when Jack called round in his uniform.

Not a soldier's uniform, though—he was still too young. He was a War Reserve Constable: part of the police force.

Jack's War Reserve Constable uniform looked just like a policeman's uniform, except ill-fitting, with the sleeves touching his knuckles and the trousers exposing his socks, but I could tell he was very proud to be wearing it.

I had not seen him in more than a year, and he was even taller and more grown-up looking than before. He must have been nearly eighteen, and I felt the familiar heart-wrench of sadness that I experienced seeing someone that I knew grow older and leave me behind.

He was cheery enough—cocky, even—when he let himself into the backyard where I was stalking an elderly chicken.

"Good morning?" he called. Mam turned first to see him in his uniform and tin helmet.

"Hello, Jack, love," she said, although there was a wary note in her voice. "Ee—look at you in your WRC stuff. He looks so grown-up, eh, Alfie?"

I grunted a reply. I was not so pleased to see him. Mam, though, was very good at being "normal."

"Have you cycled all the way here in this heat? Would you like a glass of water?"

"Yes, please, Mrs. Monk." He avoided looking at me but I knew something was up. He was being too formal.

"And you can take your tin helmet off. I divvent think Mr. Hitler will be bombing us today."

We sat in the backyard, looking up at the dense trees on the hill, and Jack drank his water, stealing glances at me.

"We were so sorry to hear about your father, weren't we, Alfie?" Mam said. I nodded. Jack said nothing.

There was a long, tense moment before Mam broke the silence again.

"So what brings you out here, Jack? Have you just come to say hello? We've not seen you in so long."

I could tell from Mam's voice that she thought something was wrong.

"Well, as a matter of fact, Mrs. Monk . . ." And that is when I knew. Nobody uses that phrase "as a matter of fact" when it's going to be good news.

". . . As a matter of fact, I have some inquiries of an official nature. If I may?"

Mam used to say that a uniform could make someone a better person or a worse person, but never the same person. Jack turned to me as he took a notebook out of his oversized tunic.

"How old are you, Alfie?"

And so it began: an interrogation of me, Mam, how long we had lived here, why official documents (which Jack said he now had access to) did not seem to match up, and more.

Mam remained calm. "I'm sure it's just a clerical mix-up, Jack, love. As you know, Alfie has a growth deficiency. Markandaya's Syndrome, type three."

This was a lie that had worked well in the past. A mysterious illness that "ran in our family" to account for my unusual appearance. It was not working on Jack.

"Ah, well, I remember you saying this before, Mrs. Monk. I've checked with Dr. Menzies in Whitley Bay and he knows of no such illness."

"Well, it is very rare," I said, but I came over as defensive, and not believable. Jack ignored me. At that moment, the chicken I had been pursuing before Jack's arrival came close to me, pecking at the ground, and in one swift movement I darted out my right hand and grabbed it by the neck.

"Take its legs," I barked at Jack as the chicken flapped around. "Go on—quickly!" Jack was flailing around, timidly trying to hold the squirming chicken's legs. "Right, hold tight and pull toward you."

As he did so, I pulled down sharply on the chicken's head until I felt a soft snap and the bird went limp. Its wings flapped for a bit and then stopped. The whole thing was over in seconds.

"Is . . . is it dead?" Jack had turned pale and was shaking a little. *Heaven help him if he ever goes into battle,* I thought.

"I hope so," I said. "Because we are going to eat it."

Mam stepped forward and took the dead bird from me, placing it in Jack's upturned helmet.

"No, Alfie. This is for Jack. Take it home to your mam, love. Come back in a month for another one, eh? But, erm . . . do not worry yourself any more about those mix-ups, eh? It happens all the time. I am certain a WRC has got far more important things to worry about." She brushed a chicken feather off Jack's shoulder and patted him on the chest.

And so Jack cycled off, his upturned tin helmet slung over his arm like a shopping basket, containing the dead chicken.

"It is war, Alve," said Mam, shaking her head when he had gone. "It does the strangest things to people. You would think we had enough trouble fighting Hitler."

For the next six months, Jack came back. He would always let himself in the backyard, and once Mam found him in our house, looking at our bookshelves. It was only years later that we discovered one of our signed Dickens novels was gone—*A Tale of Two Cities*. We always thought Jack might have taken it, but there was no way of knowing.

"He's prowling," said Mam. "He's looking for something." Each time, we gave him a chicken, until we had only three left.

Then he stopped coming and Mam heard he had been called up to serve in the air force and had been sent for training to Scotland.

We did not see Jack for many years.

But then I met his son.

CHAPTER TWENTY-FIVE

It was 1962, and the memory of the war that had killed so many people and caused so much misery worldwide was beginning to fade.

It had been more than twenty years since I had last spoken to Jack McGonagal. The shop in Eastbourne Gardens had changed hands and Mrs. McGonagal had—according to Mam—moved to the country. And then I saw Jack on the beach.

It was a day in early summer, and back then, before foreign holidays were affordable, the beach at Whitley would get packed with day-trippers, and holidaymakers from the shipyards in Scotland.

Mam loved a crowded beach. It was a thirty-minute walk along the wooded path and then down the main road until we got to the coast road, with the lighthouse at one end and barely enough space on the sand for our blanket. Mam had made herself a short-sleeved blouse, and only that morning had finished a pair of shorts for me, in rust-colored corduroy with deep pockets.

We sat on the beach in our sunglasses and blended in perfectly: "Hidden in plain sight," was what Mam said.

I read my latest library book, and we ate sandwiches, and we went for a paddle in the sea, and Mam laughed when I splashed her. Then a man approached me as I was coming out of the shallow water.

"Hiya, son—we're short of a goalie. You want to go in goal?" He looked a friendly sort. His trousers were rolled up to his knees, and he indicated a patch of the beach farther up, where there were fewer people, and a gang of boys and a couple of dads were marking out a small soccer pitch in the sand.

Mam started to answer, "Oh, I do not think . . ."

"Yes!" I said, and, before Mam could argue, I was following the man toward the group. I told him my name and he told the others: "This is Alfie."

They all nodded and said, "How's it goin', Alfie?"

The game was fast and rough. Our team ("shirts") kept our shirts on, the others ("skins") played bare-chested. Boys were tumbling into the soft sand everywhere, mainly because of the speed and power of the biggest boy playing for the skins: a wiry, muscled lad of about twelve who hacked and stamped his way toward me as I tried to defend the goal. Shot after shot went past me.

One of the dads was making a feeble effort to referee, but the most I heard him say was, "Oh, come on now, John! That's not very sportsmanlike, is it?" after John had elbowed the smallest member of the shirts in the throat. He awarded a free kick, but John just ignored him and carried on playing.

Then he was coming at me again, the ball at his feet, and I became determined not to let in another goal.

What is the worst that could happen? I thought in the seconds before I dived at his feet. *I might get kicked a little but I could be a hero.*

And so it was that as John slowed slightly in preparation for shooting at the goal, I leaped forward, head down, and grabbed the ball from beneath his feet. I did not see him tumble over me, but I heard the thump as he hit the sand and the howl of pain that followed seconds later.

"Foul!" boys were shouting.

Others were saying, "Not a foul! He got the ball!" but as I got to my feet and turned round, John's face was next to mine, red and furious.

"You broke my bloody wrist," he screamed, waving his hand in such a way that it showed it was definitely *not* broken. Then he cleared his throat with a long rasp and spat a large glob of throaty spittle right in my face.

The dad referee was running up to us. "Hey, hey—that's quite enough of that, John McGonagal. Where's your dad?"

And there he was, standing on the sandy touchline: Jack

McGonagal, staring first at me, then at his son, and then back at me. He had hardly changed in the intervening twenty years. He was still lean, his shock of black hair unmarked by gray.

Our eyes locked for a second, and he stepped onto the sandy pitch, but I was already edging away.

John's voice followed me. "You're dead, whoever you are. I'm gonna find you and pulverize you."

Then I heard Jack call, "Alfie?"

But I had already turned and run. Back into the crowds of sunbathers, back to the safety of Mam. The day had been spoiled. Soon after, the clouds gathered, which gave me an excuse to suggest to Mam that we head back home, without telling her of my encounter with Jack and John McGonagal. She would only worry.

With good reason, as it turned out. John was already at the bend of our lane as we walked back.

CHAPTER TWENTY-SIX

There were two older boys with him, the three of them lounging on an uprooted tree trunk by the side of the path.

You do not live as long as I have without sensing big trouble when it is sitting on a tree trunk thirty feet in front of you.

Big trouble, for example, does not care if there is an adult present. I spotted that in John McGonagal when he simply ignored the referee during the game on the beach. The way he swore loudly, not caring if other people heard him.

And now the fact that Mam was with me was not going to stand in the way of his giving me a beating. He simply did not care.

"Call the police, Mam," I murmured.

"The police?" she gasped. "Who are those boys?"

"They're trouble, Mam. Go on."

She turned and headed back up the lane. There was a public phone box on the main road.

Avoiding officials had been an important part of lying low for so long. As soon as I had instructed Mam to call the police, I regretted it. I should take the beating and be done with it—no one need interfere in our lives.

In a thousand years, I had never gone looking for a fight. But if someone brought one to me?

Boys now are not taught how to fight. That is probably a good thing. If people do not know how to fight, then perhaps they do it less, and that too is probably a good thing.

Me? I was taught. I have been taught fighting skills many times.

I had learned the use of a short wooden staff from a prize-fighter from Aragon who would tell me it was "the noblest of all weapons" for it was "without deceit."

His voice came back to me over the centuries as the boys in front slowly got to their feet.

"Yer mammy run off, has she?" said the biggest boy, who I guessed was about fifteen.

"She's gone to call the police," I said, and they all chuckled.

"Don't fret yerself. This'll all be done long before they get here!"

They advanced, menacingly slowly, with John between them. I stood my ground until they were about four yards away.

"What's up, soft lad? Ye just gonna stand there, are ye?"

John took another step forward, and that was when I moved.

I dipped into a crouch, grabbing a handful of the fine gravel from the path in my right fist and throwing it straight at his face, hard.

I am a good shot, if I say so myself. Rafel the prizefighter had made us practice this again and again. The gravel hit its target and John let out a yell as the grit went into his eyes.

The other two goons were distracted and before I got to my feet I grabbed a thick branch that was much less straight than I would have preferred, but at least it was the right length and weight: about four feet long, and heavy enough to take a small amount of effort to lift.

"No effort for you, no pain for him," said Rafel in my head.

With both arms, I swung it at the boy on John's right, and there was a satisfying crack as it made contact with the side of his knee. He shouted with pain and staggered backward.

"Knees first, slows him down!"

John was still rubbing his eyes, so with one end of the branch I jabbed him hard in the stomach. He did not see it coming, and doubled up with a wheeze and a squeak of pain.

By now, the goon on John's left had advanced to my right side and made contact with a well-aimed kick to my shin that hurt like heck, and he dodged the branch when I swung it at him. He was going to be trouble.

"In multiple combats, target the strongest first, when you have most stren'th. . . ."

The boy advanced again, but this time I had the club ready,

the weight steady in both of my fists. I raised it up, faking a blow, and as his hands came up to defend himself I changed direction and swung at him hard, thumping the side of his chest with a blow that knocked all the air from his lungs.

"*Now finish the job, Alfie!*" said Rafel.

There was a natural momentum for the branch to swing back, and I raised it slightly, adding my strength and smashing the wood into the side of his head, knocking him out cold. He slumped to the ground, tongue lolling.

There was no time to admire my work, for John and his other pal were both coming at me. His friend lifted his fist for a blow, and I blocked it with the branch, then kicked him in the stomach, sending him flying backward into a patch of nettles. He squealed as he landed.

That left one: John, much bigger than me and with a vicious look in his eyes. By now, though, I could tell my branch—old and dry—was weakening. I had heard it crack before, and when I swung it next at his thigh, he dodged, and as it made contact, the stick broke in my hands. I threw the pieces at him, missed, and he guffawed.

"Nice one, weirdo. Let's see how you like it." Without taking his eyes off me, he crouched and picked up one of the pieces, advancing toward me. I would be powerless against it, and raised my forearms defensively as he lifted the stick high above his head.

At that instant, I saw a black-and-white blur, and heard an inhuman, high-pitched growl, followed by a scream from John.

"Aaagh, get it off! Oww! Aaaagh!" He dropped the piece of stick, scrabbling with his hands as Biffa's claws dug deep into his skull. She mewled and growled and scratched while John McGonagal hopped about, flailing his arms and yelling in pain. Eventually he dislodged Biffa from his head, and she stood in front of him, back arched, hissing and spitting like a boiling kettle.

"You're crazy, you are! Weirdo! A psycho!" John yelled at me as he backed away up the lane.

"Go on, then," I said, pointing at his friend who was now a safe distance away. "Are you going to join him? Get lost, all of you. I do not like rubbish littering my path."

John helped his other friend to his feet and they both staggered off.

"Nice work, Biff," I murmured, but she was not listening. She took a few paces toward the retreating boys and they ran.

I felt good. Really I did. But I knew that would not be the end of it. Not by a long way.

"*In the real world, Alfie, you gotta kill 'em. Otherwise they come back for more.*"

Rafel lived in the seventeenth century. It was a different world then.

CHAPTER TWENTY-SEVEN

The police came the next day, a Monday, "investigating an assault on three minors."

I say "police." It was a policeman on a bicycle, a young one. (The uniform had changed slightly, but he still reminded me of Jack in his WRC tunic during the war.) Mam and I had sort of known the previous one, a portly, incurious man with the unlikely name of PC Sargent, who accepted Mam's assurance that I was visiting from Hexham and had a growth disorder. He simply was not interested so long as we caused no trouble, and we did not.

This one, PC Armitage, asked too many questions, and looked far too interested in everything. We sat in the backyard: me, Mam, and him. Amy the goat (who had replaced the previous Amy) bleated and the chickens pecked around. The policeman looked uncomfortable: a townie. He even flinched when Biffa brushed against his leg. He took his pointed helmet off to reveal his shiny, bald head. He was only about twenty-five.

"How old are you, son?" He was writing everything down in a little notebook.

"What's your date of birth?"

"Where do you go to school?"

"How long have you been here?"

"Tell me what happened yesterday."

I told him the lies I had practiced. I was fourteen, I said. I had left school. Back then, you could leave school at that age.

"You're a little lad for fourteen, aren't you?" he said.

I shrugged.

"And the fight? What happened?"

I told him the truth.

"So, it was you against them three, was it?"

I nodded. I did not mention Biffa.

I think the man even looked a little bit impressed. "You know one of them went to the hospital? Fractured knee."

I shrugged again.

There was not a great deal more he could ask, but I could tell he was not satisfied. It was the way he kept looking round the yard, looking at me, looking at Mam, as if saying to himself, *There's more to this than meets the eye.*

Trust me: I have lived long enough to recognize that look when I see it. Mam had seen it too. It always means that more questions will follow.

Some official, somewhere, will decide that "something's not quite right" and start finding reasons to pry. When that happens, we normally find that it is useful to move away for a while.

And so it was. A week later, Mam was questioned by a woman from the Local Education Authority while I hid upstairs. Then the policeman came back with another officer, and someone from the local council's social services department.

Which was why, six weeks later, if anyone had come to check up on my age, or schooling, or anything else, they would have found the old cottage securely locked up, its windows boarded over, and it would remain like that for almost thirty years.

Then we came back, and things were fine. Honestly they were; they were really fine. A new housing estate had been built on the other side of the woods toward the golf course. Whitley Bay was quieter in the summer, because people started to go to Spain instead, but there were lots more people generally, and they all, it seemed, had a motor car, but still—no one really bothered us, apart from the little nosy girl, and that was not what you would call "bother."

And *then* . . . the fire happened, and I discovered, for the first time ever, what it was to be totally alone.

CHAPTER TWENTY-EIGHT

AIDAN

The boy from the secret house in the woods looked at us with huge eyes, pale and terrified. The desk that I had tipped over lay on its side between us.

"I . . . I'm sorry. I was greatly in need of somewhere to shelter," he said. "The . . . the fire." He started breathing quickly, and blinking hard, as if just saying "fire" had a bad effect on him.

I stood next to Roxy, looking down at this filthy, soot-streaked creature, soaking wet and shivering. He knelt next to the overturned desk, one arm clutching the other, staring up at us, eyes flicking left and right, blinking repeatedly, his mouth moving with half-formed words and a sheen of snot covering his upper lip. I don't think I've ever seen a figure so pitiable.

Roxy spoke first. "It's OK. We're not gonna hurt you."

The words hung in the air as he continued to stare. From time to time, tiny moans escaped his lips.

"Me . . . mam . . . me . . . mam . . . ," he started again, panting between every syllable.

Roxy got down on her haunches to be level with him, and I followed suit. She reached out and touched him gently on the shoulder, lowering her head to look at his face.

"Al-vuh?" she said, and he gave a little gasp and a nod. My head spun round to look at Roxy. "Is that your name? Al-vuh?"

He nodded again. "Me . . . my old name. A-L-V-E. I usually, erm . . . Alfie. Alfie is good."

"Come on, Alfie. Come and sit down." Roxy spoke with such gentleness and such calm, never taking her eyes off his, watching his every movement.

Slowly he rose to his feet, still clutching one arm against his chest. He stumbled over to the vinyl-covered sofa and lowered himself onto it. Roxy sat next to him and turned her body to look at him while I straightened the desk and sat on that.

"Can I see your arm?" Roxy asked as she carefully lifted his hand out of the way. "Does it hurt?"

It looked like it was agony. His right sleeve was ripped, revealing a burnt forearm: deep red welts from the elbow to the wrist, with some skin peeling away. Roxy and I both sucked air through our teeth.

"You need a doctor, mate," I said. I hadn't said it harshly, but it was the first thing I'd said to him, and it was the wrong thing. He glared at me.

"No. Definitely not. Under no circumstances."

I got what he said. It was emphatic enough. But those words: "under no circumstances." It struck me as an unusual thing for a kid to say. He looked about our age.

"But, Alfie," said Roxy (using his name: *Clever,* I thought), "it's really badly burnt. It could get . . . I don't know. Infected or something."

"See? You do not really know, do you?" There was an edge to his voice, but he wasn't really aggressive. Just sure of himself. "No doctor." He sank a bit lower into the sofa and the weary look returned to his face. "Just . . . leave me be, yes? I will be fine. No word to anyone. I will be fine."

No, he wouldn't. It was obvious that this was the "I will be fine" of someone who would be anything but.

"What happened, Alve? Alfie? In the fire?" I thought it would be a good idea to get him talking, but a firm shake of the head from Roxy set me straight on *that.*

"Listen to me, Alfie," she said. "The first thing you need to do is to get clean and warm. You're shivering. We'll clean this wound for a start. Then we can dress it. It may be OK." She was looking at it carefully, touching the edges with the tips of her fingers. "Does it hurt there?" she asked once, and he winced in reply. She turned to me. "Is your dad in, Aidan?" she asked.

"NO!" said Alfie. His ash-streaked face filled with fear, and his eyes darted to the door as he made a move to get up.

"It's OK, Alfie. Sit down. You can trust us. We won't tell anyone you're here if you don't want us to." She turned to me. "You're gonna have to sneak in somehow. Stand next to Aidan, Alfie." So authoritative was Roxy's manner that he stood up next to me on her command. "Hmm. Have you any clothes that are too small for you, Aidan? You know, stuff you've grown out of?"

"No. We gave them all away before the move."

"What about your sister?"

Libby was about the same height as this weird, filthy boy standing between us.

"I'll see what I can find. It might be pink, though."

If Alve—Alfie—minded, his face didn't show it. His face hardly showed anything, really. He settled back into the sofa next to Roxy, and started trembling again, lips flapping. This was going to be tough.

Roxy got to her feet and flicked her eyes to the door. I followed her out.

Once outside, we picked our way through the mud for a few meters.

"Classic signs," said Roxy. "PTSD."

"What?"

"Post-traumatic stress disorder. He's seen his house burn down, maybe seen his mum die in the fire: it's a lot to process, hence the . . . you know."

"Odd behavior."

"Well, yeah. He needs help but he needs to trust us first. He'll run off given half a chance."

"And you know all this how?" I said. It sounded snarky, but I was properly impressed.

She shrugged. "I read a lot. Now, you go and get some clean clothes. Bring them round the front and I'll meet you at the door. My mum's in her den, working. She'll have her headphones on, probably."

"I hope so." I hadn't forgotten her fierce mum from last night.

Roxy gave me a withering look. "She's fine, my mum. She's just . . ."

"Scary?"

"Angry."

"Angry and scary."

"Whatever. You'll have to help him get clean. You know, in and out of the bath and stuff. Dry him."

"Me?" I meant to say it normally, but it came out as a squeak.

The withering look returned. "Yes, you. What with you being a boy. I don't think he'd be thrilled being butt-naked in front of me."

I decided there and then that if ever I was in a crisis, I'd want eleven-year-old Roxy Minto in charge.

Which, considering what was to come, was a wise decision.

CHAPTER TWENTY-NINE

Less than an hour later, we were back in the garage, and I had discovered several things.

1. Dad's patience was running low. I knew I'd been shirking the household jobs. I tried sneaking in the back door and up to Libby's room without him hearing, but he was sorting out paintbrushes downstairs and called me. "Where the heck have you been, sunshine?" He only ever calls me "sunshine" when he's annoyed. "I need some help: we have to get this place organized." I promised I'd help him later and scooted off. Pressed for time, I hadn't had a great deal of choice over clothes for Alfie.

2. Roxy's mum lived in the front room because she couldn't get upstairs easily. I'd have to ask Roxy what was wrong with her mum another time. (Is that what you say? "What's wrong?" Or is it something else, like

"What is the nature of her disability?" Who knows? I got the impression that it wouldn't take much to set her mum off.)

3. Alfie was a boy. That is, not an adolescent yet. (You can tell these things when someone is naked and being helped in and out of the bath.) I'd guess he was about my age, so I asked him, "How old are you, mate?" but he didn't answer. In fact he didn't say a single word all the way through the bath, while I washed his hair and he kept his arm out of the water.

4. His other arm had two small scars on the biceps, each about five centimeters long, like an equals sign. I didn't ask him about it.

5. He had a tattoo. I know! Eleven years old and a tattoo. It was on his back between his shoulder blades. It was a square cross, quite blurred, and big—with a pattern on it that was hard to make out. It looked like one that Grandad Linklater had done when he was in the navy years ago—all smudged and faded.

After he came out of the bath, I helped him dry himself and get dressed. I'd given him a pair of my underpants. They were too big, but it was better than him wearing Libby's. Her jeans fitted him OK, except they had sparkly sequins in a line down the side of each leg. He didn't say anything. The T-shirt was plain black, and what I'd thought was a sweater turned out to be a cardigan in pale blue and white, but he couldn't put it on yet because of his arm. A pair of Libby's striped rain boots completed a look that was—by anyone's standards—completely bizarre.

If Alfie minded, he didn't show it.

Back in the garage, Roxy had acquired bandages, and the gauze stuff that goes under them, some cream in a tube, cotton balls, and a bowl of water. Like the world's gentlest nurse, she bathed Alfie's burnt arm and smoothed the cream on it, pausing when he sucked his lips with the pain, then wrapped the bandage round, not too tight, securing it with a safety pin.

She had brought some apples. Alfie ate three, one after the other: core, seeds, everything.

When it was all done, he whispered, "Thank you," and then—out of nowhere—he started crying. Great heaving sobs that shook his body. All Roxy and I could do was sit next to him.

Roxy put her arm round him and said, "Shhh," like a mother would, and stroked his hair.

On and on it went, like a summer storm that eases for a few minutes, then comes back again, even more intense. In the end, Roxy was crying too, and I thought for a moment it was all going to set me off as well.

Eventually, though, the sobbing stopped, and he flopped back, exhausted, on the sofa. His mouth dropped open and his head shook slightly from side to side. And then that stopped and he was quiet.

His eyes were still closed when I said, "Do you want to come inside, Alfie? Meet my dad? We can make up a bed for you."

He opened his eyes but didn't move his head. I had said the wrong thing again.

"If you tell anyone that I am here—*anyone*—you'll regret it."

Then he closed his eyes. You would almost have thought he was sleeping—except that the tears kept coming, for a long time.

Part Two

CHAPTER THIRTY

"Quickly," said Roxy when we were out of the garage. "What's your cell number?"

She gave me this wide-eyed look of disbelief when I told her I didn't have a phone. Honestly, if I'd said I had a pet crocodile, she couldn't have looked more horrified. I didn't tell her about our money problems, about how my dad said we didn't need another monthly bill in the house. Instead I gave her our landline number.

"I'll call you," I said. "It'll be better that way."

"And remember—not a word to anyone."

"Are you sure that's right? I mean . . ."

"You heard what he said. Let's do what he asked, at least for the moment. Otherwise it might make him worse. I don't want to take that risk, do you?"

I nodded, perhaps a bit reluctantly, but it was a nod nonetheless.

I'll spare you the telling-off I got from Dad. *Lazy, selfish shirker* more or less sums it up. Aunty Alice and Uncle Jasper were out on

Jasper's boat, so it meant the rest of the afternoon was spent help-ing Dad paint Libby's bedroom walls mauve, unloading the final boxes, moving furniture around, wiping surfaces, and vacuuming so that when Mum got back at about seven from the call center the place would be shipshape, with a casserole in the oven and Dad in a good mood again.

With all the unpacking, I had found a bag of my too-smalls that hadn't made its way to the charity shop and a woolen blanket I'd never seen before that I figured wouldn't be missed. I stashed them under my bed for later.

In fact Dad's mood was good enough that—despite my promise to Roxy—I decided to tell him about Alfie.

I know. But think about it: Alfie was injured, distressed, home-less; his mum had died and as a result he was probably not even thinking straight. To heck with promises: he needed help from an adult.

I'd even worked out how I was going to say it, and probably even taken the breath that would form the words, when I heard Mum's key in the door. It would have to wait for now.

Except Dad's good mood didn't last. Mum hadn't been back ten minutes and already they were hissing at each other, and I don't even know what started it off. I heard her say, "I can do without this, Ben, after ten hours of being sworn at by idiots. . . ."

All I knew was that I didn't want to be around and there was no way I would raise the matter of Alfie right now.

"I'm just popping next door," I said, sticking my head into the living room, where Dad was leaning against the mantelpiece, head bowed, a pile of opened mail in front of him.

Bills: I could tell that much.

I'm not sure they even heard me.

CHAPTER THIRTY-ONE

Standing on Roxy's front step, I was about to ring her doorbell when I heard singing from inside: a high, wobbly voice belting out a loud hymn that I recognized from school assembly, only it was sung in a strong West Indian accent.

> *"Thine be tha gloree, risen conquerin' son!*
> *Endless is tha vict'ry thou o'er deat' has won!"*

Then there was a crash—something smashing—and a "NO!" followed by what sounded like some dialect swearing that I didn't understand. I didn't know what to do, and I stood there, hesitating, my finger hovering over the bell, when the door opened suddenly and Roxy was there, looking up at me.

"I saw you coming," she said, pointing to a tiny camera above the door.

"Sorry, I just heard . . . that is, I mean . . ."

"Oh, Mum? Yeah, she just dropped something. It gets to her.

Come on in." She about-turned and trotted back through her hall-way, calling, "Don't worry, Mum, I'll clear it up."

At the end of the hall, her mum put her head round the door-way. She was supporting herself on crutches, and she looked so dif-ferent from the first time I'd seen her. She wasn't tall, but she was heavy for her height, with bulges of fat under her clothes, and huge, dimpled upper arms. Her hair was shorter than Roxy's—a cropped Afro with a purple streak in it, matching her large, round earrings.

Her eyes, though, were exhausted. Somehow she managed to look like every picture I had ever seen of someone who is "bravely battling" a serious illness. She smiled, showing perfect teeth. It was a tired smile and forced, as if the effort of lifting the corners of her mouth drained her.

It was the same shape as Roxy's hundred-watt grin, but with none of the brilliance.

"Hello, love. You mus' be Aidan. Roxy's told me *all* about you."

"Has she? I mean . . . erm, hello, Mrs., erm . . ."

"Call me Precious, darlin'." Sorry, are you wantin' to get past? It's these damn crutches. . . ." She pressed herself against the wall as I went into their kitchen.

I wondered if she would say anything about her odd behavior last night. To my relief, she said nothing more.

Roxy was dumping the remains of a broken plate into the gar-bage. I watched Roxy's mum as she moved awkwardly round the corner, banging the kitchen door behind her by using her crutch.

"She seems"—and I hesitated fatally—"nice."

Pathetic, Aidan.

Roxy gave her little yap of laughter. "Ha! Nice? Good try, Aidan. You're such a bad liar!"

"No, I just meant . . ."

Roxy smiled, a bit sadly I thought. "It's OK. She's hard work. But she *is* nice. Underneath it all."

"What, erm . . . I mean, what is . . . how . . . the nature . . . erm . . ." Roxy let me squirm for a bit just—I think—for her own amusement. Finally she said:

"Diabetes, mainly. Plus chronic fatigue syndrome, and probably something else that hasn't been diagnosed yet. The drugs she takes for one react badly with the insulin and cause her to gain weight, which affects the diabetes and in turn causes mood swings, so she takes another medicine, and that affects the CFS." She rattled this off as if she had practiced it, and then she paused before answering the question that I was forming in my mouth. "No. There is no cure. Well, not one that's certain or that we could afford. And she's furious."

"Because there's no cure?"

"Because there's no cure, because she got it, because she can't move about, because some days she can't get out of bed, because she has to rely on me, because my dad left, because she can't get upstairs, because she has to use a wheelchair, just . . . everything, really."

Roxy had delivered this little speech leaning against the kitchen counter with her arms folded in front of her. Despite her size, she suddenly looked about forty years old, just for a couple of seconds, and her perma-smile had disappeared. I got to see exactly what she'd look like as an adult, and that was strange.

"She's got quite a singing voice," I said, and Roxy smiled.

"Yeah. If she's in a good mood, she sings."

"And the accent?" I asked.

The smile became wider. "She learned all of the hymns from my gran, who was from Trinidad. That was the first time she's sung in ages, and then she dropped the plate, so . . ." She shrugged.

"Have you been to see him?" I asked, jerking my head in the direction of the garage. Roxy shook her head.

"I had to help Mum. I've got some food ready." She indicated a Tupperware box on the counter.

"Let's go, then."

"No, Aidan. I have to show you something first. I said I had proof, remember?" She sat at the kitchen table and opened her laptop. What I saw in the next twenty minutes was to change all our lives.

CHAPTER THIRTY-TWO

"What, like you have an allergy to genies? You rub a lamp, out pops a genie, and you get a rash?"

"Sounds like it, doesn't it?" said Roxy. "But the word is *genealogy*. It's tracing your ancestors, basically. Like when they do it on TV for celebrities."

I shrugged. I took her word for it. I was still thinking of a genie allergy.

"It's what Mum does, now she can't go out to work. She creates people's family trees. Look."

She opened a web page called "Ancestral Connections" and there was a picture of Precious Minto at a desk, looking friendly, and the usual tabs labeled *About Us, Pricing, Contact,* and so on.

"Now look at this," Roxy said, clicking and typing as she spoke.

The web page she was indicating was headlined "England: Register of Births and Deaths." There was another called "British Land Registry" and a "Northumberland Directory," and as Roxy opened the pages, and zoomed in, and clicked on links, and scrolled through charts and blogs, it was as if, temporarily, she was in a little world of her own.

She hadn't said a word for about three minutes, and I was left feeling a bit awkward. It was like reading over someone's shoulder, except the book was in a foreign language. Then she stopped, flicked her eyes to the kitchen door, and said, "By the way, my mum doesn't know I've copied all her programs and memberships. She's not even authorized to see some of the sites, so if she asks . . . you know."

I nodded.

Eventually she said, "Hang on, hang on . . . here it is."

The website was called "Photographic History" and there was a grainy black-and-white photo of a lady and a boy standing in front of a stone cottage. Her long dress reached the ground, and there was an apron over it. The boy wore long trousers and a collarless shirt.

"That's it," said Roxy. "That's the house that burned down. Look at the caption."

Sure enough, the caption read *Oak Cottage, near Whitley, Northumberland, around 1870.*

I nodded. "So?"

"*So?* So look at the people in the picture."

"It's too blurry, Roxy. You can't see anything apart from, well . . ."

"They're wearing sunglasses?"

That *was* unusual, I have to admit. I couldn't recall ever seeing pictures of Victorian people wearing sunglasses.

"Were sunglasses a Victorian thing?"

"Exactly! No, they weren't!"

"They didn't exist?"

"Well, they weren't popular until the 1920s. They did *exist*. I've looked it up. People wore them for eye injuries and stuff."

I looked again at the photo. "Sorry, Roxy. What are you getting at?"

"Can't you see?" Her voice was rising with exasperation. "It's them!"

She expanded the web page as large as it would go, but it didn't really help: the details were still too indistinct. I didn't want to upset Roxy, so I said, "Hmm. I suppose they do look a bit alike."

"A bit? Exactly, more like." She hit some more keys and brought up a site called "UK Census Online." "See, the census is a record of everyone who lived in Britain in 1861." Some of the pages were in normal print; others were scans of old documents with entries in old-fashioned, curly handwriting.

"Wow!" I said, impressed. "Everyone?"

"Yes, everyone! And if we go . . . here"—she clicked on the tracker pad—"you'll see that living at Oak Cottage, Northumberland, in 1861 was . . ."

Monk, Hilda—widow—age 33—
occupation, seamstress—spouse, unknown

Monk, Alfred—child, male—age 11

Roxy's enthusiasm was written all over her face as her fingers skipped across the keys. I felt guilty for not being more excited.

"And *here*," she was saying, "is the census for 1911: fifty years later." I peered at the screen.

Monk, Hilda S.—widow—age 34—
occupation, dressmaker—spouse, deceased

Monk, Alfred—child (M)—age 11

"It's almost the same," I remarked. "But who are these people? I mean, Alfred, Alfie—it's a pretty common name, especially back then."

"It gets better. Look at the Office for National Statistics site. It has the most recent census: only seven years ago."

Monk, Hilda S.—widow—age 33—
occupation, costumier—spouse, unknown

Monk, Alfred—child (M)—age 11

"What about further back? When was the first census?" I asked.

Her fingers were a blur now, and she didn't answer me for ages.

"Roxy?"

"The first census . . . hang on . . . the first census was in 1801, and there's no mention of Oak Cottage, but look here."

She had brought up another website. "This one is searchable by name as well, and the good thing is their name is not all that common." She typed in "Monk" and a list of entries scrolled down on the screen, but before I could scan it, Roxy was typing again. "They're not there. But look what happens if I spell the name slightly differently."

She typed in "Munk," and half a page of results appeared. Roxy pointed at one.

Munk, Mrs. H S widow, Hexham, N'th'berland

Munk, Mstr. A (11), Hexham, N'th'berland

"Don't you see? 'Monk' with an 'o,' 'Munk' with a 'u,' Hilda, Alfred? *It's the same people!*"

It was hard not to be caught up in Roxy's enthusiasm, so I played along.

"So this proves, you reckon, that until last night they'd been living there—at any rate on and off—since the 1860s, so that makes her, at least, a witch?" It was hard to keep the doubt out of my voice.

Roxy's eyes shone with wonder and she grinned. "Don't you think that's *unbelievable*?"

That was definitely the word. I didn't believe any of it.

"Come on," I said, getting up. "There's a way we can test your theory. We can just ask him."

As we made our way down her back garden, I was still curious about this genealogy thing.

"So . . . people pay money to find out who their ancestors were?"

"Yep."

"Why?"

"*Why?* Don't you want to know who yours are?"

I thought about it for several seconds. "Not really. What difference does it make?"

"Would you be surprised to find out you were a descendant of Charlemagne?"

We had just done the Holy Roman Empire in school. Charlemagne was an emperor who ruled Europe in the ninth century. "I guess so. How would you know?"

"Because just about *everyone* is! Every white European, at any rate, apart from recent immigrants."

"But . . . but how?"

"I'll tell you later. Shhh!"

I shushed. We were just the other side of the fence, and I heard the door of Roxy's garage bang shut and footsteps heading into the woods.

"Come on," whispered Roxy. "Let's follow him."

CHAPTER THIRTY-THREE

We smelled it before we got there. Burnt wood, burnt leaves, all of it wet. By the time we were in sight of the ruined cottage, Roxy and I were soaked through from the still-dripping trees.

It was twilight. Between the branches of the trees, the sky was a milky royal blue with one or two early-evening stars, but no moon yet. Down by our feet it was black-dark. Here and there, huge chunks of the forest were burned away, allowing in more light, but everything was bleak and black, sorrowful and silent. Roxy used the light on her phone to show the path, but it made everything not in its beam even blacker in contrast.

Plastic tape saying POLICE LINE DO NOT ENTER was stretched round sections of the burnt-out forest. I hesitated but Roxy didn't; we ducked under it and went in anyway.

Then we heard him.

"Biff-a! Biff-a! *Komm, komm,* Biff-a!"

"What the heck's that about?" I whispered to Roxy, but she shrugged.

We approached as quietly as we could, trying not to snap twigs under our feet. I think we both saw him at the same time, sitting on the circular stone fireplace and staring at the charred ruins of his home, the dusk light making his blond hair look white.

"*Biii*-fa! *Biii*-fa!"

Have you ever seen a burnt-out house? It's pretty scary. This one still had the basic outline of a house: most of the blackened walls were still standing, and part of the upstairs, although the upper part was mostly destroyed, the floorboards hanging down into the lower rooms.

Some things, oddly, seemed untouched. Although black with soot, the big kitchen table stood solidly, bearing the weight of some metal boxes. A stone kitchen sink seemed undamaged. In one small room, a wall of bookshelves held some charred books, and loose pages drifted on the floor in the breeze, while, above, the beams of the roof stuck into the sky like a grim house-skeleton.

Other than that, though, the destruction was more or less total.

"I know you are there," Alfie said, and Roxy and I both gasped. He had not turned round. We said nothing, but stood up from our crouched position.

"You would make poor spies," he said as we approached him by the stone fireplace. "I heard you long ago."

"We . . . we didn't mean to *spy* on you . . . ," Roxy began, but he cut her off.

"It is all right. I do not mind. You are curious. It is not surprising." His tone was flat. He had not met our eyes, but remained stony-faced, staring ahead at the ruins of his home.

"I'm sorry, Alfie," I said. "About what happened. And . . . and your mum, an' that."

"Me too," said Roxy.

Something changed then. I still don't know if it was what we said, or the moment we said it, or neither, or both, but I can look back now and know that *that* was the moment our adventure started.

It was as if Alfie was making an effort to drag his eyes away from the black stumps. He took a deep breath and looked straight at us.

"Thank you."

It was a connection, a bond formed between us.

"If there's anything we can do, you know . . . to help, or, you know . . ." I trailed off. I had no idea what I was saying, really: it was just the sort of thing I had heard grown-ups say to each other.

"Do you mean that?" he asked.

Well, what could I say? *"No, not really, I was just being insincere"*? It's not that I didn't want to help, it was just that I couldn't think of a single thing I could do that would be any good in this situation.

So I said, "Absolutely," and nodded firmly.

Roxy added, "Yup!" and gave a bigger nod.

Alfie nodded back and said simply, "Good. There may be something I need help with." He got down wearily from the stone fireplace and started to walk toward the shell of the house. Then he turned back to us.

"I need to know I can trust you."

"You can trust us, Alfie," said Roxy.

I wanted to add, *"It kind of depends on what you want us to do,"* but the words dried in my throat, so I just said, "Yep."

CHAPTER THIRTY-FOUR

Alfie stepped over some charred wooden beams that had fallen to the floor.

"Erm . . . Alfie? I'm not sure that's safe in there, mate. I mean . . . ," I said, but he stopped me with a look that said, *This is my house, not yours.*

We followed him into the burnt ruin, picking our feet through the ashes on the ground, and keeping a wary eye on the beams above us. Alfie stopped by the bookcases. Close up, the damage was even more obvious. Literally hundreds of books had been destroyed; nothing was undamaged. Any pages that were not burned to nothing were covered in a film of greasy soot.

From what I could see, these were all old books, with hard, plain covers—not like the ones with illustrations and bright jackets that I had. I picked one up that seemed less damaged and flicked it open, peering at the page in the dim light. I couldn't read a word.

"What's this?" I asked.

Alfie came closer and glanced at it. "That's *Confessions* by Augustine of Hippo."

"Who's Christine the Hippo?"

"*Of* Hippo. It is a place, or was, anyway. In North Africa. Augustine is Saint Augustine, you know?" His tone suggested that he really expected me to know who Saint Augustine was.

"Never heard of her. What language is it?"

Alfie squinted at me and said in a quizzical tone, "It is a 'he,' not a 'she,' and the language is Latin." He didn't need to add "obviously," because it was in his voice.

"What's it about?"

Alfie took it from me with his good hand and fingered the sooty pages sadly. "It is probably the world's first autobiography. It is a bit heavy-going in places, by modern standards, but rather compelling nonetheless."

Rather compelling nonetheless. Who speaks like that? I said to myself. Out loud I said, "You've *read* it?"

Alfie nodded.

"In *Latin*?" I squeaked. He nodded again, a bit shyly.

Roxy was next to us by now. "Hey! Mr. Brainbox! Go on: read some out!"

Reluctantly, I thought, Alfie began reading aloud as Roxy shone the light from her phone on the page. I didn't understand a word but Roxy was wide-eyed.

"Wow!" was all she said when he faltered to a stop. "Do some more!" But Alfie placed the book back on the shelf.

"These were all mine," he said. "Mine and Mam's."

I left him alone for a moment while I checked out the yard. The chicken coop in the corner was destroyed, and several burnt chickens with blackened feathers lay among the ashes.

"I think your goat escaped," I called to Alfie, but he didn't reply, and I immediately hoped he hadn't heard. It sounded as though I was saying, *"Ah, well, look on the bright side,"* when there really wasn't much of a bright side at all.

Roxy had wandered off to the corner of the room we were in. "What's in here?" she said, kicking charred bits of wood off the top of a thick metal trunk.

Alfie said something I didn't understand under his breath and knelt down next to the trunk. There was a hinged metal closure on the lid with holes for a padlock, but no lock. He opened the lid.

"Hmm. More books!" said Roxy. "They look OK—I mean, unburnt."

Alfie closed the lid again and stood up, facing us. For the first time, I could detect slightly less sad emptiness on his face. There was something in his eyes that might have been hope.

"We have to take these. Take them away from here."

I lifted one end of the trunk by the handle. It was heavy. "You're kidding, Alfie. I can't carry this. It's far too heavy. Besides, the police or fire department or somebody will look after it. They'll take everything away and keep it safe."

Alfie shook his head defiantly.

"No. We take it now."

"Alfie, listen . . ."

"We take it *now!*"

There was no arguing with him. So, step after step, we lugged the trunk through the shadowy woods. I kept changing my carrying arm; Alfie could not and so we paused often for rests. Roxy tried to make herself useful by shining her phone on the ground and warning us of holes and roots that would trip us up.

The thin metal handles dug into my palms, and the weight pulled at my shoulders, but eventually we saw the flickering pink of the neon GARAGE sign. We dragged the trunk inside and slumped down on the chairs. I looked round: we were soot- and sweat-streaked. Somehow I was going to have to clean up before I got back into bed.

"So—are you going to show us what's inside?" I asked, flexing my aching arms. Alfie lifted the lid to reveal a stack of books, fifteen or twenty of them. They were thick volumes with stiff leather covers, and I went to pick one up.

"Careful!" warned Alfie. "Please."

I wiped my hands on my shirt and lifted one out, turning it to read the gold lettering on the spine.

"*Barnaby Rudge,*" I read out. I looked at Alfie quizzically.

"Not one of his better-known titles. Try this one." He handed me another book.

"*Great Expectations.* Oh yeah! That was a TV series. Mum watched it! So these are all by whatsisname. . . ."

"Charles Dickens," said Roxy. "He wrote *Oliver Twist* as well."

Alfie smiled. "You have read it?"

Roxy shrugged. "Sort of. Here it is." She flipped open the cover. There was a handwritten inscription, which she read out. *"To Dear Alve, with my Compliments, Charles Dickens."* She gave a low whistle. "So this is a full set of Charles Dickens's books? Are they all signed by him? But who's this Alve? It can't be you?" She peered sideways through narrowed eyes. There was a long pause and then she drawled, "Can it?"

Alfie coughed. "Ah . . . an old relative. And it is not quite the full set. One was stolen, or somehow went . . . I do not know. Suffice to say, *A Tale of Two Cities* is missing."

"What a shame. Still—I'll bet these are worth a bit!"

Alfie nodded. "Yes. But I estimate their value is probably halved because of the missing volume. Anyhow, may I . . ." He gently retrieved the books we were holding and replaced them in the trunk, closing the lid. "May I leave them here? For the time being?"

"Sure thing," said Roxy. Together we lugged the trunk under the burst sofa.

"Alfie," I said. "What are you going to do now? Where are you going to go?"

He said nothing, and Roxy flashed me a look of warning. She tried a gentler approach.

"Your mum, Alfie? Is there anyone else who, you know, you can talk to?"

"There was just us. And Biffa." His blank expression returned. It was as if the expedition to the burnt house and the rescue of the trunk of books had distracted him from his misery for a while, but now it had returned. He went to the doorway and made a kissing sound with his mouth again and called, "Hey, Biffa! Hey, Biffa!" He saw us looking. "She is a cat."

"You will have to speak to the police, you know," I said. "You can't hide here forever."

He fixed me with his ice-blue eyes. "No. Not yet. There is something I must do."

"What?"

He shook his head as if to dismiss the question like an annoying fly. "I need to stay here. You promised me you would help me."

"Well, yes, but . . ."

"Did you not mean what you said?"

"Well, yes, but . . ."

"Then I stay here, and you say nothing to anybody."

I looked across at Roxy, who shrugged.

"But your mum, Alfie . . . ," I began.

His nostrils flared with anger. "My mother. Is. Dead. You cannot change that. What difference does it make to you? You just thought she was some weird woman living in the woods. That weird woman was my mother, dead because of me!"

"Because of *you*? How . . . ?"

"I CAUSED THE FIRE!" he shouted. "I shall be lucky not to go to jail!"

"Alfie, eleven-year-olds don't go to jail," I said, trying to calm him down, but it had no effect.

"Who says I am eleven?"

"I'm just guessing you're about my age, Alfie. Look . . ."

"NO! *You* look. And you," he added, turning to Roxy, who flinched. "I *need* to stay here for a while. You *need* to help me. And, once I have done what I need to do, it will all be fine, I promise. Promise. Please, I am beseeching you, tell no one about me."

There was a long silence—I mean a *long* one. All three of us just looked at one another, shifting our gazes to each other's eyes. I was going to break it, but Roxy spoke first. I could tell she was suspicious, on some level. Because of the witch stuff, I suppose.

"OK. But you don't involve us. We could get into trouble. If anyone asks, you found this place on your own."

"All right. But I do need some food."

"OK."

"And water."

"OK."

I said, "So that *is* involving us. Quite a lot."

Alfie gave a small shrug. "You said you would help me. And blankets. And a fresh dressing for my arm. And some Tylenol. And a tin of crab meat." He paused, realizing that it had become a long list of demands. "If that is all right?"

"*Crab meat?*"

"It is my cat's favorite. She might smell it and come back. Possibly."

I sighed, already beginning to regret that empty offer of help.

CHAPTER THIRTY-FIVE

Alfie

I caused the fire. I did. Not deliberately, but it was my fault.

Now I have to face the consequences.

People in the twenty-first century say some strange things: "I shall have to learn to live with myself," or, "I shall have to forgive myself."

It is all tommyrot, which, come to think of it, is something I think you do *not* say anymore.

I have no choice but to live with myself. And I cannot forgive myself. I am not even sure it is possible.

How did the fire start?

It would have been the new wood. New, unseasoned wood—which throws off sparks. I had watched Roxy Minto walk up the lane with her bandaged head; I had tried to wave goodbye to her, hoping she would come back.

I had been too lazy to go down to the woodshed and fetch the proper aged logs, and I used the new ones that had just been cut.

So.

My fault.

CHAPTER THIRTY-SIX

AIDAN

It was late when I got back. Mum and Aunty Alice were in bed, but Dad was waiting up for me. He was furious. He's always angrier after he and Mum have argued.

"Worried sick . . . Irresponsible . . . Selfish . . . How do you think your mother feels . . . ?"

It was all the usual stuff. And then he stopped and looked me up and down.

"You're filthy," he said. "*Again!* What on earth is wrong with you? Where have you been?"

I lied and said I'd been playing football with Spatch. Dad wasn't going to check. But the whole episode made it even less likely that I was going to tell him about Alfie. I put on my very best sorrowful look.

"I'm sorry, Dad. I lost track of time. I won't do it again."

Just then, Jasper came in from the living room. "Ah! The wanderer returns!" he said. "Told you he'd be shipshape, didn't I, Ben? Been having fun, have you?" His top lip drew back to the gum line and he grinned. When Jasper smiles, he always looks as though he had to read the instructions on how to do it. It's chilling.

By trying to be jovial, Jasper had completely undermined Dad's telling-off. I should have been pleased but I wasn't. I glanced at Dad and felt almost sorry for him. He was glaring pure fury at Jasper, who just did not notice.

"Don't forget," Jasper was saying as he rubbed his bony hands together. "Early start for us seamen tomorrow!"

Oh crikey! I'd forgotten that. Jasper was taking Dad and me out on the *Jolly Roger* tomorrow. I caught Dad's eye. He was dreading it as much as I was.

"Can't wait, Jasper," I said, then I yawned theatrically. The sooner *I* got to bed, the sooner *they* might, and the sooner I could get back to Alfie with the stuff I'd promised him.

Upstairs, I turned on my bedside radio.

". . . on Radio North and here is the news. North-umbria Police say they are looking for a boy in con-nection with last night's house fire in woodland near Whitley Bay that claimed the life of one woman, named earlier as Mrs. Hilda Monk.

"She is believed to have lived with her eleven-year-old son, Alfred, who is missing from the house. Detective Inspector Maxine Ford issued this appeal last night:"

"Alfred, we want you to come forward and let us

know you're safe. You are not under any suspicion or in any trouble. Wherever you are, just go into any police station, or approach a police officer in the street and tell them who you are. And that goes for anyone who may know his whereabouts. We are very concerned for this boy's safety."

"There are fears that the boy may be injured, or suffering psychologically from the fire, which totally destroyed his home, and at one point threatened to get out of control.

"Police are conducting house-to-house enquiries to find out if a neighbor is sheltering him.

"In other news, the Prime Minister has said . . ."

I turned off the radio and stared at the ceiling, feeling sick with worry.

CHAPTER THIRTY-SEVEN

OK, stop a second and put yourself in my shoes just for a moment, because if you don't you'll end up thinking I'm either crazy or stupid or both.

- There's a kid about my age living in an old workmen's shed over my back fence, and the only other person who knows this is Roxy Minto, a girl I have more or less just met.
- The kid has just seen his house burn to ashes and lost his mother in the fire and is—according to Roxy, who sounds like she knows what she's talking about— suffering from PT-something-or-other, which is a fragile mental state.
- He has a badly burnt arm that should probably have hospital treatment, which he absolutely refuses.
- He speaks weirdly, with a strange accent that I can't identify.

- He has just begged me (backed up with vague threats)
  to keep all of this secret.

And I have agreed.

"Please, I am beseeching you" is what he said.

How much longer could I keep the secret? Was it even right to do so? The police were searching for him, so would I get into trouble if I said nothing?

All of this—and about a trillion other things—was going through my head as I snuck about the house at midnight, finding stuff for Alfie. I had unpacked a bunch of camping gear a couple of days ago, so I easily found a sleeping bag in the cupboard on the landing. I figured he might like an airbed as well, so I was holding these two items and heading downstairs when the door to what would be my room opened and Jasper came out in his pajamas and stood in the dim light.

"All right, son," he half whispered blearily. "Just heading to the john. Old man's bladder."

Thanks for the information, I thought, hoping he'd just walk past me and ignore the fact that I was two steps down the stairs with a sleeping bag and an airbed.

Fat chance.

"What the blazes are you doing with all that?" he said, scratching his beard.

Quick, Aidan. Think on your feet.

"Ah . . . I was having trouble sleeping, and . . . and I thought,

erm . . . I'd try sleeping downstairs. New house. Not used to it."
More unconvincing lies.

He said nothing, but looked me up and down before shuffling
off to the bathroom.

He hadn't believed me. I had my hoodie on over my pajamas,
and outdoor shoes.

Not knowing was agony. Why hadn't he said anything more?
Was he half asleep? Did he not care? I decided it was the last one:
he'd never shown much interest in me, so why start now? That's
what I told myself, anyhow, as I quickly scooted down the back garden, through the gap in the fence, and handed the stuff to a grateful Alfie. I'd even found a tin of tuna, which I thought was a good
substitute for crab.

Roxy had already delivered some food, and promised to bring
some fresh dressings in the morning, so it was just Alfie and me.

He looked at me with his pale, red-rimmed eyes. "Thank you,"
he said, "very sincerely." Then he added, "Pal."

Just that. "Pal." It was as if he'd never said it before. He didn't
toss off the word casually like people normally do—you know, "Hey
there, pal!"—although around here you didn't hear it so much. It
was like he'd picked it up and was practicing it for the first time,
enunciating it clearly as he did with lots of words.

Then he smiled, and despite his shocking teeth there was a
warmth that I felt all the way through me. Then the smile slowly
faded, to be replaced by a serious stare, and he said, "I am relying
on you."

I turned to go. "Aidan," he said softly.

"Yes?"

"There is something I need to tell you. But you may not believe me."

So now there's another thing to add to the list of things that will make you think I'm stupid, crazy, or both.

He reckons he's a thousand years old.

CHAPTER THIRTY-EIGHT
Alfie

I feel as though there is a space inside me. Yet the space, although it is inside me, is actually bigger than me.

It could swallow me up. If I look down into the space, I could topple over and fall down, down into the space that is not even black.

It has no color. No sound. No smell. It is just nothing.

I sat in the hut that Roxy Minto calls her garage and stared at the walls, the ceiling, the floor. Now that she had turned off the pink sign outside, it was shady, and my eyes rested. Without my dark glasses, everything outside is too bright. (Mam and I both have—had—high "photosensitivity"; bright sunlight is almost painful. For both of us, it started immediately after we had mixed the life-pearl's unguent with our blood. It must be what is now called a "side effect.")

All around me lingered the smell of the fire. I had bathed and changed clothes, but my old, smoke-reeking garments lay in a heap in the corner. It was as if the smell had entered my skin, my nose. The boy who is friends with Roxy—Aidan—is kind. He helped me in the bath. He said nothing about my scars or tattoo, although he must have wanted to ask.

And if he had, what would I have told him?

"This is a tattoo that I acquired some five hundred years ago, so it is not surprising that it has faded over the centuries."

Perhaps I should have done. Tell the truth, that is; Mam, however, would not have approved. There was a plan for what to do if either of us died, but it did not involve telling everyone the truth.

Mam.

Everything comes back to her. Every thought, every action, brings her to mind. I have already lost count of the number of times I have started to say something to her, or looked round to see if she is near, or wanted to feel her strong arms round me.

Mam would stroke my back and sing the song of the old times, in the tongue we alone shared.

And there, in the grimy hut, on the ripped sofa, I hugged myself instead and tried to imagine it was Mam. I sang the song that Mam sang, the sad notes catching in my throat, but somehow making me feel better.

When Aidan came back, it was about one a.m., to judge from the moon. I had been dozing, but could not sleep for fear that the empty space inside me would swallow me as I slept.

He had brought a long, padded bag for me to sleep in. He

asked me if I was all right. "OK" was the word he used. "Are you OK, Alfie?"

"Thank you," I said. "I am OK." It felt unusual. It is not a word I have used much before.

He sat with me awhile, not saying anything, and that was all right. Nice, even. Then he said, "How is your arm?"

"Fine," I said, but it was not. It was very sore, in spite of the painkillers I had taken.

Then, when he got up to leave, it just came out.

"Aidan," I said, "there is something I need to tell you. . . ."

"OK," he said, "shoot."

"I beg your pardon?"

"Shoot. Go ahead."

I took a deep breath and closed my eyes. I thought of Mam and our plan. Then I just said it.

"I am a thousand years old. More, actually. So was my mam."

"Say that again?" he said, so I did.

I expected him to accuse me of lying, or at least to laugh at me. But he did not. Instead he looked at me carefully and said, "How long have you lived there, in the woods?"

"On and off for about a hundred and fifty years."

"And before that?"

"We lived near Hexham, on a little farmstead. We did a bit of sewing, making clothes, repairing things. And, before that, in Wales for a time, and—"

"Sewing?" he interrupted. "Your mum was a 'costumier'?"

"That is a little grand, but yes, sometimes that is what Mam would say."

Aidan's brow had creased as he peered at me. He had sat back down on the desk and was thinking hard, I could tell.

"And . . . were you ever photographed, Alfie? Both of you? Outside the cottage?"

"Why, yes, we were. How could I forget? It was the first time either of us had seen a camera before. A man from the *Shields Gazette* came and we stood by the front door, and . . . wait a minute. Why did you ask me that?"

We talked until the sky began to get light. I told him about Da and Mam and Biffa and the *livperler*. The life-pearls. I felt a little less empty. I even think he may have believed me.

I told him about me and Mam's plan. I began to think it would work, and it might have had it not been for what happened next.

And when he finally left, I slept, and did not dream.

CHAPTER THIRTY-NINE

-: AIDAN :-

The very last thing I wanted to do—one hour after finally getting into bed at sunrise, and not sleeping a wink because of what I had just learned—was to be "woken" (although I was already wide awake) to go out on Jasper's boat.

While Dad and I were out on the boat with Jasper, Mum and Aunty Alice were going to pick up Libby from Brownie camp.

Now, ever since I overheard Mum and Dad in the car on the way back from Aunty Alice's wedding two years ago, I've known that they don't really like Jasper. But they don't know that I know.

(Adults do this thing—you must have noticed—where they kind of pretend that they're all good friends and everybody is nice, especially family. I suppose it's to "set an example" to us kids: you know, love and trust, don't make judgments, the adult world is all lovely, blah-di-blah. Except we know when they're doing it.)

In this case, it's probably so they don't upset Aunty Alice, because *she* likes Jasper. Loves him, even. And so when Jasper had said to me, "You comin' out on me ship tomorrow, young fellow-me-lad?" I had glanced over at Dad.

The way Jasper said it was more like a statement than a question, and Dad had replied, "Thanks, Jasper, we'd love to."

We.

I was relieved. I don't know what Dad imagined would happen to me—maybe he thought Jasper would sail into a storm, or make me walk the plank. I don't know. But I do know I was pleased that I wasn't going alone.

Some people have a fear of flying. I daresay some people are scared in cars. Mum won't ever go on a motorbike.

Me? It's boats. I once tried to tell this to Jasper, who scoffed and told me I had to "man up," and Dad even *agreed* with him, saying I can't go through life being scared of boats. Adults, eh? You just can't tell.

To be honest, it's not the boat. It's the seasickness. I throw up whenever I'm on a boat. (I even threw up on a pedal boat once on holiday in Majorca, though I didn't tell anyone because I was so ashamed.)

Jasper had anchored his boat and moored it to one of the two long concrete piers that curve out into Culvercot Bay like arms in a hug.

Now, I know nothing about boats, but I think his is a yacht. It's white, with a tall mast, and the sail is furled up under a blue cover along the bit that swings from side to side, which I happen to know is called the boom, so—hey!—I *do* know something about boats, after all.

There's a steering wheel, which is just called a wheel, and Jasper calls the boat a "thirty-footer," so that's how long it is.

Jolly Roger is written on the side in jaunty letters, and there's even a little pirate flag hanging over the back end. The bow. Rhymes with "snow," not with "cow." Or maybe the other way round. Like I said, I'm no expert.

When we got down to Culvercot pier, we could see a group of kids had hopped into the boat and were trying the door of the cabin.

We all saw it at the same time, but Jasper was the first to react. It was like a little bomb had exploded in his head, and he went from super-calm to super-angry in about half a second.

"Oi! Hey!" He was surprisingly fast on his feet as he ran down the pier, shouting and swearing. "You little devils! Get the hell off my boat! Geroff it now!"

Oh no. It was Inigo Delombra. Instead of being intimidated, the three boys just looked up at Jasper. The cabin door had been opened, despite having a combination lock, but they didn't go in. Inigo Delombra spoke.

"This your boat?"

"Yes, it damn well is! Get off it!" Jasper reached out and grabbed one of the boys' jackets, but he wriggled free.

"Oi, that's assault, that is, old man!" Inigo continued: "Only me dad's the harbor master, and he says there's no permitted anchorage here between April and September, so technically you're in breach of maritime regulations. We were just checkin' if you were inside."

By now the boys had clambered out and were standing facing us on the pier.

"Har-harbor master?" stammered Jasper.

"Aye. He's a stickler for regulations, my old man." The other two had begun to saunter off, but Inigo stood his ground before delivering his parting shot. "I'll do you a favor. I won't mention that you assaulted Jonesy here, but you know—y'cannit just park your boat anywhere and not expect investigation by the authorities."

Farther down the pier, the other two spluttered with laughter, but Inigo shoved his hands in his pockets and sauntered off. He turned and added:

"One more thing? Your entry code? One of the top ten." Then he looked at me and smirked. "It's a long walk for you to come back here, isn't it, Linklater? You know—from Dumpsville, where you live now?"

Dad was going down the steps of the pier and didn't hear, which I was glad about. The *last* thing you need when you're dealing with someone like Inigo Delombra is to have your dad go ballistic at them. It can only ever make things worse.

CHAPTER FORTY

So the trip up the coast to St. Mary's Lighthouse and back was grim.

Jasper was in a foul mood after his encounter with the boys on the pier, and he was concentrating hard on the sailing, barking orders like "Pull in that sheet!" and when I looked blank he'd get frustrated. "The sheet, laddie! That rope there—pull it!"

Because of the wind's direction, we had to go in a zigzag (Ticking? Tacking? Who knows?) and, more than once, Dad had to tell him, "Steady, Jasper. It's his first time."

Except by the time we turned round, just past the lighthouse, his mood had altered like a sea wind changing direction. It was bizarre and a bit scary to see how quickly his personality flipped. He reached into a cabinet and brought out a white captain's cap with gold braid and jammed it onto his head. Next he turned a knob on the console by the wheel and music blasted out. Old music—people singing, like in a church or something—and it was *loud*.

"Ah, gotta love the old Gregorian chanting," said Jasper, to no one, really. "A true elevation of the soul!" He closed his eyes dreamily for a few seconds and lifted his face to the wind.

Then, putting on a deep, posh voice, he said, "Take her to sea, Mr. Murdoch. Let's stretch her legs!"

I smiled weakly. That was a line from the film *Titanic,* which I'd seen round at Mo's.

We hoisted the foresail, which was a small one at the front, and the boat lurched forward with a force that surprised me. Dad staggered back and grabbed a handrail.

The sea wasn't rough that day, but there was enough swell to make the boat slap down hard on the waves as it carved through the shiny gray water. I had been feeling a bit sick on the earlier part of the journey, and this wasn't helping.

"Here—take the wheel," said Jasper, and he stepped aside. The ship's wheel started turning alarmingly. "Go on!" he snapped. "Take it!" and I did, while he cranked the music up even louder.

"Jasper, are you sure . . . ," yelled Dad over the chanting choir, but Jasper wasn't listening.

"ICEBERG RIGHT AHEAD!" he screamed. "HARD TO STARBOARD, MR. MURDOCH!" I didn't know what that meant. "Turn the wheel hard to the right, the RIGHT!"

His voice was so urgent that I half believed there really was an enormous iceberg looming in front of us, half a mile off the coast of Whitley Bay, and I turned the wheel with all the force I could. The boat reacted only seconds later, and lurched terrifyingly to the right. Dad was unprepared: he staggered again, banging his head hard on the low doorway, and he yelled out with pain.

"Pirates preparing to board! Hard to port!"

There were no pirates in *Titanic,* but I didn't care, and swung the boat round again. A wave splashed over the side.

"That's enough!" yelled Dad, and we both turned to look at him. "It's dangerous!"

But Jasper was having none of it. It was as if he'd forgotten that we were just ordinary people in a yacht. "I decide what's dangerous on my ship. See this?" and he pointed at his captain's cap. "It means I'm in charge!" He was smiling as he said it, not shouting, as if he and Dad were not really having an argument. But they were.

Dad pulled me away from the wheel. "In that case, you had better *take* charge," he said, grinning coldly. He reached for the knob and snapped off the music, and the difference was startling. Instantly it was just the sea and wind sounds again. And *still* he didn't give up on the "adults don't argue in front of kids" thing, by saying:

"It's all right, Aidan. Nothing to worry about. I was just a bit concerned, that's all. Call me an old scaredy-cat, eh?" He rubbed his head where he'd banged it.

And so we puttered back along the coast to Culvercot Bay, no one saying anything until Jasper turned to Dad and said, "Drink?"

"A *drink*?" The way Dad said it, you'd think Jasper had suggested he go skinny-dipping.

Jasper scratched his beard and said, "Aye. A drink." He opened up another cabinet to reveal several bottles of something I didn't recognize.

"Rum," he explained, apparently reading my mind. "A sailor's best friend!" In my side vision, I saw Dad rolling his eyes.

"It's, ah . . . it's a little early in the day for me, Jasper," he said. "But you go right ahead."

If the bottle had had a cork in it, Jasper would *definitely* have gripped the cork in his teeth to pull it out, like someone in a film. As it was, it had a screw cap, which he took off the normal way, and took a big gulp of the rum before going "Ahhhh!" and smacking his lips. Even I could tell he was faking it.

Other than that, we sailed back in silence. Dad was seething, I could tell. Jasper—after a couple more swigs of rum—had reverted to being his normal not-Jack-Sparrow self, and I threw up quietly over the back of the boat without anyone seeing.

As we were walking back along the pier, I was feeling wobbly and sleepy. Dad's mobile phone went off. His voice sounded alarmed.

"She's *what*? Police? Over the back fence? But . . . Oh. Oh. OK." Dad turned to us and said, "Libby's found that missing kid."

Well, *that* woke me right up. I staggered a little. Jasper grabbed my arm to steady me.

"Although he's run away again," Dad added.

All these ups and downs: it was like I was still at sea.

CHAPTER FORTY-ONE

My little sister had—I found out later—done a thing at Brownie camp called "Explore Your World," which involved going to places near your home that you'd never been to before. I think you were meant to go to a new park or new shop or something.

Not go over the back fence and discover a boy hiding in a sleeping bag in an old workmen's hut with a broken neon GARAGE sign over it.

But that was what Libby had done.

Now, for the second time in three days, the street was alive with people in uniforms—mainly police, but there was an ambulance with paramedics as well. The ambulance doors were open, and two paramedics were sitting on the back ledge, looking unconcerned.

Inside our house were more people, and whatever the atmosphere had been between me and Jasper and Dad disappeared. There was something much bigger going on.

Aunty Alice was making a pot of tea, the third, she said.

"Put a shirt on, Jasper, for goodness' sake," she grumbled. Jasper was still in his sleeveless undershirt, a tangle of chest hair spilling out like a burst cushion.

Two of the strangers were plainclothes police officers, a man and a woman. Another woman was something else, with the words "Child" and "Protection" in her title.

One of the police officers, the woman, was talking to Libby, who looked terrified.

"It's all right, pet. You've done nothing wrong, really y'haven't," said the woman, but it didn't look as though Libby believed her. "Now tell me again what you saw."

She was making notes as Libby spoke. The doorbell went again; phones were pinging and buzzing all over the place; the kettle gave its electronic whistle to say it had boiled; a helicopter clattered above the woods. It was chaos.

Just then, a shout went up from outside our front door, which was open.

"They've found him!"

The news got passed around and repeated. Voices barked and crackled everywhere.

"They've found him . . . found him . . . found him . . ."

"Bring him up the back way . . ."

"Injured arm, not critical . . ."

"Not confirmed his name yet . . ."

"Presume traumatized, Sarge, treat with caution . . ."

I felt a dig in my back. Turning, I saw that it was Roxy. She murmured, "Big surprise that, eh?"

Roxy didn't seem at all worried by the fact that she and I might be in big trouble for "aiding a fugitive" or whatever you call what we'd done. I couldn't share her lack of concern, and my stomach—already a bit wobbly from the boat ride—turned over again.

A uniformed officer appeared through the gap in the fence and beckoned to the "Protection" lady, who stomped out purposefully.

Then everything went quiet for about twenty minutes. The male plainclothes officer chatted quietly to Mum and Dad and Aunty Alice, while the woman took out her notebook and went round us all, taking our names and addresses, that sort of thing. She stopped at Aunty Alice.

"Do you live here, madam?"

"Oh no, Officer," and she gave her address in Warkworth, up the coast.

"And your full name?"

"Alice Hooke. Mrs. With an 'e.'" The officer wrote it all down.

Just then, there was movement at the end of the garden. A policeman squeezed through the fence gap first, followed by a very dirty and bedraggled Alfie and another uniformed officer.

They paraded up the garden and into our kitchen. The people left in the kitchen parted, creating space for them to walk through.

Alfie's whole being seemed to be weighed down by a cloak of unhappiness as heavy as iron.

And then he looked at us, me and Roxy, and the fury that burned from his eyes was alarming. He said nothing but I knew that he thought we'd betrayed him—told Libby about him, or something.

I couldn't say anything. I couldn't say, "We didn't tell on you, Alfie," because that would have revealed our deception to the adults fussing around in our kitchen. Instead we stayed silent, and Alfie looked so angry.

There was a moment—maybe ten seconds—as he stood there, shirtless and filthy, when nobody said anything while they stared at Alfie.

There was plenty to stare at: his hair caked in mud, his jeans with the sparkly sequins, the strange, faded tattoo on his back, and the scars on his upper arm.

Libby looked him up and down but didn't seem to recognize her jeans, thank goodness, probably because they were so muddy.

Then, through the throng of people in our kitchen, came Jasper, who did this weird thing. He bent down in front of Alfie and examined him like a specimen in a museum: lowering his tinted glasses, looking left, looking right, then turning Alfie round to gaze at the tattoo.

Alfie didn't seem to mind everyone looking. I thought he was just dazed—like this examination was part of being caught.

Then I noticed Jasper blinking and gawping at Alfie, and he saw me looking at him, and turned away suddenly. Alfie's eyes were cast down at the floor and he didn't notice anything, but Jasper's eyes went back again and again and I realized he was gazing at Alfie's scars. Although he said nothing, his ruddy face had gone completely pale.

He was behaving oddly, to be sure, but then, nothing about this was normal.

The policewoman intervened.

"Excuse me, sir?"

Jasper looked at her as though he was coming out of a trance. He was pulling on a shirt, and it was only then that I noticed his upper arm had two horizontal scars in exactly the same place as Alfie's.

A little equals sign.

Strange, I thought. But in the whole kitchen confusion, I didn't dwell on it.

"Excuse me, sir?" the policewoman repeated.

"Yes?" said Jasper.

"We just need some details from you, please. . . ." She took out her notebook.

I looked around for Alfie, to see if I could get him on his own and explain, but he had already been taken away to the waiting police car.

CHAPTER FORTY-TWO

alfie

It was a coincidence, surely?

The double scars, like an equals sign.

It could not be.

I just saw his arm quickly, I tell myself. *Surely I am deluded? The stress, the fire, my mam, everything . . . I cannot be thinking straight.*

I am in a police car with a blanket round me, people talking above my head into radios and telephones, a blue light flashing in the rearview mirror, and a lady with too much perfume sitting next to me, patting my arm (which is somewhat annoying).

But when everything and everybody one knows and loves is destroyed in a single night, it can affect one's judgment.

One's judgment? *Your* judgment. You see, I do not even speak like you, although I try. I am trying very, very hard.

OK?

(Mam and I listened to the wireless, although the people

on the wireless do not usually speak the same way people around here do. I try to talk like them, but I get it wrong: I can hear it myself, and I can tell when I talk to other people—which is not often—that they sometimes think I speak oddly.)

As if from a distance, there is a voice in the car: ". . . Alfie? You OK, Alfie?"

It gets louder.

"Alfie!"

I turn; it is not loud at all. It is just the lady next to me on the backseat of the car, and she is patting my hand even more forcefully. I would like to move my arm out of her way, but that would seem rude, so I endure it for a little longer before saying, "Please stop that."

She looks at her hand, startled, and then withdraws it.

Was that rude? I said "please."

"We're going to take you somewhere safe, Alfie," she is saying. "You can get cleaned up, and we'll get you something to eat. I bet you're hungry, love?"

I say nothing. I am not hungry at all. Before betraying me this morning, Roxy had brought me bread rolls, cheese, two apples, a banana, and a chicken leg in foil. I had eaten it all, like a condemned man's last meal.

Then the little girl (Liberty? Something like that) had done their dirty work for them.

I was on my own in the shed, the one that Roxy calls her

garage, which I think is quite funny. She is a clever girl. Mam would call her *wordsnoterlic* (said like "ward-snotter-lick"). It means wise and sharp.

Aidan? *Flarath,* she would have said. Traitor. I begged them both to say nothing. They told Aidan's sister. She told everybody.

Now I sit in a police car with a blanket and a lady called Sangeeta who is a Child Protection Officer, whatever that may be. She said she was working with the police to ensure my safety.

This is what she says in a breathy, singsong voice, as though I were six or something.

"Hello, Alfie? My name's Sangeeta. I'm a designated Child Protection Officer working with Northumbria Police. I've been assigned to you to ensure your safety. Do I have your permission for physical contact?"

She speaks like this a lot, I think. It is as though she has memorized phrases like the actors in plays that Mam and I liked.

Frankly, I am not really listening. My mind keeps going back to the man in Aidan's kitchen.

The double scars. A coincidence, surely, I tell myself again.

I wonder what Mam would have said. A lady in jeans and sandals protecting *me,* Alve Einarsson, who once protected Mam from a bear by shouting at it, although that was a long, long time ago when things were different from now. (For a start, there were bears. Well, at least one.)

Everything around me brings every thought back to Mam, and I feel a tear roll down my cheek. Sangeeta sees this and starts to pat my arm again, but I look at her hand and she stops.

Can we please get going? There is nobody in the driver's seat. Come on, you have found me now. What is the delay?

Here is what happened.

I was in the garage when I heard someone approaching. I had assumed it was Roxy coming back, or Aidan, so I did not bother to conceal myself. That was my mistake. I should have known better. The door opened and Libby (that is her name, I recall now) stood there, staring at me.

A little girl, maybe seven, eight years old. I knew immediately that I had been betrayed: no one would come looking for me unless they knew I was there.

So I left everything and started to run into the woods. I know those woods better than anyone. I could easily hide myself for a while if anybody came looking; then I would make my way back to the garage and restart the plan devised by Mam and me.

Ludicrous. Unworkable. A fantasy. I know—but I was desperate.

There is a hollow on the north side of the woods: a depression beneath a fallen tree that is overgrown with gorse and spiky juniper and impossible to see just by walking past.

I should have known when I heard the helicopter thudding

in the sky that I would not be allowed to escape quietly and get on with my life, our plan.

I heard the voices first, then the footsteps coming nearer. I shuffled a little deeper into my crevice. There was something else, though.

A dog.

The police dog found me in the ditch. It was sniffing furiously, then whining. I had left a T-shirt in the garage. They must have allowed the dog to sniff it, then "game over," as I think you say. I should have expected it, I suppose.

"Come on, son," said the dog's handler, a policeman in a bright yellow jacket. He held his hand out for me. "Mind the thorns."

I thought about running, but what was the point?

I would simply endure what was to come. It could not have been as bad as I was imagining.

How wrong I was there. As the driver got into the car and reversed out of the space, a journey started that was to get worse than I could possibly have dreamed.

First, though, I have to answer the question that has been scuttling around in my head like a cockroach:

Do I tell the truth?

CHAPTER FORTY-THREE

Of course I do not tell the truth. I told the truth to Aidan.

I trusted him. Hours later, I found myself in the backseat of a police vehicle, proving to me that, in situations such as this, telling the whole truth is—to say the least—unwise.

Besides, they probably already know. Why would Aidan— and Roxy, since he certainly told her—have held back the information about my age when they betrayed my whereabouts? They would not have, would they? It would have been:

"We know where the missing boy is, and you'll never guess what! He says he's a thousand years old!"

So I say nothing, nothing at all. That was the tactic that had saved me and Mam countless times over the years. If you say nothing, then nothing can be used against you.

Fortunately, this Sangeeta lady does not fire a lot of questions at me. In fact she says very little at all, other than factual stuff, instructions. Such as:

"All right, Alfie. We're going to the police station at North

Shields first, but it's nothing to worry about. You haven't done anything wrong. There's a clinic there, and we'll get that arm of yours checked out by a doctor, all right?"

I nod. I have a headache. I lost my dark glasses in the fire and the daylight is hurting my eyes.

If all this were not strange enough, no sooner had the car's engine started than that man came out of Aidan's house, the bearded man who had been there in the kitchen when I came in. A relative? A friend?

The double scars.

He brushed past everyone and tapped on the car window. I shrank back into the car seat. At that point, a policeman's arm came between him and the glass.

"Excuse me, sir?"

"I need to speak to Alfie," he said. Turning back to me, he leaned down at the window. "Alfie! Alfie!"

"Sir, sir. Sorry, but . . . you can't just—"

"Unhand me, Officer!"

"Sir, I must stop you. Are you a relative?"

"No. No. I just need . . ."

"Sir, if you continue to struggle, I'm afraid I'm going to have to—"

"Jasper! What on earth is going on?" A woman—Aidan's mother, I think—had appeared in the doorway and was yelling at this Jasper character.

By now, we were backing out of the driveway. As we turned,

I craned my neck. The man was being spoken to by a police officer and the woman, and he seemed quite agitated.

"Who was that?" asked Sangeeta. I shook my head.

"I have no idea," I said, which was true.

Yet, through my daze, I kept thinking of what that man had said: "Unhand me, Officer!"

Nobody speaks like that. Do they?

There was something else, though. Some *thing* I could not identify, because it was not a *thing*. It was a *feeling*. It was a feeling that lasted a moment, a second, when he stared into my face through the car window and our eyes met. When I tried to recall the feeling, it slithered away, as if I were attempting to catch a fish in a barrel with my hands.

It was the feeling that I had seen him before, and it did not feel good.

CHAPTER FORTY-FOUR

The rest of the day was to be like this: a seemingly endless parade of people talking gently to me, pretending they were my friend in order to find out everything about me.

At the police station, I was taken to a room labeled FAMILY SERVICES, where there were sofas and a television playing a cartoon film about a little fish to the empty room. A plastic ride-on police car was next to a bookshelf with mainly picture books and one or two battered children's paperbacks, and a box of soft toys.

Sangeeta pointed out the books before asking, in a voice that proved she had practiced sounding as natural and relaxed as she could, "Can you read OK, Alfie? And write?"

The truth? This would be the truth:

"Thank you, Miss Prasad. I am proficient in Old Norse, Old English, Middle English, and Modern English, plus French, Latin, Greek (ancient *and* modern, although they are not *so* dissimilar), and a smattering of Welsh and Scots Gaelic."

I did not say that, of course. Instead I just nodded. I was not insulted. I knew she was just doing her job.

She showed me the shower room, and left me with soap and a towel, and a pile of clothes from Marks & Spencer, all new, with the labels attached, that appeared in the changing area as if by magic. They must have had a cupboard full of them. I had never worn proper boys' jeans before. They were thick and stiff, with machine stitching, quite well made. The white shoes were nice. Trainers? Sneakers? I think they are sneakers.

Lunch was something in a box called a Happy Meal from McDonald's, which I have heard of, of course, but I have never had before. For some reason, there was a plastic toy with it. The food was nice but the drink was too sweet and I had water instead from the tap.

The doctor was all right, but she asked more questions than Sangeeta. As she removed the bandages that Roxy had put on, she said, "Hmm. Not a bad home dressing, Alfie. Who did that for you?"

I said nothing as she set about cleaning the burn. It hurt like flaming hell, but I gritted my teeth and made no sound.

"You're a tough lad, Alfie."

I wished they would all stop using my name so much. I know it is to make them seem friendlier, but it is annoying.

"How did you come by this injury?"

I stayed quiet.

They cannot force me to talk.

She gave me a thorough checkup: head lice, blood pressure, saliva samples, height, weight, everything.

"And how old did you say you were, Alfie?" she asked, her pen poised over a printed sheet, which she was filling in.

I had not said. I could have said, *"One thousand and eleven."* If I had, what then? Would things have been different?

"I'm eleven," I said.

"Uh-huh. OK. And your date of birth."

This was trickier but I had worked it out earlier. I told her the year that would make me eleven, and added, "September the first." Everything was part of the plan.

Then, as I sat there with fresh bandages and a full stomach, the questions began in earnest. I knew they would.

Sangeeta came into the sofa room with another woman, who introduced herself as Vericka from North Tyneside Social Services. She was older, with short white hair, glasses on a chain round her neck, and a face that looked permanently slightly annoyed.

They both had thick notepads and sheaves of forms. *We may be here a while*, I thought.

"All right, Alfie. We have to ask you a few questions, do you understand?"

I nodded, and it started. Gently at first. Name, age, and then:

"Can we ask you about your mum, pet?"

I nodded and told them her name and age, all according to the plan.

They wrote in their pads.

"Where do you go to school, Alfie?"

"I do not go to school. I am home educated. Home-ed."

Home-ed. That is the slang, is it not?

"I see," said Sangeeta. "Only you don't appear on the home-education register."

I shrugged, as if to say, *"That is your problem, not mine."* Sangeeta and Vericka exchanged a glance.

"And who is your family doctor, Alfie?"

Shrug.

"Do you ever see a doctor?"

I shook my head.

"Don't you ever get sick?" asked Vericka, a bit crossly, I thought.

I shook my head again, only this time my answer was more or less true. Coughs, colds, occasional tummy aches, but nothing you would bother a doctor about. Mam had remedies for most things.

"Do you have any family, Alfie? Anybody you can stay with?"

I shook my head. That was the truth. There was just Mam and me.

Sangeeta pressed on. "No one at all? An aunty, an uncle? Maybe living somewhere else? Family friends?" She was getting desperate. "Anyone at all?"

Shrug. Another look between Sangeeta and Vericka.

And so it continued for another hour, and I still stuck to the plan.

I was left alone for a little while after that, and then Sangeeta came in with yet another woman, and I was beginning to forget all their names now. Began with an "L." Anyway, she was a "Child Bereavement Counselor" who asked me if I wanted to talk about Mam, and, when I said no, proceeded to ask me all about her anyway, forcing me to remember, and that made me cry, which I hated.

She said she would meet me another time, and told me I could always call her up, or ask to see her anytime (which was unlikely), and that she would inform me about Mam's funeral.

After she left, in came a man. Almost the first man I had spoken to all day. I do not know, really, why I was pleased about that, but I was.

He was called Robbie. He was a Fire Investigations Officer. He wanted to know about the fire. I told him everything I knew.

Well, almost everything.

CHAPTER FORTY-FIVE

Mam had been on edge the evening it happened, and all because of Roxy Minto's appearance in our backyard that afternoon.

The evening had turned chilly, as I had predicted, and we
were indoors with a wood fire going.

"Do you remember the first time you met a black man,
Alve?" Mam said. I suppose because of Roxy. We had recounted
this story to each other a few times over the years, but we still
brought it out now and then.

It was not long after this story began. It was in the sixth
or seventh year of the first King Henry's reign, or 1107 as you
would say now. By then, Mam and I were living in Jarrow,
where there had been a great monastery, but by that time it was
almost in ruins.

There was one old prior remaining—a senior monk—and a
handful of older boys and young men, including me, who were
learning and reading and training to become monks ourselves.

It was a sleepy, empty place: no one asked too many questions about me or Mam. Mam would visit the old prior, Paul, to keep him company.

Monks were not allowed, of course, to have wives or girlfriends, although many did, secretly. Everyone knew about Mam and Paul but nobody really minded. Or if they minded, they said nothing. I asked her once if she was in love with Paul. She smiled and said, "In a manner of speaking."

Paul knew our secret too. The legend of the Neverdeads was still alive in those days.

He kept our secret; we kept his.

Back then, we had seen many people from different countries. There were the Danes, obviously, the ones who stayed. There were also lots of Scots, who were not so popular in our part of the world, although it depended on which dialect they spoke. For some years, we had heard more people speaking the Frankish tongue—they had come from what is now France with the conquering king, William, who had later been so cruel to so many people in the north of England, but who had not come as far north as us.

But in quiet Jarrow? Not for several years had anyone passed through from another country, until the arrival of Johannes at our priory.

He was young, with dark skin, the color of the coal dust that lined our seashores, and none of us had ever seen anyone like him.

He had come to learn with us, to pray with us, to join our community. He arrived on foot from Monkwearmouth, down by the coast, and, when he entered the village, people stared. People literally stopped and gaped. An older lady gave a little shriek of surprise. He was not wearing a monk's robe, just a normal tunic and breeches, with a woolen wrap secured by a leather belt.

I think that is what astonished people: he was dressed just like us.

Old Paul had been expecting him, of course, and came out to greet him, and he grinned, and they clasped hands and came into the monastery. But I had heard nothing of the young man who was to join us.

I knew about black people, of course. The faraway place that we now call Africa was well known to be populated with men and women and children who had black skin, but whose blood was as red as mine. Then again, I had heard all sorts of things from travelers.

How could I be sure about Johannes, then? Like Saint Thomas, who doubted the reappearance of Jesus after his death on the cross, I required proof. I reached out and tried to rub the color from Johannes's face. I looked at my fingers for smudges, but there were none. I rubbed his arm, and he laughed: a good-natured laugh, not mean at all. This had happened to him many times before, he told me later.

"*Scholasticus bonus es, o amice!*" he said to me in Latin. "You are a good student, my friend!" He told me, "Scholars must ask questions and discover answers!"

All men of learning (and back then it was nearly always men) spoke Latin. It was the way that educated people from different countries could communicate.

We all spoke our own languages too, of course. At home with Mam, she and I still spoke a form of Old Norse; with many of the monks in Jarrow we spoke a dialect of Anglo-Saxon that is now known as Old Northumbrian.

We could understand other types of Anglo-Saxon as well. I was learning how to speak Frankish and had already mastered Greek, because it was the original language of so much of the Holy Bible that I copied many times as a young scribe.

Mam and I laughed at the memory of Johannes. He had been a good friend to us. He stayed a few years in Jarrow and then—as was the way with monks—he moved on, taking his learning and the Word of God with him.

About three decades later, Johannes passed through Jarrow again on his way to the cathedral in Durham.

He was a middle-aged man now, no longer slim, and with graying hair, but his smile was as warm as ever, and he sat at our hearth, looked at us both, and hesitated a little before saying, "Neverdeads?"

He knew. We trusted him, we nodded, and he smiled, shaking his head slowly. "Of all the Lord's holy miracles!"

We smiled too, although we knew it was not a holy miracle but science. Or *al-kimiya*, as we called it then. Alchemy.

Back at our fireside in Oak Cottage, I did my Johannes voice for Mam, because she thought it was funny and she liked to remember him.

"Of all the Lord's holy miracles!" I said, and Mam chuckled for maybe the two hundredth time at that.

I put another log on the fire. They were poor logs. I had been lazy that day and picked an armful from the pile nearest the house. They were not yet seasoned properly.

Wood that has fallen naturally because the tree or branch is dead is often good already. This wood, though, was from a tree that had blown over in a storm in the early spring. Mam tutted gently. "Alve! You brought in the new wood, didn't you?"

Robbie would know all about fire, so I did not tell him that bit, nor the stuff about Johannes. But I told him the rest.

CHAPTER FORTY-SIX

Mam had gone up to her bed, I told Robbie the fire investigator. I had gone out, as I often do, to shoot rabbits.

It is all right. I do not shoot them for fun. I shoot rabbits in order to eat them. I know some people in the twenty-first century are squeamish about things like that, especially those who live in towns: that is why I point it out.

(I have a sling to shoot with. You do not use them nowadays, but slings are a very effective weapon. Mine has a small pouch in the middle of a long leather cord. I made it many years ago and I am quite accurate. I also have Da's knife, the steel blade darkened with age and worn thin through centuries of sharpening.)

I told none of this to Robbie, however. I just said that I was going for a walk.

"At night?" he asked, but he tried not to sound surprised.

There is a huge field to the north of our woods, which on cool spring nights is full of rabbits. Until quite recently I had never seen anybody there at night. Not until the new estate was built, and then some people walked dogs there. I had stopped going so often. I would not want to hit someone's dog by accident, or even a person.

I had the big light, on a head strap, that I take with me, but the moon was so high—almost full—that I did not need it to see the way. Instead I turned it on when I got to the field, and swept the beam at ground level. That way, the eyes of the rabbits shine back and you have your target.

I spotted one immediately, and slowly withdrew my sling and put a ball bearing, about half an inch across, in the pouch. I kept the rabbit's eyes in my sights, not moving my head while I began the "windup"—spinning the pouch round on the long strings. That is when I noticed something different. A different kind of light to the south: very faint, a different color. Orangey, grayish.

The color of fire.

Forgive me, but I do not suppose you have been greatly exposed to seeing things on fire: buildings, towns, boats?

I have.

I knew immediately what it was. Terror mounting, I sprinted back to the woods, batting away branches, skidding on moss, my breathing rapid and shallow. I nearly tripped over Biffa, who came pelting out of the woods. I knew then that something was badly wrong.

"Biffa! Biffa! *Kum-a, kum-a!*" I cried, but she did not even look back. Terrified, she ran across the field as if pursued by a dog.

Even then, I heard in my head the voice of my old combat teacher, Rafel: *"Calm, Alve. Your heart, she needs the air!"* and I tried to make my breathing slower and deeper, but it was not easy.

In the dense woods, I could not see the orange glow, nor smell the smoke, until I got much nearer, but soon it was unmistakable. A few yards farther and I could hear it: a sort of high-pitched whoosh, and crackling.

And there it was below me as I stood, wheezing, on the wooded slope: my house, *our* house, a roaring, terrifying inferno, yellow-orange flames licking the trees that seemed to be shrinking back from the heat.

I had one thought only, and I screamed it again and again at the top of my smoke-filled lungs:

"MAAAAAAAAM! MAM! MAAAM!"

I could not even get near to the house. Some of the chickens had got out, and one flapped by my feet. Others were still trapped in the coop. Amy the goat's stall door was banging open.

I watched in powerless horror as a glass window cracked and shattered with the heat. Could I get closer? What about Mam? I jumped down into the yard where only that day Roxy Minto had fallen and hurt her head. I knew it was dangerous to try to save Mam, but I was not thinking straight, and I ran to the corner of the burning house, grabbing a bucket of water on the way.

I threw the bucket at the back stairway, thinking maybe I could get upstairs, which was already ablaze. It sizzled, and for a brief moment I thought there may be a chance, but then, seconds later, the water had evaporated and the flames were advancing again.

Then it fell: the wooden lintel above a collapsed door came away without warning and thudded into my arm, singeing my flesh and causing me to scream out.

I retreated, shouting again, "MAM! WHERE ARE YOU?" I collapsed in a coughing fit as thick smoke enveloped me.

In the back of my mind, a hideous, ugly thought was forming. Looking back, it seems rather strange to me that at that moment of terror at least part of my mind was considering matters in a calm and detached way.

I think it may be a little like those people who say that at a time of great drama, "everything seemed to slow down." For me, things did not slow down, but instead some things became clearer, like a camera lens focusing on one part of a blurry picture.

So this is what I thought:

Is it time to enact the plan?

Through the smoke and the astonishing heat and the noise of destruction all around me, that thought, that thought *alone*, was as sharp and clear as a monastery bell on a winter's night.

The heat and the flames forced me back, farther and farther. My arm was hurting, my eyes were stinging so much that water was streaming from them. I cried out again for Mam. Had she escaped? She would find me, surely?

Then I heard the sirens, and I ran uphill, up the slope. I ran in terror and in panic. I ran until I came to the shed that had been there for months, and I let myself in with the key that I had seen the little girl put under the stone before.

That was it. That was how it happened, the night my mother died.

I looked up at Robbie. He had stopped writing, and his eyes were full of tears, which alarmed me a little.

He sniffed loudly and looked at his shoes, shaking his head. "I am so, so sorry, Alfie. Truly, son, I am."

He seemed very shaken. The silence was uncomfortable, so I said, "My mam?"

He looked up. "Yes?"

"Did . . . did she . . ." I could not form the question to which I so wanted an answer. Robbie helped me.

"Did she suffer, you mean?"

I nodded.

He seemed to weigh his words. "No," he said, eventually. "No. I don't think so."

I swallowed hard. "Thank you." Then I added, "Have you seen a cat? A black-and-white cat?"

He shook his head. "Sorry, son."

I had forgotten that Sangeeta was sitting in the corner until she got up and said, "Thanks, Robbie. I think Alfie has had enough now," and for once I was not annoyed by her presuming to know what was good for me.

I had had enough.

CHAPTER FORTY-SEVEN

Sangeeta drove me to a house on the terraced seafront in Culvercot—a big white villa with a name: Earl Grey House. There were square pillars either side of the front door. Inside, it had high ceilings and smelled of food and cheap air freshener.

A children's home. My home.

I am a thousand years old and I live in a children's home.

I miss my mam. I miss Biffa. Somehow nothing seems quite so bad when you are stroking a cat.

Yet, for several hours now, I have been thinking only about the man with the beard and the scars, just like mine. Surely I imagined it.

Surely?

I was certain now that I recognized him. From somewhere. Then, once again, the memory wriggled from my grasp.

CHAPTER FORTY-EIGHT

AIDAN

Well, *that* was odd.

I mean—Jasper running out of the house and all that, and Mum going after him, and practically dragging him away from the car before he got arrested or something.

Dad had been watching from the house. "He's nuts. Honestly, Marie. I knew there was something not right about him."

"Shush, Ben," said Mum, because Aunty Alice—who had seen nothing of this—was approaching with Libby behind her.

"Poor lad!" said Jasper as he came back into the house. He grinned his long-toothed grin, and then raised a hand to wave at the police officers who were still milling around outside. "Thanks, fellas!" he said, as if they'd done him a favor. Which I suppose, by not arresting him, they had.

Jasper seemed relaxed and confident, but he was faking it, I was sure. Perhaps it takes a bad liar to spot a bad lie.

"Aw, that poor wee lad. I just wanted to wish him all the best, you know?"

"Oh yeah?" said Dad. It came out a bit aggressively, but Jasper either didn't notice or had to keep up the pretense.

"Yes. What an inconceivably rotten thing to have happened to him! I wanted to tell him that the situation would get better."

Aunty Alice had missed all of this. She'd been talking in the kitchen with a policewoman she'd been at school with. "What's up?" she said innocently.

Jasper got in first. "Ah, not much. I was just trying to reassure that young fellow. He looked so lost, you know? Police said it wasn't the time or place, and you know—they were probably right in hindsight." He turned and headed upstairs. "Anyway—look at the time! We'd better be on our way, Alice, me old fruit pie."

I kid you not—he talks like that. They were out of the house and back to their boat in Culvercot within half an hour. Jasper refused Dad's offer of a lift and phoned for a taxi.

It was the strangest atmosphere. Everybody was *behaving* normally, but nobody was *feeling* normal. Libby had gone upstairs and did not come down to wave them off.

As soon as the taxi had rounded the corner, Dad murmured, "Blimey! Don't want to see *him* again for a very long time."

Mum slapped his arm playfully. "*Ben!* That's my brother-in-law."

Dad tutted. "Brother outlaw, more like."

CHAPTER FORTY-NINE

Alfie

Night after night, I slept badly. When you are as old as I am, there are a lot of memories that can turn into bad dreams.

The man's face kept coming into my mind, when he leaned down at the car window, and each time I would reach for the memory, but it would elude me and I would wake, sweating, in the hot nights. My bed was covered with a "duvet." I was used to sheets and blankets.

I ate little. Mam and I used to have simple food. I do not know why, but at Earl Grey House we are served things like curry, and spaghetti, and peri-peri chicken, which burns my lips.

Pizza is all right. I do not mind pizza.

I had been in Earl Grey House for a week and everybody from Sangeeta, whom I saw daily, to the children's-home staff (led by a slightly scary lady who was introduced to me as Aunty Reet) was being very gentle and sweet. There were eight other children there of assorted ages. Two of the girls smiled at me, but I did not feel much like speaking. The last person I had spoken the truth to betrayed me to the police. Now I had to learn to live in my life of lies.

I do not suppose that the man with the Neverdead scars knows where I am now, and besides, I tell myself that I was probably imagining it all anyway.

It is easier that way. For the time being, anyhow.

Then the subject of Mam's funeral came up. I knew it would, of course. Sangeeta asked me if I wanted to go. I said yes. I have been to more funerals than almost anyone I have ever met, including old people.

I had seen a headline in the local newspaper two days earlier:

WOODS FIRE VICTIM:
"SIMPLE" FUNERAL FOR TRAGIC MUM

Sangeeta also asked me if I wanted to help organize it, but I said no.

So there we were, me and Aunty Reet, on a Saturday morning outside Earl Grey House, waiting for Sangeeta to take us to Whitley Crematorium, where dead people are burned instead of putting them in a grave.

I think Mam would have approved. We once saw a funeral for a Viking thane, or lord. I say Viking: he was Danish, at least, but he liked the old Viking ways because it was his family heritage. By then, his family had lived peacefully up the Tyne for four or five generations.

A floating platform had been constructed on the beach at Culvercot, although there was no village there then. The thane's body was placed on it and surrounded with wood and sea coal, set alight, and pushed out to sea.

We all gathered and sang the old songs and ate meat that the thane's family had provided. In truth, everybody knew that only the most important people were ever buried on an actual burning *ship*. For a start, you had to be able to afford a ship to burn. Ealdor Sveyn—the dead lord—was certainly not that important or that rich. He was, though, what you would now call a "snob." He imagined himself to be grander than he really was. But we did not mind: the funeral feast was free.

So the platform was set alight and pushed into the bay, where it drifted out beyond the rocks. It soon collapsed in a hiss of smoke. The following morning, Ealdor Sveyn's charred corpse was washed up on the shoreline. His grandson took it away and buried it in the ground somewhere.

All of this was flashing through my head as I stood outside Earl Grey House, looking out over the bay. It was warm, but there was a slight breeze coming off the sea.

I could see the exact spot, a little way out into the bay, where Ealdor Sveyn's raft collapsed and sank, taking his half-burnt body with it. I could almost hear the chants and sad songs that were being sung by everybody on the shore. There was one by Bede that I remembered:

> *"Foruh them neidfaerae, nenig weirthit*
> *Thonk-snottura than him tharf sie . . ."*

"Are you all right?" It was Sangeeta's voice, and I turned round. She said it again. "Are you all right? You were lost in the clouds, then, Alfie!"

"I am sorry. Were you saying something?"

"No. But you, you . . . were singing something! What was it?"

"Nothing, Sangeeta. Sorry."

She looked at me, eyes narrowed, for a moment. She has done that a lot in the past few days. "OK, then. I was asking if you've ever been to a funeral before."

I must still have been in my half-dream state. I said, "I have attended far too many."

"I thought you said you had no relatives, Alfie? Is that because they've all died?" She did not say this aggressively. Was she trying to catch me in a lie? It felt that way.

I was thinking of a reply when Aunty Reet came down the steps of Earl Grey House and ushered us along to the waiting car.

I will avoid a long description of the funeral, because nothing happened until the end.

There were not many people there.

There was me, obviously, Aunty Reet, and Sangeeta. I had a pair of non-jeans that Sangeeta had bought me, and a dark pullover.

There was Vericka, and Robbie the Fire Investigations man. He winked at me and gave a tight little smile. That was nice of him. But I wished there were people I really knew. Friends. Of course, that was impossible. I had even lost my cat.

There was a reporter too, with a camera, which she put away after Sangeeta had a quiet word with her. I am not sure what a reporter was expecting to see. Probably more people, I should imagine.

There was a vicar, obviously.

After all the words had been said, and Sangeeta had squeezed my shoulder until I almost asked her to stop, and the coffin disappeared behind a red curtain like an especially sinister magic trick, that was it. We turned to go, and I saw them.

Roxy Minto and Aidan Linklater, standing at the back of the little chapel.

CHAPTER FIFTY

"Who are they?" murmured Sangeeta slowly.

Well, what could I say? "I do not know" was not true. Nor was "Friends," for I certainly did not think of them as such. They had betrayed me, which is not what friends do. Had they not, I might already have acted upon me and Mam's plan.

We were walking up the chapel's aisle, and would be level with them soon.

"I, erm . . . Just give me a moment, will you, Sangeeta?"

I was left in the chapel with Aidan and Roxy.

"Hi," they both said together, in a flat tone, appropriate to the circumstances.

"Hello."

"I . . . ," said Aidan. "I thought, that is, *we*—Roxy and me—we thought we'd come along and, erm . . ."

I should have helped Aidan out here. I should have recognized that he was trying to be kind but was struggling for the right words. I should have said something like "That is all right. Thank you for coming."

Instead I cocked my head and waited for him to stumble through.

"It . . . it's just that your mum, your mam . . . well, erm . . . she was all you had, and erm . . ."

Roxy had taken a breath to say something, but I turned to Aidan first. "Listen. I know you mean well, but frankly I do not—"

He cut me off. "Alfie. We believe you."

"I beg your pardon?"

Roxy said, "We believe you, Alfie. The thousand-year thing. Or at least we don't *disbelieve* you."

"There is a difference?"

"There's loads of stuff that doesn't add up, but there's evidence there if you look for it, at least back a few hundred years, and, if it's true for a few hundred years, then why not for a few hundred more?"

I stared at them both. I felt breathless. I glanced over at Sangeeta, who was having a quiet conversation with the vicar but still watching me out of the corner of her eye, I could tell.

"Thank you," I said, eventually. There was a long pause, and then I said, "So why did you tell the police where I was?"

A shocked look passed across Aidan's face. "Is *that* what you think? Alfie, I didn't. It was my little sister. Honest. She was just . . . She's only seven. I never told a soul!"

Roxy too looked horrified. "You're our friend, Alfie. Friends don't—"

But she was cut off, because at that point Sangeeta came over, all smiley and funeral-gentle.

"Hi," she said to Roxy and Aidan. "I'm Sangeeta, Alfie's CPO. Do you know one another?"

"A bit," said Aidan.

"That's nice. How do you know Alfie?"

"Oh, erm . . . through, erm . . . school."

Why did he say that? I had sort of edged behind Sangeeta now, and I was frantically shaking my head at Aidan, and at the same time Roxy's description of me as a "friend" was echoing round my brain.

Do I believe her? Does she mean it?

"That's strange," said Sangeeta, turning to me. "I thought you said you were homeschooled, Alfie?"

"Not school!" yelped Aidan, picking up on my signal. "No— not school. No. That is, erm . . ."

Aidan was not a convincing liar, or a good actor. The panic was in his voice. All over him, actually. You could practically smell it.

Sangeeta, genuinely curious, I think, said, "Yes?" and thank heavens for Roxy Minto.

"You mean school*work*, don't you, Aidan?" she drawled, as if to a rather slow child. "You helped Alfie with his schoolwork occasionally. But you only visited him once or twice. Maths, mainly, wasn't it?" Aidan did not respond. "*Wasn't it*, Aidan?"

"Oh. Yes. Maths. Yes," Aidan intoned, nodding on each syllable. Either Sangeeta is easily fooled or she decided not to pursue it at that time.

"Well, that's nice of you," she said. "Thank you for coming today. It was very thoughtful."

Walking back to the car, Sangeeta and I were a few paces ahead of Aidan and Roxy.

"Why did you say you had no friends, Alfie?" she asked quietly.

I had begun to say, "Because I thought it was true," when her telephone started ringing in her pocket and she stopped. That was when I saw a thin man, with a thick black beard and big eyebrows, wearing a long dark overcoat. When he was about thirty feet away, he abruptly turned and walked quickly in the opposite direction.

It was definitely him.

Sangeeta was hunched over her telephone and did not see this.

I looked behind: Roxy and Aidan were just coming out of the chapel, talking to each other. I immediately worked out that the man was going to approach me until he saw them, at which point he had turned and hurried away between the overgrown graves and mossy headstones. Seconds later, he disappeared behind a line of long black hearses that were awaiting the next funeral.

Something stirred inside me. That memory from long, long ago, rising to the surface and taking a gasp of air.

His face, leaning into mine, and growling, *"Holl munnen!"*

Shut your mouth.

The smell of cheese, and sealskin, and ship's tar.

His long teeth snarling at me to be quiet as I cried for my da.

The man from the boat to England.

Aidan's Uncle Jasper.

CHAPTER FIFTY-ONE

Did you know a shark can detect blood in the water up to five miles away? I sometimes feel that way with danger: I can notice the faintest traces. It is like a smell. An aroma of something from the past, and it was playing in my nose when I said to Sangeeta, "Can we go now?"

"All right, Alfie," she said. "What about your friends?"

"*Now.* We need to go now." I hurried, head down, toward Sangeeta's car with Sangeeta trotting behind me to catch up. When I glanced back, I saw Roxy and Aidan looking puzzled and hurt, and I wanted to go back and explain, but I could not, because I did not understand it properly myself.

I am certain Sangeeta thought it was delayed grief that had made me hurry off and so she left me alone in my thoughts as we drove away. But it was not grief. Well, not only grief.

It was Jasper.

It was fear.

Plus the realization that Aidan and Roxy had lied to San-geeta. For me. They had done that for *me*.

Sangeeta had stopped the car outside Earl Grey House and was saying something. I had not been paying attention until she took something black from her handbag and put in it my hands.

". . . It's just for safety, you know. I've put my number in al-ready, and Aunty Reet's."

A cell phone. I had never owned one before. Or even used one, for that matter. I turned it over in my hands, examining it.

She must have thought I disapproved, because she said, "Yeah, I know. Sorry it's not a smartphone, but it does the job."

Instead of asking her how to use it, which would sound odd, I thought I would figure it out myself.

Later I lay on my bed in my room at Earl Grey House. I stared at the ceiling. For the first time in a week, I thought about Mam and did not feel the hole of emptiness opening up inside me. Instead I felt a cold, sickening fear.

Jasper.

I had it all worked out. He did not know where I lived, so he had waited for Mam's funeral, knowing—or hoping—that I would be there. Then he would approach me.

Why, exactly, I could not figure out—but it could not be good. The memory of his bearded face leveling with mine on the creaking cargo boat all those years ago kept coming back, and it scared me.

Fear had replaced grief—and it was about to get worse.

CHAPTER FIFTY-TWO

Mam and I survived because we stayed together.

It was a strange life, indeed, but we had each other. Neither of us would leave the other alone in the world. You see, there was only one *livperler* left. If either of us took it, we would be able to live and die as normal—we would restart the aging process. But by doing so, we would abandon the other. That was our dreadful reality.

Mam would not take it and let me watch her grow old and die. Nor would I do that to her. Neither of us would make the other live on without the other.

Yet we each knew that we were not immortal. *Ageless* and *immortal* are different things, so we lived with the understanding that one day an accident might befall one of us and leave the other still living.

Neither of us liked the idea of being alone, and each of us thought that suicide was both terrifying and repellent.

Instead whoever was left would immediately enact the plan:

1. Locate the sole remaining life-pearl.
2. Administer it straightaway, and thereby . . .
3. Restart the process of aging, and . . .
4. Begin again to grow up.

It sounds simple. It is not. For one thing, I have to get to the life-pearl, and that is not an easy thing, because Mam and I hid it, long ago, in a secret, hard-to-reach place. But I am going to have to do it.

I long to grow up, to be a man. I long to be in a hurry to do something, before time runs out. I long for the feeling that life is precious, that I have to cram as much as I can into every sun-drenched day and every frost-filled night; to know that child-hood is special because it does not last forever; to have friends, like Aidan and Roxy, who will not look at me strangely, and then turn away from me when I fail to age like them.

In short, I long to grow older, and if that means that one day I will die, then I will make sure that I do not waste any more of my life.

That is what my plan is.

As soon as I can get the life-pearl.

Although, for that, I am going to need a boat.

CHAPTER FIFTY-THREE

A.D. 1140

We had left the monastery at Jarrow several decades before. Old Paul had grown old, and retired from his post. He had made enough money—we knew not how—to buy a small farm on what we called Cockett Island, just off the coast.

In those days, monasteries—or at least some monasteries—were incredibly rich. Some of that money ended up being used to buy land and houses for retiring monks.

Paul asked Mam and me to join him, she as his housekeeper and me as his scribe: someone who would write for him, as his eyesight was becoming very poor. He was also fond of Biffa, probably the world's only Neverdead cat. He promised her an endless supply of the island's plentiful crabs. He would mash them up for her, because already her teeth were getting worn like mine and Mam's, and she found it difficult to bite through crab shells like she used to.

Mam and I had now been living for more than a hundred

years. Throughout that time Mam had kept with her the single remaining life-pearl.

It was—is—stored in a small clay box, about the size of a modern cigarette package, surrounded with sheep's wool and fine sand for extra protection. The box bore no marking. The lid fitted closely, and was sealed with a mixture of tallow, beeswax, and pine resin.

That box lived with us, almost as if it were another member of our little family. Mam always knew where it was. We seldom traveled, but if we did, Mam would carefully unpick the seal and lift the tiny sphere out and swallow it for safekeeping. It would reappear about a day or so later, expelled in the manner dictated by nature.

Glass—in case you did not know—is extremely resistant to almost all forms of chemical reaction, so the little ball was completely undamaged by stomach acids and other internal processes. At the end of the journey, the glass ball would be cleaned, replaced in the box with some sand, resealed, and buried in a place that only Mam and I knew.

Thus did the clay box containing the life-pearl come with us to Old Paul's farmstead on Cockett Island.

The choice of burial spot for the box was always crucial. The ground should not be too damp. Nor should the box be buried too deeply: we had to be able to get at it quickly in an emergency. If we could not for any reason, if we had to leave in a hurry, then it would need to remain undisturbed and undiscovered for as long as it took to come back and retrieve it.

It was Old Paul who suggested the cave on the eastern side of the island: one of two caves high up the beach that were dry year-round. He knew about the pearl, and he knew we needed to keep it safe from those who might want it. The cave was deep and dark. There was a crevice behind a large boulder at the back that I could squeeze my arm into. Inside the crevice, out of sight, was a sandy ledge. It had been used in the past to conceal treasures from the Vikings, its location passed from one prior to the next.

It was perfect. Anything put there would be safe: completely hidden forever from anyone who did not know of it. The only people who did know were me, Mam, and Old Paul.

We had encased the clay box in more tallow and resin and beeswax for extra protection. When it hardened, it was wrapped in rough cloth, and this is the package that Mam extracted from her shawl as we stood in the cave at twilight.

The wind howled around us and the island's puffins—the squat black birds with the comical beaks—skidded and swooped in the sky above us. Old Paul, almost blind by now, intoned a prayer that he had made up for the occasion.

"Lord, through whom we may all find eternal life . . . ," it began. His voice was quavery, and the prayer droned on. Finally, as we were starting to shiver in the cold breeze, he said something that I noticed—through my half-closed eyes—caused Mam to look up. She caught me peeking.

"Lord," Old Paul was saying, "be merciful to those who choose to take the mighty power of life and death into their own hands. If it be a sin to prolong a life beyond its allotted span, look not with anger upon those who do."

Do you understand? Old Paul was asking God not to punish Mam and me for being Neverdeads.

Mam gave me the cloth-wrapped package and I shoved it in the space between the boulder and the cave wall.

It was safe forever.

"How long have you thought that? How long have you thought that the Lord may punish us for . . . for being what we are?" Mam asked Paul as we walked into the wind back to the farmhouse, with Paul holding my hand for guidance.

"It has troubled me for some time," he said. "I sought clarification from the bishop, who guided me in his wisdom."

There was a pause as Mam stopped walking and the wind howled.

"You told the *bishop*?" Mam was horrified that Paul had broken our pact of secrecy.

"Do not worry," Paul said, trying to reassure her. "I said nothing about you or Alve. Our discussion was restricted to what might happen *if* someone had such a power."

"But still," I said, "he might have thought it was a strange question. He might have wondered . . ."

"Fear not, young Alve," said Old Paul firmly. "The bishop had no suspicions. Your secret remains a secret. And the Lord will love those who love Him."

I was not so sure.

CHAPTER FIFTY-FOUR

Not long after, Old Paul died and was buried in the garden of the island's tiny chapel, where his bones lie to this day. Mam and I, and Biffa, stayed on in the farmstead.

A little while after that, a church official came to tell us we must move out, as a new priest was coming to live there. That is when we decided to leave the life-pearl box in its place.

"It is safe here," declared Mam as we walked down the steep and rocky cliff path to the cave. "No one will find it."

It had been about ten years since we had performed the little ceremony on that windy evening with the puffins skittering overhead. Nothing had changed.

"Should we check?" I asked Mam. "You know: that it is still there?"

She smiled her wise smile. "Why would it not be?"

"Because . . ." But I dried up. It was impossible for it *not* to be there.

"So I think we should just leave it, Alve. We both know it is there. We are the only ones who do. It can come to no harm. I feel easier in my heart when it is not in our home. This island is not going anywhere; that stone"—she was pointing at the large boulder—"is going nowhere, either.

"And if one of us should be called to the Lord"—that is what Mam used to say: instead of dying, you would be "called to the Lord"—"then the other will come straight here, administer the contents of the life-pearl, and begin the process of growing older. If that is what he or she wants," she added.

It was a thought that filled me with awe. That this immense power—the power both to create and to end immortality—lay in a small clay box buried in a dry sandstone cave on a windy island in Northumbria.

And lies there still. Undisturbed for centuries.

CHAPTER FIFTY-FIVE

In the children's home, countless questions jostled for position in my head, demanding answers that I could not give.

Where has Jasper been for a thousand years?

Why did he turn up now?

What did he want from me?

Was it the life-pearl?

It had to be. That must be what he was after—he was ageless; the scars on his arm made that clear. And, like me, he wanted to end it.

He could not possibly know where it was, though. But there was a more frightening possibility. Perhaps he knew that *I* knew and planned to use me to get to it.

I stared at the new school uniform hanging on the back of my bedroom door. Sangeeta said she would take me to school tomorrow, and after that I was to make my own way.

Make my own way.

Make friends. Grow up with them. Be normal.

Except that I could not. Not unless I managed to get to the pearl—before anyone else.

Part Three

CHAPTER FIFTY-SIX

AIDAN

The first day back at school, and the term had already started badly. It would get worse by the end of the week.

I'd been looking forward to catching up with Spatch and Mo, but something had changed.

I guess it had been happening for a while without me noticing. But now I did. Their holiday together at Spatch's grandparents' house in Naples had made each of them much better friends with the other than they were with me.

Spatch had got such a deep tan that he was even browner than Mo, but he said they hadn't been able to go to the beach much, owing to a sewage overflow closing it halfway through the holiday.

"That'll be why you're so brown, then!" I said, punching his arm gently.

He didn't get it, and pretended my punch had hurt him (which it can't have done). "Ow! What do you mean?"

"You know—you're brown 'cause you went swimming in the sewage!"

Now, I know it's not the sort of joke that could be described as "sophisticated," but *I* thought it was pretty funny, and started laughing, but they didn't join in. Spatch rolled his eyes at Mo.

"You're so lame, Linklater."

That's when I knew that, although we weren't enemies, our threesome had become a twosome, and the one left out was me.

Besides, what could I say about my Easter break?

"Guess what happened to me over the holidays? I became friends with Roxy Minto. She's my next-door neighbor."

"Wow, cool."

"Yeah, and you know that fire that was on TV? Well, there's a kid who escaped it and he's called Alfie and he says he's a thousand years old."

"Oh, how interesting. I'd like to meet him."

Instead I would be teased about whether I was in love with Roxy, and mocked for believing (even temporarily) someone who claimed to be a thousand years old.

As it was, I had to be content with telling the story of the fire, and the fire trucks, etc. They liked that, sort of. The rest of it I kept to myself.

I hadn't seen Alfie since the funeral a few days before. To be honest, he had been a bit weird, suddenly hurrying off without saying goodbye. Imagine being his friend might be pretty difficult. (I cannot imagine him laughing at sewage jokes, for example.)

I don't think he quite understood that we were trying to make up to him and convince him that we had not told the police.

Then, on the first day back, he turned up in afternoon assembly, at the end of the row, with the rest of shouty Mr. Springham's rowdy class. He was two rows in front and hadn't seen me, but I had a good view of him.

Brand-new school uniform, haircut, and a pair of those glasses like my Uncle Jasper's that get darker in the sunshine but which were now semi-tinted.

It didn't look like anyone was talking to him, but that was normal for a new kid.

By lunchtime, word had got around.

1. New kid called Alfie Monk.
2. He's the boy orphaned by the big fire in the woods.
3. Very quiet.
4. Speaks strangely, like English isn't his native language.
5. Shocking teeth, like he's never been to the dentist.

I didn't see him at break or at lunchtime, even though I was looking out for him. It wasn't until the next day that our paths crossed.

The first week of term was Local History Week. According to the letter sent out to parents, local history is the Head's "lifelong passion," and he's determined to share it with—that is, inflict it on—everyone else. Some people get totally excited about it. That's some people for you.

This year we were going to The Saxon Experience, which the letter home said was:

A vivid re-creation of life in Anglo-Saxon times, peopled by larger-than-life characters in authentic clothing. A unique chance to live the life led by our ancestors of more than a thousand years ago.

And here's the strange thing: until I read that, I had had *no idea* what Alfie had been talking about.

A thousand years? Might as well have been a million. But now I had what the Head, Mr. Landreth, calls a "frame of reference." Alfie was from Anglo-Saxon times. Even thinking that was strange.

I was secretly hoping that the trip would be a chance to rebuild ties with Mo and Spatch, but, after just one day, Mo was off sick. (He was skipping, I'm certain. He just needs to cough and his mum keeps him at home.) Worse, Spatch was banned from the trip for "persistent non-completion of homework." He'd be spending the day in Mrs. Spetrow's office, finishing his biology project from last term.

There were about a hundred kids—all of our year, more or less— waiting in the school playground before getting on the coaches for The Saxon Experience, and it was pretty noisy.

I felt a poke in my back. It was Roxy, and next to her was Alfie, a nervous, gappy smile on his face.

"Look who I've found," she said.

Before I could say anything, Mr. Springham popped up next to us and said needlessly loudly:

"YOU THREE. COACH ONE, SEATS 18, 19, 20, GO!"

Assigned seats? Oh great.

It was an hour on the coach to The Saxon Experience. An hour in which I discovered:

1. That Alfie was living in a children's home in Culvercot.
2. It was very strict and had imposed a curfew on him: in by nine p.m.
3. Sangeeta and the council were trying to find him a foster family, but these things take time, apparently.

And he kept asking about Jasper. I mean, more than once. At first, it wasn't weird. It was just, "How's your Uncle Jasper?" which sort of surprised me a bit because, if I'd mentioned him at all, it had only been in passing.

"He's, erm . . . fine. I guess. Why?"

"Oh, no reason. I was just asking."

Alfie's tone was unconvincingly casual, so I asked, "Have you met him before or something?"

"No. Never in my life. Never met him, no. Not at all."

Hmm. Too many denials there, I thought. Once again, a bad liar spots a bad lie. Did this have something to do with Jasper's odd behavior the day Alfie was found? But I thought I'd let it go.

Then, a few minutes later, he said: "How did he meet your aunt?"

"Who? Jasper? Blimey, Alfie—online, I think. Why? What's it to you?"

"Nothing, Aidan. Just small talk."

And there we left it because the Glasses Incident happened.

Inigo Delombra was sitting behind us, and he is someone you just steer clear of. He's not *exactly* a bully, because—as Mo discovered once in elementary school—he'll back right off if you stand up to him. The problem is he's already as tall as the women teachers (and Mr. Green) and weighs about 175 pounds, easy. He's huge, in other words, and standing up to him takes courage.

So when Inigo stuck his head over the back of our seats and said, "Hello, new boy!" I sensed trouble.

Roxy and Alfie were seated together. I was across the aisle. I could see Inigo Delombra's posse of supporters (all two of them) chortling at what might come next.

"Wanna Haribo?" Inigo said, looking directly at Alfie.

"A what?" said Alfie.

"A Haribo."

"What is one of those?"

Oh no.

Inigo grinned at his sneering followers. "New kid doesn't know what Haribos are!" Turning back to him, he said, "Here! Have one." He showed him a packet of gummies. Alfie looked dubious.

"Go on! Have one! Have two! I've got another packet. Where you from then?"

"I was, well, my father was from Gotland, but then he lived in, erm . . . he . . . he is sort of Danish." The fear was written all over Alfie's face.

"Oh! So you're from, erm . . . Danishland. That'll be why you talk funny, eh? Anyway, let's have a look at your specs then?"

"My spectacles?"

"Yeah! Your glasses—come on!" He reached out and plucked them from Alfie's nose. Roxy had been quiet up to this point, but now she piped up: "Hey. Give it a rest."

"Oh, Little Girl speaks, does she?" Inigo leaned in close. "Shut it, squirt, or the rest of your term is gonna be H-E-double-L. Now what about these specs, eh? They are cool. Let's see if they go darker."

He had put them on and was staring out of the window.

"Wow! They do. Here, Jonesy: check these out." He passed them back to his pal, who held them up to the light and put them on and then passed them to someone else, and then someone else.

One boy said, "Where are these from? Are they unbreakable?"

I glanced across at Alfie, and the pained expression on his face was unbearable.

I got out of my seat and made my way to the back of the bus. By now, the glasses had become just a thing to be passed around. Half of the people at the back had no real idea where they'd come from, or that they'd been stolen from Alfie. It was comparatively easy for me to say:

"Here! Let me have a go!" I had to say it a couple of times, but then they arrived in my hand. I put them on, posed, smiled, and headed straight back to my seat.

"Hey! Bring them back!" shouted Inigo. "Linklater, you're dead! And you, too, Danish boy!"

It was only a small victory but my heart was thumping.

I was back in my seat when Mr. Springham got out of his, and bellowed down the coach:

"QUIET! I SAID QUIET! DELOMBRA—WHAT ARE YOU DOING OUT OF YOUR SEAT? GET BACK AT ONCE! YOU'RE A DISGRACE, ALL OF YOU! SIT DOWN AND EITHER READ OR PLAY SOME BRAIN-ROTTING GAME ON YOUR PHONES! I DON'T CARE, BUT I WANT SILENCE UNTIL WE GET THERE. IS THAT UNDERSTOOD?"

There was a murmuring of "Yes, sirs," during which I handed Alfie's glasses back to him across the aisle. If that didn't convince him that our offer of friendship was sincere, then nothing would.

"Thank you," he whispered, but he knew what had just happened. You don't live as long as he has without knowing that making an enemy of Inigo Delombra is a bad idea.

He was about to find out just how bad.

CHAPTER FIFTY-SEVEN

I'll say this for The Saxon Experience: they tried their hardest to make things interesting.

The problem was the kind of thing they thought a bunch of kids from Percy Ack would *find* interesting. Everything was aimed at six-year-olds, with signs in bright colors featuring cartoon figures and speech balloons saying things like:

Can you spot the biggest house?

How many animals are in this picture?

That sort of thing.

Alfie, Roxy, and I ended up together in one group. There was a visitor center, a café, and the education room, where a man dressed in Saxon clothes gave us a welcome talk. Mr. Springham only had to shout at us once to QUIET DOWN!

"Greetings and salutations, children of the twenty-first century!" said the man in the old-fashioned clothes. "My name is Eckfrith, and I own a small farm on the banks of the Tyne . . . ," and so on.

All the way through, Alfie kept quietly tutting and shaking his head slightly. I thought nobody had noticed apart from me, but the man who was giving the talk had obviously seen it as well, and suddenly stopped.

"Aha! I see we have a disbeliever among us!" he said sort of good-naturedly. "Tell me, young man—what is wrong? What makes you think I am not a genuine Anglo-Saxon farmer?"

Without missing a beat, Alfie said, "You are too clean," and the class erupted in laughter. The man didn't seem to mind.

"Well, young man, you're probably right. Soap was very expensive in those days!"

"Practically nonexistent, you mean? And no one said 'salutations'—that is a French word that was not common until long after 1066," said Alfie.

"Well, erm . . ." The man was floundering.

"Also your tunic would not be red."

The man looked down at his simple cotton overshirt. He was clearly a little surprised.

"Ah, really?"

"No. Unless you were a very wealthy farmer, you would not be able to afford a red tunic. Red was a very expensive dye."

"Ah, well," said the man, grinning. "Then I am an exceedingly wealthy farmer!"

"So why are you wearing a poor man's boots?"

More laughter from the class until Mr. Springham shouted, "ENOUGH!" and gave the evil eye to Alfie, who shut up.

Behind us, I heard Inigo Delombra mutter, "Think you're clever, don't you?"

The nudges and giggles continued, though much quieter. Alfie had got himself noticed, that's for sure. Whether that was a good thing or not, I couldn't tell.

But it was nothing to what came next.

CHAPTER FIFTY-EIGHT

What came next was the "authentic reproduction Anglo-Saxon village," which was a collection of round huts with thatched roofs, and Alfie started sneering even at the sign. It was like being with a grumpy adult.

"How can it be authentic and a reproduction?" he said. "It is either one or the other."

Roxy was humoring him. "Stop it, Alfie. You'll love it. It'll be just like when you were, erm . . . younger."

Looking round, I saw that we had lost the rest of our group.

"Great Scott," Alfie said. "Who built these? An army of dwarves?" We crouched to go through the doorway.

"I think they were smaller than us back then," Roxy said by way of explanation.

"Only a bit," said Alfie. He looked at the hut's fireplace and then up at the roof. "Where is all the smoke going to go? There is not a smoke hole. People would choke."

"All right," I said, a bit irritated by his know-it-all attitude. "It's probably just a mistake. Look." I pointed out the window slit at the next hut along. "That one has a smoke hole. There's smoke coming out of it."

He looked and humphed in reluctant agreement before turning his attention back to the hearth, which was a ring of stones. "There is not even a proper fireplace. Most homes had one, built up to about this high, at least." He held his hand level with his knee.

"What was the point of that?"

"I do not know," he said, irritated. "They just did. Only the poorest people would not have one, because you had to buy the stones, but the poorest people did not live in houses like these."

"They'd *buy* stones? But stones are free."

"They are not just any stones. If you get a stone from the beach or a river, it might crack apart under the heat and explode. You do not want that happening when you are huddled round the fire for warmth in the winter. You want granite or limestone, and that means paying for it if you do not live near any. And as for *that*"—we were outside now and he was pointing to another fireplace, next to the hut—"it is much too close to *that*." He pointed at the straw and twig roof. "It could go up at any time. No one would put a fire there. In fact I am going to tell them."

He marched off in the direction of the man in the Saxon costume who had spoken to us before.

"No, Alfie. No!" Roxy said. I was curled up, embarrassed. He turned and stared at us both intensely.

"Why ever not? Not only is it historically inaccurate, it poses a significant danger right now."

I couldn't bear to watch. He was like one of those busybody old ladies who'll tell off a young policeman if his shoes aren't shiny enough. Roxy and I peered out from behind what seemed (to me) a very authentic-looking wheeled cart as Alfie strode up to the guide and tapped him on the shoulder, while he was talking to a group of people.

Alfie pointed. The guy looked over, then looked down at Alfie and shook his head, making a "go away" gesture with his hand before returning his attention to the group. So Alfie tugged his sleeve. The man was annoyed, I could tell, but Alfie didn't care, and I sort of admired him for that. The group of people began to wander off and this annoyed the man even more, so with a furious expression he followed Alfie to the fire and I overheard part of their conversation.

". . . significant incendiary risk . . . extinguished . . ."

". . . I'll go and speak to my supervisor. . . ."

The guy in the Saxon tunic wandered off in the direction of the visitor center. Just then, Inigo Delombra and one of his hangers-on appeared from round a corner, each holding a bundle of twigs.

"Go on, lads," said Inigo, and before we could stop them, they each chucked their armfuls onto the fire, which instantly burst into life. "Hey, that's cool, that is! I love a massive fire, me! Whoa!"

The fire had gone up alarmingly and was by now dangerously

high. When the smoke had cleared, Inigo Delombra and his pals were nowhere to be seen.

"Look at that," Alfie said. "One stray spark, and that whole roof will go up. It is as dry as . . . as . . ."

"A dry straw roof?" said Roxy, with a straight face.

"Yes. And it will spread to the others. I do not suppose you have seen a whole village burn?"

"No, Alfie," I said. "Surprising as it may seem, I haven't. Have you?"

The words were out of my mouth an instant before I realized what I'd said. Alfie—who'd seen his own house burn down only weeks earlier—knew more than anyone the true horror of a fire, and I started to apologize.

"Hey, that came out wrong. . . ."

But he had gone, reappearing a few seconds later with a wooden bucket.

"Have you seen a tap anywhere?" he asked, the urgency in his voice clear.

"There'll be one at the visitor center, or in the café."

"Too far. There is only one thing for it."

By now, the flames were really quite high. Alfie had his back to me, but I could see he was fiddling with his trouser fly. He turned his head and called to me over his shoulder.

"Come on! What are you waiting for? We have got to put it out somehow!"

"Alfie, you're crazy! It's a museum. You can't just . . . pee all over the exhibits."

"If they want to have any exhibits left, then it is my duty. Yours too, Aidan. Come on."

He had already started. There was a noisy hissing, and a vast cloud of yellow-gray smoke started to rise from the fireplace.

"Come on!" he shouted over the noise of the hissing fire. "I do not have enough urine in me. I went after lunch."

I had not been after lunch. In fact I'd been halfheartedly looking for the toilets for a while, so, when I finally started, I released my bladder in a blissful gush. The smoke and steam doubled and rose high above the tops of the huts.

Alfie had finished and done up his fly when we heard the guy in the tunic shout, "Oi! What the hell are you doing?"

"Run!" said Alfie.

I was midstream at that point, and I couldn't possibly stop.

"I can't!" I wailed, but he was off already and the guy was getting closer.

"You little toe rag!" he bellowed.

The group of tourists had returned and at least two of them were taking photos of me in a cloud of pee smoke at the fireplace, and *still* it kept coming, making me curse the extra-large Coke I'd drunk.

There was only one thing to do. With all the effort I could summon, I managed to slow the stream so I could tuck everything back into my pants, and I started to run, pee dribbling down my pant leg. The only way I could get away from the Saxon guy was to push through the tourists, but as soon as I got near, they parted for me and that's when I tripped.

I stumbled forward, half turned, and landed on my back in a puddle. My flies were open, *everything* was hanging out. I was being watched by a group of astonished tourists and, a couple of seconds later, by a man dressed in a woolen tunic and fake chain mail.

"All right," he said, throwing down his plastic axe and grabbing me by the arm. "Come with me."

A camera flashed, and my humiliation was complete.

CHAPTER FIFTY-NINE

Alfie and I were in trouble, although, owing to Alfie being a new kid, and what had happened to him recently, the teachers were inclined to go easy on him, and, luckily for me, I think they saw the unfairness of being gentle with Alfie and tough with me. We both got off fairly lightly.

Of course, no one believed us when we said we'd been trying to stop the roof catching fire, and I didn't say anything about Inigo and his pals fueling the flames, because just about the worst thing you can do at school is to snitch. Alfie seemed to know that, because he kept quiet about that part too. Roxy, very wisely, pretended she hadn't seen a thing.

We sucked up the telling-off and being sent to sit on the bus for the rest of the trip. There was talk of a visit to the principal, and a letter home, and Alfie's social worker being told and all of that, but it was obvious they were just threats.

"I simply do *not* understand you," said Mr. Springham, for once strangely quiet (which made it even more menacing). "Were you showing off? Did you think it was funny?"

I hung my head to display a sorrow that I just did not feel. "No, sir."

"No, sir," Alfie repeated.

"Exactly," said Mr. Springham.

"Although we did avert a fire which might have caused significant damage to property and people," said Alfie.

Mr. Springham controlled himself, and it was such an effort it turned him a weird sort of purple color.

CHAPTER SIXTY

alfie

Going to school is exhausting. It is also one of the most exhilarating experiences of my long life.

I have never been to one before. Not a school like a twenty-first-century school, anyway.

I have been to many "schools," where I have learned many things.

But a huge building containing more than a thousand children, all learning the same things, which they do not have to pay to attend? No.

By the time it became the law to send your children to school (I have looked it up—it was 1880), I had been reading and writing for centuries.

At first, compulsory education was for children up to ten years old, so—as a boy living as an eleven-year-old—I did not have to go. Then the age was raised to eleven, then twelve, but, so long as you could prove that you could read and write and so on, you still did not have to attend.

By 1918, the year the Great War ended, the education age was again raised, to fourteen. That is when things started to get difficult, and Mam and I had to begin deceiving the authorities about my age and why I was not at school. We became very good at it, always helped by the fact that I was quite obviously well educated.

And now I find myself at Sir Henry Percy Academy, or "Percy Ack" as everybody—the teachers included—refers to it.

The other children are loud and lively. They are rude to the teachers, and the teachers do not seem to mind, although there is one who shouts a lot. The pupils often look at me suspiciously, but nobody is actually unkind, not to my face. Except, that is, for one boy called Inigo Delombra, who seems to eat sweets all the time. He passed around my glasses, and he imitates my way of speaking. He pretends it is what he calls "banter," but it is not.

And then there are Aidan Linklater and Roxy Minto, my friends. It feels good to be able to say that.

It is all keeping my mind off Aidan's Uncle Jasper. I have not seen him again, and I am beginning to think I imagined it all. It is possible. I have been in a strange state of mind.

At school, we are given books for free. Can you believe that? There is a library where you can have any book, and some of the stories are wonderful. Everybody is given a meal at midday. Some children go to a "Breakfast Club" where they are given free food. Imagine!

I am not in the Breakfast Club. Instead I get breakfast at Earl Grey House. The other children all eat "breakfast cereal" from different colorful boxes. They tip it into a bowl, and then pour milk all over it and eat it with a spoon.

(You probably know this already, but I am just saying in case you do not.)

The breakfast cereals taste too sweet to me, so Aunty Reet normally makes me eggs.

Sangeeta took me in on the first Monday. She parked the car opposite the school while other children mingled on the pavement, and looked at me closely.

"You OK with this, Alfie?" she said. "It's pretty soon after everything."

For a moment, I had a dreadful fear that she was about to say that I should not go. That I was not ready, or something. For years and years, I have seen children going to school in their uniforms, laughing and shouting. Surely she would not stop me?

"It is the law, is it not? I have to attend school regularly," I said.

She gave a half smile. "Well, yeah. But you know . . . we're not . . . that is, it could wait. A bit."

"What else would I do?"

She sighed through her nose and tucked a lock of hair behind her ear. "I know. Look, Alfie . . ."

"Yes, Sangeeta?"

"Is there anything you're not telling me? I'm just worried that . . ."

"No, Sangeeta. I will be fine. Thank you for the drive."

"The ride, Alfie. It's called a ride."

"The ride."

When I glanced back, she was watching me go, biting her bottom lip. She knew something was up.

But that was a problem for later. I was about to learn something much worse and much more immediate.

The time to enact the plan was about to run out.

CHAPTER SIXTY-ONE
AIDAN

I'm not sure I have ever seen anyone actually turn white before. It's one of those things that people say, isn't it? Like "I nearly died," or "I peed myself laughing" (although that did happen to Valerie King once, a few years ago).

But generally nobody *really* turns white. Except Alfie Monk during a talk at school for Local History Week.

He's pale to begin with, and with all the sunshine we've been having lately he's even got a bit sunburnt, but this was something else.

The lady giving the talk said something, Alfie gasped, and when I looked across at him, the color had disappeared from his cheeks. It was horrible. He was whitish-gray and his mouth started moving as if he was saying something, but there was no noise.

What happened was this.

It was a warm afternoon and the school assembly hall was boiling hot, and it still smelled of school dinners. Everybody was a bit restless, and nobody was all that interested in listening to someone give a talk called "Northeastern Archaeology: From Yesterday to Tomorrow!"

(It was the exclamation mark that did it: a sad attempt at cheeriness.)

Mr. Springham announced the speaker, Dr. Susannah Heinz, and I immediately swung my head round to look for Roxy. Had she recognized her? Roxy grinned back.

It was Sue from our street. Sue of Sue and Pru—the cat ladies! She wasn't wearing her huge sweater and jeans, but a sensible pantsuit.

Even before the talk had started, Mr. Springham had already had to shout "BE QUIET!" twice and make Inigo Delombra swap places so he could keep an eye on him. Worse, the blinds were down so Dr. Heinz could show us some slides, and she had a quiet, reedy voice with that strong foreign accent.

I felt sorry for her, really. She looked as though she'd be a sweet old aunty.

Worst of all—for her—was that she was nervous, and it was obvious. It was like our class was a wild dog that could smell fear.

"Hello, children," she began, and I thought, *Bad start.*

"Who can tell me vot an archaeologist is?" she asked.

"A boring old fart," said Inigo Delombra, not *quite* quietly enough. I swear Dr. Heinz heard, and I felt awful for her. No hands went up.

"Vell, er . . . erm . . . archaeology is . . . is the study of human history through the excavation of the sings ve have left behind. These can be sings zat are dug up, or sometimes ruined buildings and monuments. In fact I often say to my friend Prudence that I'll never be rich because my career is in ruins!"

She grinned and waited in vain for a laugh. Instead 120 blank faces stared back at her. Five seconds later, Alfie said, "Ruins! Ha!" and everyone turned to look at him.

Awkward.

Alfie was *definitely* the only person in the whole room who was interested. He leaned forward in his seat, hanging on Dr. Heinz's every word as she went on and on about digging up stuff.

She showed us a trowel. *Woo-hoo.* And a paintbrush that she said was used to brush dirt off stuff.

And then the slides. Endless slides. And still Alfie didn't get bored.

"So here we have a site zat I helped to excavate back in 1990, in ze village of Saxton, near Towton, vich is about ninety miles from here, so not *werry* local."

It was a picture of another hole in the ground so far as I could see, and next to it was a grinning young Dr. Heinz with thick glasses.

"And who can tell me vot happened in Towton?"

Alfie's hand—alone—shot up. "The Battle of Towton!" he yelled.

"Indeed—sank you. The Battle of Towton. It is often called ze most deadly battle in British history, vere upward of twenty-five sousand men are said to have died in a single day, although my personal belief is that zis is a vild exaggeration—"

"Excuse me?" Alfie's hand had gone up again.

"Yes?"

"It was more like forty to fifty thousand people. It was huge." People turned to look at the kid who was daring to contradict the expert.

But he had learned his lesson from the day before at The Saxon Experience, and now he began to retreat. "That is, erm . . . so I have heard."

"Well, ze various records are not in agreement, but I know vot I sink," said Dr. Heinz, with an air of finality.

"And I know what I saw," said Alfie. People had started to chortle, so he added, "On television once." It prompted Mr. Springham to stand up.

"That's enough, Alfie Monk! Pipe down and show some respect!"

Alfie blushed bright red, which was a contrast to his color only two minutes later.

It was nearly at the end of the talk and Dr. Heinz said, "And finally . . . ," prompting a relieved *"Yessss!"* from a few people, which she *must* have heard.

"After all zis, you're probably wondering vot's next for northeastern archaeology? Vell, let me tell you briefly about our project on Coquet Island, werry near here."

At that, Alfie—who had shrunk into his seat a bit thanks to his telling-off from Mr. Springham—sat bolt upright as though his chair was electrified. Another picture popped up on the PowerPoint, of a little square lighthouse and some surrounding buildings, painted white with crenellated walls, like a cartoon castle.

"Zis, children, is ze lighthouse on Coquet Island, but it is believed to be built on ze site of a medieval chapel. Back then, it vas known as Cockett Island. . . ."

I actually yawned. If this was interesting to Alfie, it wasn't to me. On she went for a minute or so.

". . . vill be commencing our dig zis summer, excavating an area from *here* to *here* . . ." She was pointing at a map now. "Ve expect to unearth artifacts from early inhabitants of the island and perhaps even . . ." She paused for effect, then added, in a spooky voice, ". . . a *skeleton* or two!"

Nobody reacted. We were past caring. I glanced across at Alfie, and that's when I saw that he'd turned pale. Was it the mention of skeletons? I mean, he was still mourning his mum: this may have been too close to home.

It was what she said next that prompted Alfie's biggest reaction.

". . . before all zat, though, I vill be conducting a personal excavation of some caves beneath the main site. It vas not unknown for caves to be used for hiding treasures, and after all, the vords 'excavate' and 'cave' are both derived from ze Latin *cavare*. . . . "

With a loud scraping of his chair, Alfie got to his feet and stumbled to the door. Once again, everyone turned to look. I saw Mr. Springham draw a breath to shout at him, but Alfie got in first. "Sorry, sir. I do not feel well."

Without waiting for a response, he pushed open the hall door and went out. I followed him as Mr. Springham said to me, "Go and check he's all right."

He wasn't all right. Nowhere near all right.

CHAPTER SIXTY-TWO

Alfie

Nothing could have prepared me for what I learned in the school hall that day.

I had been struggling to hear the archaeologist over the constant fidgeting and murmuring. I understand why people might not be interested, really I do. But the poor woman was being ignored.

I suppose I did not help with my interjection about the Battle of Towton. I wanted to tell her, "I saw it with my own eyes! Field after field of unburied corpses and bloodstained snow, memories that come back to me in dreams even now . . ."

But of course I could not, and I stopped myself.

Then she showed the picture of Cockett Island (now called Coquet, rhyming with "poke-it," though I have no idea why), and I felt a lurch deep inside me, a quickening of my heart.

In the twenty-first century, nowhere is secret. Coquet Island is a bird sanctuary, Dr. Heinz had said, and people cannot normally go there in case they disturb the puffins and other seabirds.

But now more people will be visiting, and digging and excavating.

Somebody may find the skeleton of Old Paul, and they will say things like ". . . believed to be a man in his seventies . . . bone samples sent for DNA testing . . . possibly a farmer . . ."

And I will be shouting, "No! It is Old Paul, the prior! He was like a father to me! He was eighty-two, which then was like a hundred and twenty now!"

It was not, however, the skeleton that concerned me most.

Buried deep in the dry cave was the only possibility that I might ever escape from the prison of my deathless life.

I can imagine the reports on the wireless: *"A mysterious artifact of glass . . . appears to have been buried on purpose . . . radiocarbon dating . . . expert analysts . . ."*

By the time Aidan came out to check I was all right, I was shaking and sweating, but I knew what I must do. I pushed my way through the crowd of students as they came out.

"Alfie! What the heck?" called Aidan, but he did not follow me.

The archaeologist was still there at the front, packing up her trowel and things, and her little computer.

"Dr. Heinz! I must ask you something!"

She looked up, surprised, and smiled. "*Ach,* hallo, young

man. Our Battle of Towton expert, I see." She was being friendly, which I was glad about.

"Yes, but your excavation of Cockett Island. When does it start?" I sounded too eager, too desperate, but I could not help it.

"Vell, let me see," she said, taking out a mobile telephone and tapping it a couple of times. "Ze main dig is not due to start for anozzer month or so, although I have been on site already, setting up some initial—"

"Yes, yes, what about the cave?"

"Goodness me, young man! Aren't you ensusiastic? It is so nice to meet someone vith a keen interest in archaeological pursuits. I remember—"

"*What about the cave?*" I was being rude, I could tell, but I was panicking. "I mean, that is . . . what are you looking for?"

Dr. Heinz stopped her packing and came round to sit on the edge of the table. She pushed her glasses up her nose and leaned in close. She looked at me so intensely that I felt myself shrinking back.

"Zere is a legend. Zere are references to it all over Europe, although it is werry little explored. A legend of a race of people who were immortal. Zey were known by different names. 'Over-death' is one: they had 'overcome death,' do you see?"

I nodded. My mouth was dry, my heart hammering.

"Some say zis legend gave rise to ze stories of vampires:

nocturnal beings who never died. Zere are at least two references to a place called *Karparty,* meaning the Carpathian Mountains in Romania; zat, of course, is where the story of Count Dracula arose. Oh, I'm sorry—you look scared!"

"No, no—go on!"

"Anyhow, there is a mention in an ancient document by a medieval Northumbrian bishop, Walter. It is in ze British Museum now, but *my* interpretation is zat zere may be artifacts associated with ze legend buried or hidden on Coquet. Perhaps it was a semi-religious cult. Bishop Walter was unclear. Or perhaps . . ." And here she paused and winked at me. "Perhaps it vas all true! What do you sink, young man?"

I was speechless. Literally speechless. I managed to stammer, "Th-thank you," and walked in a dreamlike state out of the hall into the sunshine, where I shaded my eyes until my glasses had adjusted their darkness.

A month, she had said. That was long enough to work out a plan, I told myself.

How wrong could I have been?

CHAPTER SIXTY-THREE

I saw him that night.

In front of Earl Grey House, across the seafront road, are benches overlooking the bay, and he was there: Jasper.

It was late, about ten p.m., and quite dark. The streetlamp cast a little pool of light that nearly reached the benches, and he sat, hunched over, occasionally stealing a glance at my window.

Well, it seemed like that, but he cannot have known which was my room, and my blinds were closed, so he could not see me. I was scared, though, and there was nothing I could do about it.

I could, I suppose, tell Aidan. *"Aidan, your Uncle Jasper is following me."* I did not think that would be well received.

I could tell Aunty Reet, or Sangeeta. *"There is a man on a bench outside."*

It is hardly a crime, is it, sitting on a bench in the evening?

I kept looking, keeping my light off, carefully opening my blinds. Once I saw him get up and cross the road, and I thought he was coming to knock on the door, but he did not. Instead he walked down the street and got into his car and drove away.

I felt sick. I hardly slept. But at least it answered one question. *I knew now that I was not imagining it.* Jasper was watching me.

Sometimes knowing the worst can be a relief.

CHAPTER SIXTY-FOUR

⸗ AIDAN ⸗

Alfie was acting weird. All that stuff during the archaeology talk? If he was trying to keep a low profile, he was going about it the wrong way. I would have to tell him.

As for me, when I got home, my heart did this little dance when I saw Aunty Alice and Jasper's car parked outside our house.

I'm always happy to see Aunty Alice, quite apart from the fact that she nearly always brings her homemade flapjacks. I'm less happy to see Jasper, especially after the strange boat trip.

As soon as I walked in the door, though, I could sense something was wrong. Aunty Alice was sitting in the kitchen and gave me a hug as usual, and as usual, she smelled of laundry and Juicy Fruit chewing gum, but her eyes were red and she tried to turn her head so that I wouldn't see.

I hate thinking about grown-up people crying. It doesn't seem right.

Mum ushered me out of the kitchen before I'd even got my

jacket off. In the hallway, she said, "You need to go next door for your supper."

"To Roxy's? But her mum . . ."

"Her mum's OK. Libby's already there. It's your Aunty Alice, she's . . ."

"What's wrong?" I was really worried.

"It's Jasper. He's kicked her out."

"*Kicked her out?* You mean, like . . . she's moved out of their house?"

"Well, yes . . . but not by choice. He changed the locks on the doors and told her he no longer wanted to live with her."

I was stunned by this. "But . . . but they're married."

"That doesn't matter. For the time being, your Aunty Alice is going to be with us. Right now, though, we need a little time alone, so you have to go next door. Mrs. Minto's expecting you."

When I came in, Precious Minto was standing at the cooker, frying fish fingers and singing a hymn under her breath in her wobbly falsetto. We ate more or less in silence, our conversation not stretching far beyond "Pass the ketchup, please."

Roxy, Libby, and I did the washing up while her mum went to rest. Roxy explained that her mum was "in remission," which is when an illness goes away temporarily, but it isn't a cure.

"It does mean she sings more, though," she added with a comic eye roll.

We hadn't talked about Aunty Alice and Jasper, but now we did.

"I hate him," said Libby. For once, I didn't feel like reminding her what Mum says whenever we say the word "hate": "It's a strong word that can scar your heart."

She said, "He swore at me. He told me to *something* off, you little *something*." (Libby can be quite prudish at times. She would never repeat a swear word, even in front of me. Especially in front of me, come to think of it.)

Jasper had said that to Libby? Roxy and I exchanged glances. "When? When did that happen?" I asked her. She was doing her annoying thing of restacking the dishwasher, that I had already loaded, into an arrangement more to her liking. You wouldn't think she was only seven.

She looked up, apparently surprised at the question.

"That day when I came back from Brownie camp. The day I found the boy . . ."

"Alfie."

"Yeah, well, everyone was in the kitchen, all those people, and Jasper wasn't."

I had forgotten that, probably because I hadn't thought it was important, but, now that she mentioned it, I suppose it was unusual not to want to know what was going on.

"Aunty Alice was seeming a bit lost, so I went looking for him. He was in your room."

"*My* room? Well, that's where Aunty Alice and him were staying."

"I know, but listen to this. He didn't hear me come in. He was sitting at the window, looking at the police car driving away, muttering to himself and moaning."

Roxy and I had stopped clearing up. Roxy said, "Moaning?"

"Well, moaning, tuneless singing, and mumbling; I couldn't understand what he was saying. It sounded like Latin. *Ackoom tay-am,* he was saying, *Ackoom tayam.* Then he saw me in the reflection of the window and he was really shocked. That's when he told me to . . . go away."

Roxy murmured, "Say that again. The thing he was saying."

"What, *Ackoom tayam?* I've no idea what it means."

"I do, though," said Roxy with a little shrug. "*Acum te-am.* It's a Romanian folk song: we learned it in drama class last year." She said it so casually, as if everyone should have at least *some* knowledge of East European traditional music.

"What does it mean?"

"It means 'Now I've got you.'"

I looked carefully at Libby to judge her expression. I was incredulous. "You didn't tell this to anyone?" She shook her head and I saw her chin make the very beginnings of a tremble.

"I was scared, Aidan."

The last thing we needed was a sobbing seven-year-old. It was Roxy who stepped in and—to my astonishment—put her tiny arm round Libby (who was taller than her) and said, "It's OK. I'd have been scared as well."

Roxy's little squeeze had opened up something in Libby and she carried on: "He gave me a hug afterward and he did this." Libby demonstrated with Roxy, stooping a little to hug her, then whispering in her ear:

"Not a word. Not a single word, do you understand?"

"He said that?" I asked, amazed. Libby nodded, and her chin started to go again.

We stayed at Roxy's and watched TV, although I didn't pay attention to any of it. Nor did Roxy, I don't think; every time I looked over at her, she wasn't even looking at the screen. When Libby and I got back, Aunty Alice had gone to bed.

Acum te-am.

Now I've got you.

What on earth did Jasper mean by *that*?

CHAPTER SIXTY-FIVE

alfie

The next day was the School History Exhibition, apparently one of the highlights of Local History Week. I was distracted, thinking about Jasper and the upcoming archaeological dig—how was I going to get to the pearl before they found it?

But something soon happened that took my mind off all that.

The idea behind School History Exhibition day was that small "teams" were tasked with finding an old object at home and researching where it came from and what its significance was to local history.

Each team was allocated a table in the playground where they would display their object and a poster. The whole school would then be invited to the exhibition. People had brought in old photograph albums; one girl had her great-grandmother's christening shawl—that sort of thing.

By the time the exhibition was in full swing, the heat wave had persuaded the school to allow the boys to go tieless. One or two had taken the chance to unbutton their shirts to the waist.

"Oh my Lord," said Roxy, who had already done a quick tour of the playground exhibition. "Wait till you see Inigo Delombra!"

We did not have to wait long. His exhibition, which he was manning with two of his friends, was close to us, and I saw him from a distance. He had taken the opportunity of not wearing a tie even further than others, with the addition of a large, shiny cross on a thick chain to decorate his bare chest. Dark glasses completed the impression of small-time con man.

He seemed in a cheery mood as we pushed through the throng to make our way over to his exhibition.

"Ah—look who it isn't!" he said, grinning wolfishly. "Verily and forsooth, 'tis thou, the fancy-talking fop!"

"That is not the right meaning of 'fop,' Inigo," I retorted. "Indeed it means someone given to fancy, showy dressing. Such as the sporting of ostentatious jewelry." I indicated his cross and chain.

His two friends thought this was hilarious. "Owww! Delombra, you is *burned*!" said the one called Jonesy, in an American accent, and clicked his fingers. Inigo curled his lip in response.

(I think this was what everybody calls "banter," and by the way people smiled, I was good at it, on that occasion, at least.)

Until then, I had not even seen what his display was, but I looked down and immediately felt sick and breathless at the same time.

It is as well that his friends were distracting him or someone might have heard me gasp. As it was, Aidan said, "Oh wow! Look at this, Alfie," and moved to pick up a book from the desk.

"Hey! No touchin'! That's valuable!" said Inigo Delombra.

I stared, dry-mouthed, at a copy of A Tale of Two Cities by Charles Dickens, and I knew—I do not know how but I just knew—that Inigo Delombra would say what he said next.

"It's autographed, you know! Look!" He opened the front cover of the book, and there it was, in extravagant, curly handwriting.

> To the dear Reader, Alve, with my Compliments,
> Charles Dickens

Roxy pointed at the inscription and said, "Hey—it says 'Alve.' Just like—"

"Yes," I cut in. "It is a very unusual name."

"Never read it meself, mind," said Inigo. "Borin', if y'ask me. But he wrote loads, did Charles Dickens. An' I love the title. If you say it the wrong way round, you get A Sale of—"

I interrupted him. "H-how did you get this?" I tried to sound relaxed and interested, but I do not think I succeeded, because Roxy's and Aidan's heads both snapped round to look at me. Inigo had been distracted by a friend chortling at some joke he had made, which I had missed in my astonishment, so I said it again, a little too loudly.

"How DID you get THIS?"

"All right, all right—keep your hair on. It's been in me family for years. I got it off me Great-Uncle John."

"And what is his name?"

"I've just told you, man. It's John. First name—*Great-Uncle*. Jeez. He got it off his dad, an' I haven't gorra clue where *he* got it. It was years ago. You all right?"

I pulled myself together. "Yes, fine, splendid, actually. Thank you," and I wandered off in a daze, with Aidan and Roxy following me, and the sound of Inigo Delombra imitating me in my ears: "*Splendid*. Who the heck says 'splendid'?"

I turned to Roxy. "Do you trust me?"

She narrowed her eyes. "Where is this going?"

There were people all around us. "Do not ask. Just answer my question. Do you trust me?"

"Yes, Alfie. I trust you."

Aidan added, "Me too. What is all this?"

"Faint," I said to Roxy. "Right now. Just faint on the ground and stay fainted for as long as you can. I promise you it is important. Just do it."

"Faint?"

"Yes. Imagine you are the lead actress in a play and the script requires you to faint in the heat of a . . . a jungle or something."

That got her. "Right here, right now?"

"Yes. You will be brilliant, I promise."

"Why, though?"

"I asked you if you trusted me. . . ."

She needed no further coaxing. With a little moan, she fell back into Aidan's arms in the middle of the crowd. Aidan was good as well.

"She fainted!" he yelled. "Everybody clear a space—Roxy Minto has fainted!"

Everyone stopped to look and formed a little circle round her. As I slipped away, I heard someone say, "It's the heat—she's fainted!" and then—inevitably—Mr. Springham's booming voice:

"CLEAR A SPACE! GIVE HER SOME AIR!"

Inigo Delombra's table was deserted as they gawped at the fainting victim, leaving the book unattended.

My book. Ten seconds later, I had it in my schoolbag, and thirty seconds after that I was out of the school's back gate, trying to walk fast but naturally, and breathing as if I had just run a mile.

CHAPTER SIXTY-SIX

⸱⸴ AIDAN ⸴⸱

It was just getting worse. The amount of trouble we were building up for ourselves was pretty terrifying.

I mean, when it was me and Roxy keeping the secret of the weird kid who claimed to be a thousand years old, it was OK. Fun, really, in a way: you know, us against the world?

I was even cool with being the friend of the new weird kid at school and the tiny girl with the squeaky voice. Not that I had much choice, what with Spatch and Mo being pretty much inseparable these days.

But now we were thieves. Except we weren't really, because I hadn't stolen anything, nor had Roxy. And nor, for that matter, had Alfie.

We sat in Roxy's garage, the three of us. The copy of *A Tale of Two Cities* lay on the desk and we stared at it, silently, for ages. The rest of the collection of Dickens books was still in the metal trunk beneath the battered sofa. Eventually Alfie spoke.

"It *is* mine. You do believe me?"

"I believe you, Alfie. It has your name in it," Roxy said, staring at the floor.

"Yeah, me too."

"Tell me again," said Alfie. "What happened after Roxy pretended to faint?"

By the time Mr. Springham had made it over to the gathered crowd, Roxy still hadn't recovered. Any longer, and I was getting scared they'd call an ambulance or something. Soon afterward, she "came round," and I accompanied her indoors with Miss Newton, where she was made to sit in the library with a glass of water.

Miss Newton started filling in some form about Roxy fainting, and she was asking questions like "Do you have a headache? Did you injure yourself when you fell?"

School was finished for the day, anyway. Miss Newton offered to take Roxy home in her car, which was nice of her, and because I live next door, I got a ride as well. It was only when we were sitting in Miss Newton's car that Roxy's mobile phone starting pinging like mad.

"You're popular!" said Miss Newton, smiling, but Roxy's face was expressionless.

"Oh my goodness!" she said, reading her messages. "There's been a theft at school. Some book has gone missing or something."

I've got to hand it to Roxy. If I hadn't known she was acting, I just could not have guessed. Her tone was pitch-perfect: surprised but not personally concerned. I knew I couldn't act as well as she could, so I just kept my responses to the minimum I thought I could get away with.

"Gosh! A theft! Wow!"

Roxy shot me a sideways glance and rolled her eyes, smiling.

Miss Newton said, "I'm sure someone's just misplaced it. These things happen all the time. Is this your house, Roxy?"

And now, an hour later, all three of us were in the garage, staring at Alfie's book.

"It is *not* theft," he said when we'd filled him in. "It was mine to begin with. You cannot steal something you already own."

"But how did Inigo have it in the first place?" asked Roxy, fanning herself with the hat from her *Oliver!* costume. "He said it had been in his family for ages. His Uncle John or something?"

I started saying, "Couldn't you, you know . . . ," but she was already out the door.

"Back in a minute!" she said.

We sat in silence for a bit, Alfie and me. Eventually I picked up the book. "Is it any good?" I said.

"*Any good?* It is his best! He told me himself it was his favorite."

"What's it about?"

"Do you remember the French Revolution?"

"No, but I suppose you do."

"Sort of. It did not affect us directly. Not at first. But I do not think there is anyone left in the world that it has not affected by now. Anyway, the two cities of the title are London and Paris, and there is a man called Sydney Carton who is a brilliant lawyer—"

He was cut short by Roxy returning with her laptop. As we watched over her shoulder, she logged into the same genealogy sites she had shown me a few weeks ago.

"Thank heavens for people with unusual names," muttered Roxy as her fingers tap-tapped on the keyboard. "Here we go: Inigo Delombra. There's his birthday, born at North Tyneside General Hospital . . . father Alfonso Perera Delombra, born in Spain . . . mother Anne Janette Mac . . . erm . . . McGonagal . . ."

"Wait," said Alfie. "Did you say *McGonagal*?"

"Yeah, look. Why?"

He didn't answer her straightaway. Instead he said, "Check *her* parents, can you, please?"

More tapping, then, "Here we go. Anne Janette McGonagal, second daughter of James McGonagal and Carol Downey Adams, who were married at . . . hang on . . ."

"No, do not bother with James," Alfie snapped. "Who is this John McGonagal? Who is Great-Uncle John?"

Roxy gave him a look as if to say, *"Calm down with the commands,"* but she could tell that he was excited, so she kept on searching.

Moments later, up came a scanned page from an old census.

"There! John McGonagal, born 1951 in South Shields. He's the brother of James."

"Yes," Alfie said. "That's Great-Uncle John!" He was practically shouting.

"And this is relevant why, exactly?" murmured Roxy, clearly baf-
fled by Alfie's excitement.

"I knew him!"

We both stared at Alfie.

"You *know* these people?" I gasped.

He nodded slowly. "It was John's father, Jack, who stole the book
from me in the first place. I always suspected but I had no proof.
Now I know."

We were letting this sink in when Roxy's phone pinged.

"It's Mum. She wants me to go in."

She had hardly finished speaking when we heard Precious
Minto's ear-splitting screech from her back door: "*Rrrr-o-xyyyyy!*
You come in now! An' bring your friends!"

This did not sound good.

CHAPTER SIXTY-SEVEN

The email from the school principal was open on Precious Minto's iPad, and we passed it around.

TO: All 6th Grade Parents
FROM: Mr. D. J. Landreth, Head of School
SUBJECT: Exhibition Theft

Dear Parents/Caregivers,

It is with sorrow that I report what appears to be a serious theft on the school premises today, and with equal sadness that it appears very likely that the perpetrator(s) is/are fellow students at Sir Henry Percy Academy.

As you may know, an after-school exhibition was held today in the school grounds for Local History Week at which students showed items from home of local historical interest.

One valuable item—a book signed by Charles Dickens—was stolen at around 4:10 p.m. from the exhibition stand of Inigo Delombra, a Year Seven student.

There will be a school-wide assembly tomorrow morning in which I will address the students personally. In the meantime, I would be grateful if you would ask your children if they know of any information that may be of help in tracking down this item.

The police have been informed and are working closely with me and the school authorities.

Naturally I would prefer an outcome that did not further involve the police, and take this opportunity to reassure you that, if the book is returned, the matter will be handled within the school's own disciplinary procedures.

With thanks

D. J. Landreth (Mr.)

Principal

CHAPTER SIXTY-EIGHT

The "school-wide assembly" was something that usually only happened on the first day of the school year, in September, because it was virtually impossible to fit all the students into the assembly hall.

The early summer heat wave made it even worse. The hall actually smelled bad, with everybody's odors mingling and amplifying in the crush.

I won't bother telling you the whole of Mr. Landreth's speech: you can probably guess most of it.

"Serious theft . . . letting the school down . . . letting yourself down . . . thoughtless crime . . . police informed . . . Come forward anonymously with information. . . ."

All of that.

Roxy, Alfie, and I looked straight ahead at the stage where Mr. Landreth was speaking. We didn't dare even glance at one another in case we gave something away.

And then Mr. Landreth said, "Of course, as you all know, we

have CCTV cameras in the school grounds, and we will be examining these closely. Believe me, if we find out that the culprit has NOT volunteered to come forward, then the consequences will be much worse."

That's when we did break our gaze and glance at each other.

CCTV cameras? None of us had thought of that. Could one have picked up Alfie's theft? Surely not.

Surely yes.

CHAPTER SIXTY-NINE

alfie

I did not even think of security cameras when I made my oh-so-clever plan to get back my book—stolen all those decades ago by the boy I thought was my friend.

Who would? Who would think that a school, of all places, would have cameras placed on the gates, in corridors and stairwells?

On the way to the science block for "double biology," I looked up at the walls that may have held cameras overlooking the playground, or "the scene of the crime."

There were none, and I relaxed a little—enough to pay attention in class, at least. Of all the lessons, biology was my favorite. In most of the other subjects, I was quite far ahead of the other students, and the main effort I made was not to be *too* clever, or to contradict the teachers when they made idiotic statements like "Shakespeare's audiences found these jokes hilarious." Well, not that I remember. Mam and I liked plays, but William Shakespeare's jokes often fell flat. For years, women were not allowed to act in plays (I cannot remember why—probably another king's order), so the women's parts were played by young (and not so young) men. That was often very funny, but not, I think, as Mr. Shakespeare intended.

I had not studied modern sciences very much at all, however.

Anyway, it was biology with Mrs. Murphy, and I was paying attention because I have decided that I want to be a doctor when I am older. That is, *really* older.

There was a knock on the classroom door, and Mrs. Farrow, from the administration office, came in. This, it would appear, was very significant, to judge from the looks exchanged among my classmates.

She looked at me and said, "Alfie Monk. Would you come with me, please?" There was a low murmured *"Oooh"* from the rest of the class.

In the Head's office was Mr. Landreth, Sangeeta (whom I had not seen for a few days), and a police officer.

This was going to require a cool head.

CHAPTER SEVENTY

Mr. Landreth stood up when I came into his office. Sangeeta nodded at me and gave a nervous smile. The police officer fiddled with her notebook.

"Mr. Monk," Mr. Landreth said. "Take a seat." He indicated a chair facing the desk, interrogation-style. This was probably deliberate.

Mr. Landreth rocked on his heels a bit and clasped his hands.

"You know Sangeeta Prasad. This is Officer Gayle. Do you know why you are here?"

Obviously, I did. Equally obviously, I was not going to admit to anything until I knew what they knew, so I answered, "No, sir."

"I'd like you to take a look at this." He reached over to his desk and adjusted his computer screen so that I could see it. The picture was grainy, but it was clearly me: ten seconds of security film showing me walking quickly to the school's rear gate. A counter in the bottom corner showed the time: 16:12:30.

And that was it. The book, which I had *not stolen* but simply *reclaimed*, was nowhere to be seen, because it was in my schoolbag over my shoulder. I had taken it to Roxy's garage, and then brought it with me to Earl Grey House because I actually wanted to read it again.

"Before you say anything, Alfie," said Sangeeta, "I want you to tell the truth."

"Of course," I said solemnly.

"Well?" said Mr. Landreth.

I looked at all three and kept my face steady. "What?"

"This film shows you leaving the school at more or less exactly the time that the apparent theft of Inigo Delombra's book occurred."

They were desperate, I could tell, but I had to stay calm.

"You are right, it does." *No! Too impertinent.* I added: "I . . . I mean, yes. Sir."

"Why were you leaving the exhibition so early?"

"I am sorry, sir, but I did not find it of great interest to me."

"And why did you choose the rear gate? You live in the opposite direction."

Hell's fire. I had to think quickly.

"I . . . erm . . ." *Quick, Alfie.* "I wanted to avoid some boys who had threatened me. From another school, from Monkseaton High."

This, I thought, was rather brilliant. In just a short while at this school, I have noticed that everyone on the staff is terrified of bullying, of accusations of bullying, and especially of not seeming to take bullying seriously. There is even a plaque on the wall of reception declaring the school is a "proud supporter of the Anti-Bullying Schools Initiative."

"Are you being bullied, Alfie?" asked Sangeeta.

"Not exactly. But I wanted to avoid them." I hung my head but could see that the adults were exchanging looks. This had thrown their investigation off track. Involving another school was genius, and I was feeling rather pleased with myself.

Too soon.

The police officer said the first words she had uttered so far. She flipped back a few pages in her notebook.

"What's your full first name, Alfie?" she said. She had a pen ready to write it down. I thought she was just checking details.

"Alve. A-L-V-E. Mam's idea."

(Sorry, Mam. I just thought that a reminder of my orphan status would be helpful here. It was not.)

The police officer addressed Mr. Landreth. "What was the inscription inside the book, sir?"

She knew. She did not need to ask. Mr. Landreth played his part. "It read, *To the dear reader, Alve, with my compliments, Charles Dickens.*"

"A remarkable coincidence, wouldn't you say, Alfie?" said the police officer.

I said nothing. Without the book, they could not prove anything. There was no evidence. Coincidence is not evidence.

"Do you have anything to say, Mr. Monk?" Mr. Landreth's tone had hardened. His eyes narrowed, and he pursed his lips.

"I do not, sir." I looked at him with an expression of what I hoped was puzzled hurt.

He turned to Sangeeta. "Very well. Miss Prasad?"

Sangeeta looked at me sadly as she bent down to her bag and took out *A Tale of Two Cities*.

"It was in your room at Earl Grey House, Alfie. I didn't even have to look hard."

Well, that changed things.

CHAPTER SEVENTY-ONE
AIDAN

Sitting outside Mr. Landreth's office, I could hear voices inside, but I couldn't make out what they were saying.

Next to me was Dad. Next to him were Roxy and her mum. Mr. Springham was sitting opposite, stony-faced.

This was super-serious, and I was very scared.

Fifteen minutes earlier, Roxy and I had both been called out of our classes by Mrs. Farrow, who walked us, wordlessly, to the principal's office, where Dad and Precious Minto were waiting with Mr. Springham.

While Mr. Springham's back was turned, Dad mouthed at me, *"What's up?"*

I shrugged and adopted a look of bewilderment, but I knew what was up all right. And then Alfie came out of the Head's study, followed by his social worker, Sangeeta, and a policewoman. Alfie kept his eyes fixed on the ground.

I glanced across at Roxy. Her skin looked dull and even a bit pale, and she stared straight ahead, not meeting my gaze.

Then we trooped in.

I'll give you the short version. The long version is too horrible to remember.

We were rumbled.

If you want to convince somebody that you've fainted, you don't do what Roxy did, apparently.

1. Don't fall backward. That's what she did and I caught her. Mr. Springham didn't see that bit, but he heard descriptions of it. Real fainters nearly always fall to the side, or forward.

2. Watch out for the "hand-drop" test. The paramedic (or Mr. Springham, in this case) holds the fainter's hand above her face and lets go. A genuinely unconscious person allows the hand to fall and hit their face. A faker, like Roxy, makes it fall so that it doesn't hit her face.

I didn't know any of this until it was spelled out by Mr. Springham.

"I thought it was just a silly girl seeking attention," he said. "But when I realized it had happened at exactly the same time as the theft, it was obvious that you were working together with Alfie Monk."

"Helping somebody else to commit a crime is a crime in itself— you do realize that?" said Mr. Landreth.

"We didn't know he was going to take the book," I protested. That was the truth.

"So why did you do it, then?" snapped Dad.

We had no good answer. At any rate, not one that didn't involve saying stuff like "Alfie had his book stolen back in 1940 by Inigo Delombra's great-grandfather." That was the truth, obviously, but the truth was not going to help us here.

It was Roxy who dug us out of the hole. After the longest of pauses, during which Mr. Springham had said "Well?" three times, with increasing volume, she looked at her shoes and said:

"It was revenge, I think."

And she told the story of how Inigo Delombra had teased Alfie on the coach to The Saxon Experience, and taken his glasses. She exaggerated it brilliantly. She said that Inigo had called him "Four-Eyes" and "Zombie Mouth" (a reference to his bad teeth). Alfie was secretly crying, she said.

All four adults in the room were silent until Mr. Landreth said, "I see. And presumably Alfie didn't tell us this because he feared being labeled a 'snitch,' am I right?"

We both nodded. My eyes were directed at the floor, but I did see Mr. Landreth and Mr. Springham exchange a long look.

It had worked. Once again, I was left in awe of Roxy's quick thinking in a crisis.

CHAPTER SEVENTY-TWO

Dad and Mrs. Minto left shortly afterward.

Roxy and I were made to wait outside Mr. Landreth's office again, while Inigo Delombra and Alfie went in. I tried listening with my ear pressed against the door, but Mrs. Farrow kept walking past. I think she knew what I was up to and she told me to sit down.

Eventually we were both called in.

1. Prompted by Mr. Landreth, Roxy and I apologized for staging the fake faint.
2. Alfie apologized for taking the book.
3. Finally Inigo Delombra apologized to Alfie for taking his glasses.

(Incidentally, I have never heard three less sincere apologies. Inigo's especially was delivered in a quiet monotone: "I-am-sorry-I-took-your-glasses-and-I-won't-do-it-again-there-can-I-go-now-weirdo?" He didn't *actually* say the last bit, but he managed to imply it.)

As we turned to leave, Inigo mouthed a swear word at Alfie and waved *A Tale of Two Cities* triumphantly under his nose. Alfie gritted his teeth and said nothing.

Alfie and I were heading back to class when Sangeeta, the social worker, said, "Alfie?"

We both turned. "It's just Alfie I need to speak to," she said. I carried on, but stopped round the corner so that I could listen.

"Do you have any personal belongings: in a desk or locker or anything?" she asked Alfie.

He must have shaken his head, because I then heard her say, "All right, then, come with me. You're not going back to your class."

I saw him again only a few hours later, and *everything* changed after that.

CHAPTER SEVENTY-THREE
Alfie

"Do you want to go for a drive, Alfie?" Sangeeta asked outside Mr. Landreth's office.

I had grown to quite like Sangeeta. She would talk straightforwardly about Mam, and encourage me to do the same. She no longer hushed her voice, or put her head on one side in a "poor little boy" sort of way; that always made me feel worse.

We drove in her car, making small talk: How was my arm? (Almost better, thank you.) How was Earl Grey House? (OK, but I did not like the food much.)

The roads were more or less empty. It had rained a little at dawn: a quick, violent shower that had come and gone in half an hour, and the thirsty earth had sucked up the water like a dry sponge until only a few puddles remained in the shade. The sun would dry them out soon.

We drove to Tynemouth. Sangeeta had promised to buy fish and chips. I knew something was up, something bigger than the controversy about the book. Obviously. You do not get taken out of school for lunch normally.

We ate our fish and chips from the packet, sitting side by side on the large stone plinth at the base of the monument to Lord Collingwood. The tide was out, exposing flat brown rocks, small pools, and seaweed in the small bay below us.

Sangeeta looked up at the cloudless sky and tutted. "We need rain," she murmured. I knew a tricky question was to follow. I had noticed this in Sangeeta: she preceded difficult discussions with a remark on the weather, like she was warming up.

Sure enough: "Alfie?"

"Mmm?" I said, through a mouthful of cod.

"You know that I've tried to be straight with you, ever since I met you, don't you?"

I did not like the sound of where this was going.

She continued: "Only, I don't think you're telling me everything you know."

I looked at her, furrowing my brow to express puzzlement, or interest, while secretly thinking, *Sangeeta, if I did tell you everything I know, you would not believe me anyway.*

"The thing is, Alfie, we've been asking around. We believe you *do* have family. I mean—I understand you and your mam led pretty private lives, and that's nothing to be ashamed of. But there are people who talk of boys just like you living in your house, with your mam, before you were even born."

"What people?"

"Come on, Alfie. Nobody lives their lives completely cut off from other members of society. The vicar of St. Mary's on Ilfracombe Gardens, for a start. He was at your mam's funeral? He says that when he moved here twenty years ago, he visited your mam, and there was a young lad of about your age living there. Is this a cousin or something? Or an older brother?"

I said nothing, and ate some more chips.

"Come on, Alfie. Don't go all silent on me."

I stayed silent.

"We've looked at local records, Alfie. We can do that, you know. Council tax, the census, the electoral roll. There've been members of your family living there for years and years. You're even in the phone book. Monk, H., Oak Cottage, Whitley Bay. That was back in the 1950s. Who was that—your grandmother? Great-grandmother? Where is the rest of this family, Alfie? Why all the secrecy? You have to help us here."

She took out her cell phone and tapped it a few times until a photograph appeared. I had to struggle not to gasp. It was the one Aidan had told me about from the *Shields Gazette*. Mam and I stood in front of Oak Cottage, me clutching Biffa and grinning.

As I stared, Sangeeta said gently, "Who are these people, Alfie? He looks so like you, doesn't he? Look—the dark glasses, the erm . . . gappy smile. He even had a cat! Didn't you say you lost your cat?"

"I am sorry, Sangeeta. I do not know."

Sangeeta clicked the telephone off and put it away.

"And I'm sorry too, Alfie. I don't believe you." Her voice had acquired a harder edge. We were both quiet for a moment. Below us, on the wet sand, a collie chased a stick into the sea, and a seagull screeched.

"Alfie. *Talk to me!*"

I said nothing.

"I have another theory, Alfie. I wonder if, in fact, you're much older than you say."

I stared out to sea, and swallowed hard.

CHAPTER SEVENTY-FOUR

Our fish and chips were finished, but we stayed at the base of the monument, looking out toward the sea.

"I looked it up, Alfie," said Sangeeta. "At first, I thought you might have damaged your thyroid at birth. It's a medical condition that can prevent you growing properly. There used to be a comedian on the radio . . ."

I don't know why I blurted it out but I did. "Jimmy Clitheroe."

Oh no. Why did I say that?

"Why, yes, Alfie. But . . ." She shifted in her seat to look at me more closely. "How on earth does an eleven-year-old boy know about a comedian from sixty years ago?"

I shrugged again. "Mam liked him. *Said* she liked him, when she was younger."

"When she was *younger?* Alfie, your mam was born in 1980-something. Jimmy Clitheroe was big in the 1950s. Also— how did you know I was going to say Jimmy Clitheroe?"

"I was just guessing. He had a growth condition, that is all."

(It was true. Mam and I had loved Jimmy Clitheroe. He was a man-boy who never grew up, because something had gone wrong when he was born. We thought he was hilarious. He would say, "Oooh, flippin' 'eck!" when something went wrong, only it was funny when he said it. He was on the wireless, and on the television when television was in black-and-white.)

Sangeeta narrowed her eyes. "Anyway," she continued slowly, "turns out there's nothing wrong with your thyroid. But might it be something else?"

"Like I said, I do not know, Sangeeta."

"Only if it turns out that you are *not* eleven, and are a lot older, that would change things considerably."

Now I was really nervous.

All I want is to grow up normally. Have friends my age. Go to school. This suspicion could ruin everything.

And then I saw him. He did not see that I saw him, but he was there, sitting on a bench farther along the headland. Had he been watching all this time?

Jasper.

Did he follow me?

"Can we go now, please, Sangeeta?" I said.

He must have followed me.

"You can't dodge these questions indefinitely, Alfie."

Why is he following me?

"Do you hear me, Alfie?"

I cannot tell anyone. It could expose everything.

"Alfie? Earth to Alfie!"

But what if he means to harm me?

"Over there, Sangeeta. There's a man who . . ." But he had gone. "Sorry, Sangeeta. I am not thinking straight."

We were back in the car and I had strapped myself in when Sangeeta turned her whole body to me and looked at me solemnly.

"Alfie. I need to tell you this. I have submitted a request to the head of Child Services that we perform a DNA age test, which should clear up any doubts."

"A DNA test? Why?"

"An analysis of your DNA can reveal your age to within a few years, maybe a few months. It's pretty new, and they'll need fresh cell samples. You know what DNA is, Alfie?"

"Yes, of course. It's the name given to the molecule within the nucleus of a cell that carries all the genetic information in every living organism." I caught myself sounding knowledgeable and ancient, even though we had just learned this in school, so I added, "I think."

Sangeeta shook her head and smiled. "You *think*, eh, Alfie? You know what the dentist told me? He reckoned you have the teeth of someone *much* older than eleven. I think I can tell that just by listening to you."

"And what if I do not want to have this cell test?"

She had started the car but turned the engine off again to emphasize her point.

"Well, here's the curious thing. If you're over eighteen, you can refuse, and we would have to go to court if we wanted to pursue it, which is a hassle, frankly, and probably not worth it if you've already admitted to being an adult. But seeing as you say you're a minor—that is, someone under eighteen—we, for the time being, are your legal guardians."

"And?"

"And you're booked in for cell sampling next week. Meanwhile you've been withdrawn from school pending a confirmation of your true age."

My heart dropped. It was as if I could see everything that I had aimed at reversing over the horizon. "But, Sangeeta . . ."

"No buts, Alfie. Imagine the trouble I would be in if it was discovered I was sending a grown man into a class full of children."

CHAPTER SEVENTY-FIVE

Unfortunately for me, I *can* imagine the trouble Sangeeta would be in, and it meant that I was silent all the way back to Earl Grey House, my ancient mind dancing, fighting, arguing with the task ahead of me.

I would need help, that was for sure.

I would need to act fast, of that I was equally sure.

I had thought I could wait a week or two—maybe a month—to plan everything and beat the archaeologists to the site on Coquet Island.

Now things were different.

I knew that the second application of the life-pearl would start the aging process again. From the moment I took it, I would start to grow up again. That was assuming it still worked after centuries underground.

What I did *not* know was whether it would "reset" my age. If I took it, would the DNA test of my cells, which Sangeeta was insisting upon, still reveal my *true* age? Or would it show me to be eleven?

I also knew that if I did not act before I had the test, then everything would be lost.

The only hope I had was to act soon.

And by soon, I mean tomorrow.

Staring out of the car window, I looked in the side mirror. The car behind was a black BMW. I could not see inside because of the sunshine reflecting off the windshield, but I knew it was him.

Then I saw his car indicator light flashing; he turned up Beach Road to the left as we continued on toward Culvercot. He was just checking that we were going back.

I think.

I needed help and I needed friends—and I needed them both fast.

CHAPTER SEVENTY-SIX

By four-thirty, I was in Roxy's garage, the pink sign still flickering -AGE outside.

Roxy had this shy grin as she opened her laptop and beckoned me over to look. I was expecting more of the genealogy sites that she was so keen on, but this was different.

www.pet-locator.com

Have YOU lost a pet? We'll find it—

guaranteed!

"For Biffa. Your cat," said Aidan. "We thought, you know . . ." But I was ahead of him.

"Yes. It is brilliant, and thank you. Only . . ."

I wanted to say, "Only we cannot do this now. I love Biffa but there is something even more important." But I was so touched by their friendly concern, and they were so enthusiastic. I said, "How much does it cost?"

"It isn't cheap," said Roxy quietly. "For the full service: posters, house-to-house, web support, everything, it's, erm . . ." She hesitated and coughed. "Two thousand pounds."

I felt my shoulders slump. "And where will I get two thousand pounds from?"

Roxy and Aidan said nothing, but their eyes both drifted to the burst sofa and the trunk underneath it containing my (almost) complete set of Charles Dickens books.

Ah.

There was, of course, no question that the books would be worth two thousand pounds. Much more, probably. But how would I sell them? How soon could I do it? Biffa meant more to me than any amount of books, but it was a long time since the fire. Would she even be alive? How would she eat? We had to mash up her food because her teeth were so bad. Would she even be able to hunt?

It was another hot evening, but the air was damp. It hadn't rained now for weeks, not really, and the ground was dry and cracked. Even the birds in the woods had gone quiet, as if their usual chirping were too much effort.

"Rain is on its way," I declared, by way of breaking the silence, and Roxy took out her cell phone and jabbed at it.

"Not according to this it's not," she said, and she showed me a chart on the screen with a weather forecast on it. But it was wrong, and I told her so, perhaps a little abruptly.

"Wow, Alfie. You're jumpy. What's up?" asked Aidan.

And so I told them about Sangeeta's suspicions about my age, and the cell test I was to undergo next week.

Roxy and Aidan fell silent. Eventually Aidan said, "I'm really sorry, Alfie. That'll mean . . ."

"It will mean the end of everything. I will not be able to go to school. I just want to grow up *normally*. You have to help me."

Roxy got up from the torn sofa, leaving two patches of sweat on the vinyl where her legs had been. "Thing is, Alfie, what can we do? Realistically?" She opened the door of the little fridge and a waft of cool air came out but soon disappeared.

And then we sat, or stood, or walked about, discussing and dismissing how I could get to Coquet Island.

Tomorrow.

Even if we could get to Amble on the mainland, up the coast—how would we get to the island about a mile out to sea? It is a nature reserve now, and tourist boats are not allowed to land because of all the rare birds whose eggs, hundreds of years ago, Mam and I would collect to eat.

It was the thought of Mam that set me off. That and Biffa starving to death somewhere. My head sank into my arms in despair. I felt the sobs rising in my chest when Roxy came over and patted my back.

"Why don't you just wait, Alfie? You know, in a few years' time, who knows what scientists might discover, especially if they're able to test you? And anyway, you could make your own way to Coquet Island one day to find the pearl thing, no?"

The sobs stopped in my throat and I lifted my head.

"You do not understand, do you? I CANNOT WAIT! Once the archaeologists start their digging, it is only a matter of time before the life-pearl is either destroyed, or found and stuck in a museum, or opened and sent for analysis, and then what hope do I have? I will be stuck this age *forever!*"

I was shouting, but I could not stop, especially when Aidan said, "But we'll be here for you, Alfie. . . ."

"NO, YOU WILL NOT! You will grow up, you will leave me behind: the 'strange kid, who talked funny, who had a tattoo, who reckoned he was a thousand years old.' You will be the same as everyone else, the same as Jack, and I will be left like this." I looked down at myself, an ancient man in the body of a boy.

I got to my feet and walked off without a further word.

CHAPTER SEVENTY-SEVEN

I arrived back at Earl Grey House forty minutes later than I should have, because I simply could not summon the energy to walk fast. Every step felt like my feet were sticking to the ground. I was expecting Aunty Reet to be furious, and I had already decided that I did not care.

Instead she said, "There's someone to see you, Alfie."

"Who?"

"Apparently they know you from years ago."

I nearly threw up on the spot. It had to be Jasper.

My hand was shaking and I steadied it on the doorknob before opening the lounge door.

CHAPTER SEVENTY-EIGHT

He faced the window, a dark silhouette, hands clasped behind his broad back. "Hello, Alfie," he said before turning round. When he did, it took a few seconds and then I gasped aloud.

I had not seen John McGonagal in nearly sixty years. Not, in fact, since I fought him in the lane all those years ago. There was no mistaking him, although his hair was now mostly white, and his eyes had a sadness and emptiness that was almost heartbreaking. He nodded slowly. I had not said anything.

"I thought it was you," he said in the same Geordie accent that he had threatened me and Mam with, and I was instantly on edge, the memories flooding back.

"You're crazy, you are! Weirdo! A psycho!"

And then Rafel's words: *"In the real world, Alfie, you gotta kill 'em. Otherwise they come back for more."*

Had he come back for me? What was he saying? The silhouetted figure was talking and the words were swimming in my head. . . .

"It couldn't be anyone else," John was saying, and my thoughts came back into focus, back into the twenty-first century. "When my great-nephew—Inigo, you know him—told me about the book incident at his school, I knew it had to be you."

I stood there, blinking in amazement.

"It's all right," said John, shaking his head. "I know exactly what Inigo's like. There's a good lad in there somewhere but it's hidden underneath layers of lazy, stupid, swaggering. . . ." He stopped himself. "Well, that doesn't matter. What matters is that I'm here."

I spoke for the first time. "I can see that. But . . . why?"

He turned back to the window and stared out, taking his time to answer.

"The doctors gave me six months to live—about six months ago. Don't worry," he said, giving a short laugh. "I feel fine. Tip-top, in fact. Mostly. But there were some loose ends to tie up—before I go, you know?"

I nodded, even though he was not looking at me. I had sat down on the hard sofa, but I did not take my eyes off him. He turned back and looked at me with his sad old-man's eyes.

"I deserved that beating you gave me, Alfie. Deserved it one hundred percent. Took me a while to realize it, though. Years. And by the time I did, I wanted to—I don't know, apologize, I suppose. But you and your mam had moved, hadn't you? All because of me, I expect.

"And you left no trace. I'll bet you're good at that, eh? Moving on without a trace?"

I shrugged, wondering, *Where is this going?* It sounded very much as though he *knew*. Knew my secret. I got an uncomfortable prickling sensation down my neck.

"So I left it, and lived with it. Only you moved back, didn't you? People talk, Alfie. And there's lots to learn if you're prepared to listen. I wrote to your mam but I got no reply. I thought I should probably just leave it alone. Then I heard about the fire."

He paused. I think he was being really careful to sound measured and gentle. "I'm sorry, Alfie. About your mam. And . . . you know . . ." He looked around the sparsely furnished room with its hard-wearing paint and classroom smell. "This . . . and everything."

"Do you . . . do you know? About me? And Mam?"

He smiled, and, for the first time, his sadness seemed to lessen. "Oh aye. I know. Your secret's safe. Well, there is one other person that knows. The person that told me, in fact."

"Hello, Alfie," croaked another voice, and I spun round on the sofa. Sitting hunched in the corner of the room, in shadow, was a figure I had not seen when I came in, who had been sitting there all this time.

He was ancient, shrunken, with wild white hair and a permanent tremor in his chin. But there was a sharp look in his eyes that told me he was a *long* way from mental decline.

Staring at me and shaking his head was the person I was used to thinking of as the last friend I ever had: Jack McGonagal.

CHAPTER SEVENTY-NINE

"I'm sorry as well, Alfie," Jack said eventually, but his voice was so quiet it was hard to hear. I moved close and pulled up a chair. "You've been badly treated by our family, eh? First me, then John there and now that young good-for-nothing Inigo."

"You . . . you have not told him, have you?" I said, a note of panic in my voice. "About my . . . age thing?" I looked between old Jack and John.

They both shook their heads, and I gave a relieved sigh.

"You get to your nineties, Alfie, and you have had a lot of time to reflect on things you could have done better. And by then you're running out of time to put them right. Sometimes you can." He stopped for a long, painful-sounding cough. "And sometimes all you can do is try to say sorry. I stole, I mocked you, I told people your secret. And I am very, very sorry."

For several seconds, it was so quiet between the three of us that I felt I could almost touch the silence, and then a telephone bleeped shrilly from the office down the hall.

They were waiting for me to say something, but I did not know what to say. Instead I gazed at Jack and—for just a moment—it was as though eighty-something years had not happened.

"What happened to Jean?" I asked him.

He gave a snuffled half-laugh. "Jean Palmer? Ha. Dumped me for a Polish sailor."

I nodded slowly. He did not seem upset. Instead he started a wheezy laugh, but within it was the laugh of the young boy I had known. Suddenly I could see him in his big shorts, with his bony legs; I could see his hands, grimy from bicycle oil, digging into our shared bag of chips. . . .

And then the image was gone and I was back in the clammy front room at Earl Grey House.

"Tell me, son," he whispered, and I moved in even closer. "This . . . thing that you have. Is it . . . I don't know . . . is it *good*? Do you like it?"

I do not think that anybody had ever asked me that, and I thought hard before answering.

"It was, I think. But not anymore. It hasn't been good for a long time."

He nodded. "Old age is no walk in the park, son," he said. "But I thank the Lord every day that I've been granted the gift of growing old. Because I would not want your life, Alfie, my friend. Not in a thousand years."

Do I want to be as old as him, though? I thought at that

moment. And if Jack had not said what he said next, everything could be different.

He paused, and he was panting, as if the effort of speaking— even softly—was huge. He took a rasping breath. "Look at yourself. *Listen* to yourself, Alfie! If you know of a way to reverse whatever it is that's wrong with you, so you can have real friends and a real life, then do yourself a favor, eh? I was your friend, once, I think. I hope. But now you need friends who will not . . ." He paused for breath. The tremor in his chin stopped and he looked straight at me. "Who will not leave you behind."

"Thank you, Jack," I said. I put my hand out to shake his, and he extended his thin hand in response. His handshake was gentle, but not weak, and I felt his papery skin move beneath my fingers. He smiled and his shoulders seemed to lose a little of their hunch, as though a weight had been lifted from them.

"There is one more thing . . . ," he began, but at that moment Sangeeta stuck her head round the door.

"Everything all right, Alfie?" She came into the room without waiting for an answer. "Are you going to introduce me, then?" She strode forward to John, hand extended. "Sangeeta Prasad, I'm Alfie's social worker. And you are?"

"Ah, erm . . . hello. John McGonagal. This is my father, Jack. We . . . erm, we were friends of Hilda's. Alfie's mother. Just wanted to, you know, say hello to the young fellow."

Sangeeta smiled but I was worried. How long had she been

there? Was she listening at the door? Aunty Reet must have called her and told her that two old men were visiting me. *I do not like this*, I thought.

Whatever mood we had had in that stuffy lounge was now shattered completely. John said, "Come on, Dad. Probably time we were on our way." He helped old Jack out of his chair. "Nice to meet you," he said to Sangeeta, and old Jack said, "Cheerio."

"I'll see you out," I said, and followed their slow progress to the front door, Sangeeta looking at me suspiciously.

In the hallway, John lowered his voice and said, "Is everything all right, son?"

I nodded. Everything was *not* all right, of course, but I couldn't say that to him. Not with Sangeeta close by. Then Jack reached into his jacket pocket and brought out something wrapped in a carrier bag, which he gave to me with a quivering hand.

"It's time you got this back, Alfie," he said with a smile. Inside was my copy of *A Tale of Two Cities* by Charles Dickens.

"Thank you!" I said.

"Good luck, Alfie. You were a good friend. I wish I'd been a better one."

And with that, Jack and John made their way carefully down the worn steps and into John's car that was parked on the seafront street.

I turned away from the door, and Sangeeta was standing in the hallway, arms folded, watching.

CHAPTER EIGHTY

"You're up to something, Alfie Monk," Sangeeta said, managing somehow to keep her voice gentle and friendly, and razor-sharp as well. "I've got my eye on you, young man. Or *not* so young. You'd better—"

She was cut off by Tasha and Melanie—two of the other young residents of Earl Grey House—hurtling down the stairs, laughing loudly, one of them bumping into her.

"Sorry! Sorry! Hey, Alfie—you comin' for a plodge?"

A few of the other children had adopted a habit of going for a paddle—a "plodge"—in the bay on warm evenings. This was the first time I had been asked along. I was secretly rather thrilled.

"Yes, I will see you there presently," I replied, and they both giggled at something and ran out the front door.

Sangeeta nodded at me. "Be careful, Alfie. I'm watching you." Then she too departed, leaving me in the hallway with its bulletin boards and hard-wearing carpet and smell of disinfectant.

Jack was right. I had to reverse this.

Looking down, I noticed the bag and took out the book. I frowned. There was something inside, something making the book fatter than it should be. I opened the book to see the envelope that Jack had slipped under the front cover.

Written on the front were the words "For the chickens" and inside were two fifty-pound notes.

An idea began to form in my head.

Upstairs in my room, I took out the telephone that Sangeeta had given me, and turned it on to compose the first text message I had ever sent.

> Dear Roxy,
>
> I have an idea for getting to the place we talked about. I will meet you and Aidan at the Metro Station at 8 a.m. tomorrow.
>
> Yours sincerely,
> Alfie

Seconds later, my telephone went *ping*, and I read the message. It said: **LOL OK.**

It seemed a bit abrupt, but I was fairly certain it meant yes.

For the third night in a row, I hardly slept, but this time it was not because of fear or sadness, but excitement.

I had worked out how to get the world's only remaining life-pearl back.

As a plan, it would definitely be considered "audacious." But it was the only plan I had.

I was going to bribe someone to break the law and take us to Coquet Island.

CHAPTER EIGHTY-ONE

AIDAN

The journey up the coast—Metro to Newcastle, bus from the Haymarket—takes nearly two hours, and by the time we arrive in Amble, the morning has turned chilly. A church bell is chiming ten and a large lady in an apron is rolling up the shutters on the Neptune Café.

Amble is a sandy-colored low-rise seaside town, which seems to have its back hunched against the North Sea. There's a permanent, faint salty smell in the air, and I hear a couple saying to each other, "Eeh, it's turned, hasn't it?" and "Won't be long before it rains."

Coquet Island is there, lying off the shore, its little lighthouse the only visible feature.

Alfie has hardly said a word, apart from to outline his plan, made possible by the two fifty-pound notes he shows us. After hearing it, I'm not at all sure why he even wants us here, but he said it was for "authenticity." He's going to pretend to be an adult, and the presence of children will "aid the illusion," apparently. I'm not convinced. To be honest, I think he just wants us there for "moral support." Roxy, on the other hand, sees it as a chance to star in her own drama, I'm fairly sure of that.

The weather app on her phone puts the chance of rain at ninety percent by this afternoon. So Alfie was right. Anyway, by this afternoon, if everything goes according to plan, this will all be over.

The fact that we have made it this far without a hitch should have put us in a good mood.

Instead we all feel like the weather: chilly and brooding, as if there's worse to come.

The three of us sit in the Neptune Café, staring out of the big window at the pedestrians in their shorts and windbreakers. Alfie has a cup of tea, Roxy and I each have a can of Coke, but none of us is drinking. The café owner eyes us suspiciously as if she expects us to steal something.

It's Roxy who breaks the silence by handing her backpack to Alfie and saying, "OK, then. Time for your transformation, Superman." Silently he takes the bag and goes into the café's restroom to get changed into his old man gear.

She's so relaxed about it all, it's a bit infuriating. It's probably because she's in no danger of setting off any alarm bells at home.

"Easy-peasy," she said on the bus when I asked her how she had explained her early absence. "Drama Club trip to York!"

"And your mum didn't wonder why you were starting at, like,

seven on a Saturday morning?" I asked. "She didn't wonder why there was no letter or consent form to sign?"

She shrugged. "My mum's got enough problems. If I tell her I've signed the consent form to save her the trouble, she's grateful."

I envied her casual deception. If I'd tried to pull off something like that, Mum or Dad would have seen through it instantly. They'd have wanted to see the email, or the schedule of events. Mum would have nagged Dad into getting up early to run me to the drop-off. It would never have worked.

The note on my pillow would have to do, and it worried me.

Gone to Mo's. Back at teatime. X

There's a distinct risk that my dad will drive round to Mo's flat and haul me back home to help him fix the bathroom tiles/clean out the guttering/put boxes in the loft/all of the above. It's what I'm supposed to be doing today. He'll think I'm shirking again.

As for Alfie, he couldn't have cared less. The doors at Earl Grey House were locked and alarmed, but he'd discovered it was a simple matter to get out via the fire escape.

"Shall we go?"

The voice behind me makes me jump. I spin round to see Alfie, in a long coat and man's brimmed hat: Roxy's *Oliver!* costume. It's pretty convincing, I have to admit. The woman behind the counter gives us a funny look—as anyone would if a boy had gone into their bathroom and emerged dressed up as an old man.

As we leave, the shop bell tinkles above the door. The lady still hasn't taken her eyes off us. I see her reach into her pocket and take out her phone, and I have a sinking feeling in my stomach that something is not quite right.

I say nothing.

CHAPTER EIGHTY-TWO

Roxy can't stop giggling at Alfie's old-man impression. Under any other circumstances, I would be laughing too: it really is good. He stoops *very* slightly—barely more than dropping his neck forward a little—and tugs the brim of the hat down over his eyes. Stooping any more would make him look very short because he's not especially tall. He makes his legs slightly stiff, and slaps his feet flatly and gently on the pavement, as if bending them any more would cause him discomfort.

It's only a hundred yards or so from the Neptune Café to the little wooden kiosk on the harbor front with a big, colorful sign saying:

PUFFIN TOURS LTD
NEXT SAILING 12:00

There's a man smoking a huge electronic pipe behind the glass front of the kiosk. As we approach, he puts away a phone, and I just know it. I don't know how, but I do.

"Guys!" I say. "We're not going to get away with this."

In an annoying singsong voice, Roxy says, "You're defeatist!" and carries on walking right up to the kiosk, Alfie shuffling alongside her.

There's a rectangular hole in the glass for tickets and money, and a wisp of smoke is emerging. It's only vape smoke, but there's so much of it that it's almost like the kiosk is on fire.

Alfie lowers his head to the gap in the glass and says in his deep voice, "I wonder if I can make it worth your while to venture a landing on the island, mate?"

For a moment—a tantalizing moment—I think we've got away with it. The man takes a long drag of his vaping pipe and murmurs, "You what?" and he pauses before exhaling a long plume of smoke.

Alfie extracts two fifty-pound notes from his jacket pocket.

"I was wondering if I could persuade you to make a landing on the island, mate? You know, on the east side, out of sight? My kids here are keen to see the puffins close up, you know wha' I mean?"

The man eyes the two large banknotes. Alfie pushes them toward him beneath the glass. "It will be worth your while."

The man reaches out two fingers with bitten nails, and pulls the notes toward him and puts them in his pocket. Alfie turns to us and grins.

"Get lost," growls the man. "For a start, I'd lose me license. Second, do y'think I was born yesterday? You lot were in the Neptune earlier on, weren't you? Go on—away with you."

"Is that a no?"

"What did it sound like? Course it's a no. Get lost!"

I see the dismay as Alfie's shoulders slump. He half turns away, then straightens up and turns back again.

"May I have my money back, then?"

There's a dreadful pause while the man takes a drag of his pipe, blows the smoke out again, and then says, "What money?"

Alfie's whole body sinks and, without looking back at us, he slouches down onto a nearby bench.

He's been quiet all morning, but, for the first time, poor Alfie really does look a thousand years old.

CHAPTER EIGHTY-THREE

Alfie

I sit on the bench and gaze out at the violet-gray sea. High above me the seagulls caw their lonely cries to the white sky, hanging in the wind that is beginning to whip up tiny white tops on the waves outside the harbor.

Below where I sit, the masts of the yachts in the marina sway in the swell, the sail pulleys clanking in the wind.

It was a ridiculous idea.

But now I have ruined it, and there is no way that I can do what I have waited hundreds of years to do.

To grow up.

To have a twelfth birthday. A real one.

To have friends that grow up with me, and then to fall in love, and marry, and have children, and watch them grow up and have children . . .

And to feel that life is valuable, precious. To yearn for each day to be longer, because I do not have an endless number of them . . .

Because I understand, by now, one thing more than anyone else on earth: without death, life is just existence.

And, for what seems like the millionth time since Mam died, the tears stream down my face, chilling on my cheeks in the cold breeze. At first, I do not even notice that Aidan and Roxy have sat down on either side of me. Aidan puts his arm round my shoulders and squeezes, and Roxy rests her head on my arm, like I used to do with Mam.

We stay there for a long time, I think.

Then, from behind us, I hear someone say, "Wow! Look!" I turn, and they are pointing out to sea, where a flock of birds are diving repeatedly into the sea and coming up again.

"Are they seagulls?" the little girl asks her mum.

"I don't know, pet."

The girl giggles. "They look like . . . like flying footballs!"

Their voices act like a winch, dragging me from my despair.

"They are puffins," I say to her. "You do not often see them this close to land. There must be a shoal of mackerel running, or sprats. Sprats are their favorite."

The mum smiles. "You know a lot."

I shrug. Modestly, I hope. Then Roxy pipes up.

"How cold do you reckon that water is, Alfie?"

Aidan scoffs. "It's the North Sea, Roxy. It's freezing."

"But it's nearly June."

"So?"

"So I've got an idea."

CHAPTER EIGHTY-FOUR

Roxy's idea is so outrageous and outlandish, so bold and brave, that there is no *possible* way it could work.

It is also my only—and my last—hope.

We are going to steal a boat. Well, by "we," I mean "I," basically.

In a small, busy marina, in summer, surrounded by other people, I am going to steal a little yacht (or any yacht, for that matter: I am not sure I will have much of a choice) and sail it to Coquet Island, about a mile off the shore.

I know. Sheer folly.

But the alternative is not to try, and that is not much of an option.

I can remember a time when nobody stole very much at all. Indeed, I can remember a time when stealing as much as a basket of fish would get you hanged—however old you were.

So . . . stealing a *boat*?

Sitting there on the bench, the three of us observe the marina and work out the plan that—even if it works—is guaranteed to get us all into a great deal of trouble.

If it does *not* work—which is highly likely—the consequences are too grim even to think about, which is what I say to Roxy.

"So we don't think about them!" says Roxy, too brightly for my liking. "It's simple," she goes on. "Either we try and *probably* fail. Or we *don't* try and *definitely* fail."

In that tiny sliver of chance, between "probably" and "definitely," lies my future.

Roxy is on her cell phone, jabbing away with her fingers. Suddenly she is Roxy-in-Charge: tiny and *very* impressive.

"There are two Coast Guard stations near here," she says, looking at her telephone. "The first is Amble, right there." She points across the harbor to a low building facing the water. "The other is in Seahouses, up the coast. We've got to hope that you reach the island before either of them can catch you. Seahouses is easy—it's way too far. This one, well . . . I dunno, really."

If this were not discouraging enough, I am struggling to identify which sailing boats I could handle by myself that would have the speed I require.

There is only one: a thirty-foot, white, single-masted yacht. It is moored on the last jetty of the marina, closest to the open water, which is good, but a long walk past other boats, which is bad. I will be noticed. I will have to walk by dozens of people, who all know each other and the other sailors, and have to hope that they pay me no attention.

"That one," I say to Aidan, pointing to the yacht, which has a little pirate flag flapping over the stern. He says nothing. "Did you hear me?"

"I heard you. Does it have to be that one?"

"Why? What's wrong with it?"

"That's my Uncle Jasper's boat," says Aidan.

CHAPTER EIGHTY-FIVE

Our only chance of sailing a boat out of the little marina is to do it in full view. "Hidden in plain sight," as Mam used to say. Even then we are going to need a massive distraction.

That is why Roxy asked about the temperature of the water.

First, though, we have to call out the Coast Guard.

We have moved away from the bench to a quiet part of the harbor where there are no passersby, but we can still see both the Coast Guard station and the yacht I am about to steal.

The three of us face each other. I cannot speak for them, but my heart is thumping like a blacksmith's hammer, and my throat is so dry I feel like I could drink the whole harbor.

In the entirety of my long life, I do not think I have ever felt more thankful for friends like these, but it is not something I can easily say. I look at Aidan and he has turned *very* pale.

"Is something wrong, Aidan?" I ask him, but he shakes his head.

"No," he says. "Let's do this."

"Are you sure?"

He smiles. "What are friends for, Alfie?"

And so begins the rest of my life.

CHAPTER EIGHTY-SIX

Roxy has turned off "caller ID," which she says is a way that the recipient of a call can identify you.

She has given a false name and (presumably) a false number to whoever answered her emergency call, and then wails, "It's me dad! He's in trouble! He's on a windsurfer and he's miles out to sea!"

She is good. Very convincing. I look at her face and it is contorted with worry, as though she really is making an emergency call about her dad.

"He went in off Low Hauxley Beach," she says. "You've got to help! Thank you. . . . Yes, I'll stay here."

We do not have to wait long. Within a few minutes, three figures in yellow oilskins run out of the Coast Guard building and climb down a metal ladder on the harbor wall to a waiting rescue boat: a large, gray, rigid inflatable.

By the time the boat has started, Roxy, Aidan, and I are

down by the marina. I am breathing so hard with nerves that it is making me a little light-headed.

"Will you hurry, please?" says Roxy into the telephone. "I've got no battery left on my phone. You are comin'? . . . Thanks, I've gotta go 'cause—" And she shuts the telephone off mid-sentence.

"Are you OK?" asks Aidan, but I can only nod in response.

He turns to Roxy. "All right. Time to do your thing." She tightens her jaw and marches behind a shuttered ice-cream shed, emerging seconds later in a T-shirt and underwear.

There are people on the jetties—yachties, mainly—but no one seems to take much notice of us. Not yet, anyway.

"Jolly good luck, Roxy," I say, and I offer her my hand to shake. Her face breaks into a grin.

"You, Alfie Monk, have to be the weirdest kid ever!" she says. "Come here!" She throws her tiny arms round me and squeezes hard. "*You* are the one that needs good luck. All I have to do is pretend to be drowning. *Jolly good luck*. Ha!"

With that, she descends some steps from the jetty into the water and slips in without even gasping at what must be *very* cold water. She is clenching her jaw so tightly that thick sinewy cords run down her neck, and her eyes are so white and wide open that I fear they may pop out.

I tell you: Roxy Minto is the toughest girl I have ever met.

She begins her swim out into the middle of the harbor, and nobody even notices her tiny dark head bobbing through the water.

CHAPTER EIGHTY-SEVEN

Aidan and I must work quickly.

I have taken off the stupid coat-and-hat costume and am back to looking like a child. There are some empty lobster pots and a blue plastic crate lying in a heap at the side of a jetty, and we both pick up an armful and head toward the far end of the marina.

Look as though you have a purpose, and people will ignore you. It is one of many pieces of advice that have helped me over the years.

Only not this time. A thin woman in a thick sweater, with a red, windswept face, steps into our path.

"All right, lads?" she says, not unpleasantly. "Where you's headed with all that?"

"I . . . erm . . . ," says Aidan, and I glance across at him. He has turned almost as red as the woman in front of us.

"They're for his uncle," I say.

"Oh, who's that, then? I'm the harbor warden on duty today. I have to keep an eye on things."

"It . . . it's Jasper. Jasper Hooke," says Aidan eventually.

The lady's face softens. "Ah, Cap'n Hooke, eh? We've been seein' a lot of him lately! Goin' after the lobsters now, is he?" She glances up to the sky, which is turning from white to gray, with a darker purplish bruise moving closer. "I wouldn't go out now, though. Tell Jasper that Natalie said that. Look—people are coming in."

She indicates the approach to the harbor, between two long piers, where already four sailing boats are heading back. There are others in the open water. The wind is getting stronger, and there are one or two sharp, cold raindrops. We hurry along the jetty, past the yachties securing their boats against the coming storm, and I can just see Roxy's head, way out in the middle of the harbor.

Right on cue, we hear her cry—*Help! Help!*

Only it is very quiet. Surprised, I look around me. Nobody else has heard. Even Aidan has not heard.

"Did you hear that?" I ask him.

"Hear what?"

The idea was that Roxy would cause such a disturbance that everybody would be distracted while we quietly slipped out of the harbor.

But it is not working. Nobody is paying any attention to the tiny speck way out in the water. The noise of the wind, and the sea sloshing the sides of the boats, and the rattling rigging and the slapping sails . . .

"Help!" It sounds genuine, but then, Roxy is a very good actress.

I drop my blue plastic crate and run back along the jetty toward the red-faced lady.

"Someone is in trouble!" I yell, pointing in the direction of the faint scream that comes again.

"Help!" shouts Roxy.

"Ee, is that someone *swimmin'*? You're not allowed to swim in the harbor. Hey! Hey!"

Now I really am scared, because I cannot make out Roxy's head in the water any longer. The swell of the sea has increased and even her raised arm disappears from sight. Natalie has taken out a small pair of binoculars and is sweeping them from side to side. Eventually she says, "Yes! There is someone!" and we both hear the cry again:

"Help me!"

Then Natalie is off, her rain boots thudding against the wooden planks of the jetty as she runs for help. I am running in the opposite direction, back toward Aidan, who has stopped by his Uncle Jasper's boat.

"Come on—we do not have superfluous time, Aidan!"

The boat is tied to the iron mooring and Aidan is already unhooking the long rope. He is about to unravel the last loop when he stops, his brow furrowed and a concerned look on his face. He is looking at the boat's wheelhouse.

"What is it?" I ask.

"The keys. Look. They're in the ignition." He is whispering.

Sure enough, a key is sticking out of the boat's control panel, with a large cork float dangling from it.

"Why would—" I start. Aidan is ahead of me.

"—anyone leave their keys in a boat? Unless . . ."

". . . they were already on board?"

The swell of the water has made the yacht rise and fall, and the last yard or two of rope has become disengaged from the mooring. Already the boat is drifting from the jetty. I put my fingers to my lips and leap onto the stern of the yacht as quietly as I can. Aidan follows, landing lightly. We creep toward the wheelhouse.

Next to the ship's wheel is a tiny open doorway leading below deck to a little kitchenette with a table and, beyond it, a bed.

Lying on the bed, arms outstretched, eyes closed and with headphones covering his ears, is Aidan's Uncle Jasper, an empty bottle of rum lying next to him. He has the music turned up so loud that it is seeping out of the headphones: I can even hear that it is old church music, what we used to call plainchant, voices chanting and singing.

There is a length of rope neatly coiled, hanging from a hook next to the wheel, and it seems as though Aidan and I have the same idea simultaneously. While he shuts the door as quietly as he can, I loop the rope over the door handle and stretch it tightly round the metal handrail. I come back and loop it again, and once more round the handrail, finishing with as secure a knot as I can. There's a broad grin on Aidan's face and he holds up his open palm. I do the same, and he hits my hand, which is strange but fun.

We have drifted quite a few yards out into the harbor by now, and the swell is taking us toward another boat.

"Hey! Look out!" we hear from the other vessel, and it turns to avoid a collision by inches. "You idiots! There's a storm coming!"

A couple of hundred yards away, a boat with a little engine is puttering toward Roxy, and clusters of people have gathered on the pier and on the jetties.

There was never a hope that we would get very far without rousing Jasper. Any significant movement would alert him, so we just have to get on with it.

I for one have nothing to lose. If I have to sail to Coquet Island with Jasper held prisoner in his own boat, well . . . that is what I am going to do.

It is not as though I have any choice.

We had planned—if "plan" is the right word—to get out of the harbor under sail power, but the key in the ignition means we can use the engine, so I turn it, and it powers up. I steer the boat toward the open sea.

And then we hear it.

"Hey! What the blazes is going on?"

There is no window in the door that Uncle Jasper is rattling with all his might. He has no idea who is stealing his boat.

How long will the rope hold the door shut? Can he break the door down? How long until we reach the island? We have not yet cleared the two piers and there is at least another mile to go—and then what? On the island there is no harbor, no pier, no nothing. Where will we land?

Perhaps the plan could have been polished a little more.

Together Aidan and I start hauling up the mainsail, and before it is halfway up, the wind has caught it and the boat lurches strongly to one side. I grab the wheel, Aidan secures the sail, and in seconds we are cutting through the silver water and heading for the open sea with breathtaking speed.

"What in the name of God Almighty are you doing? I hope you realize the seriousness of your crime, you thieving scum!"

I have no idea how long the door will hold. It is not looking good.

CHAPTER EIGHTY-EIGHT
AIDAN

I almost feel sorry for Jasper. The sheer panic in his voice shows that he's terrified. There he was, relaxing on his boat, listening to some music on his headphones, when suddenly he's locked in and—so far as he knows—kidnapped.

Alfie, though? Alfie is as cool as can be. It's as if he's got one thing to do, and nothing—*nothing*—is going to stop him. He's steering the boat, jaw tight, eyes screwed up, peering through the gathering rain.

I don't know how fast we're going. Boat speeds are measured in knots, and I've no idea how big a knot is. Looking at the water rushing past us, though, we're going *at least* as fast as a car driving through a town. The wind is deafening and the sail is a huge white curve, filled completely. We're in luck with the wind: it's coming straight off the land and taking the yacht directly to the island. We'll be there in a matter of minutes.

"Hello? Hello? This is Delta Foxtrot One Niner. Delta Foxtrot . . ."

It's Jasper on the radio. He's screaming for help.

"Hello—do you read me? . . . Is that Dave? Dave! Are you in the lookout? It's Jasper Hooke. My boat's been stolen, looks like we're heading straight for the island, and I'm on board, trapped below. I've been kidnapped, Dave. Call out the Coast Guard. Call the police! Call anyone! Over."

Dave's voice crackles back.

"Coast Guard just returning from an abortive mission, Jasper. Hoax call, we reckon. Blimey—is that you out there? You'll win the America's Cup goin' at that pace, Hookey. Get 'em to turn round—it's not safe. Over."

"I can't, you idiot, I'm . . . I'm *kidnapped.* They're not gonna turn round just because I ask politely! Call the Coast Guard station; tell them to divert the rescue boat to the island and intercept us! Over!"

"Who's kidnapped you, Jasper?"

"I don't know, Dave! I'm locked in, I can't see them."

"They may be armed, Hookey."

"For heaven's sake, Dave! They may also have a man-eating tiger with them for all I know. Just do something before this thing capsizes with me in it. Over and out!"

There are footsteps on the stairs leading to the door, followed by a loud banging as he tries the door again.

"Let me out! You're gonna be in so much trouble. This is piracy. You'll hang for this!"

Then it goes quiet. It's an uneasy silence, as if the silence itself is planning something. The steely water is rushing past the hull, and by now the rain is coming at us almost horizontally, but the sail is taking all of the wind and there's a sweet spot in the wheelhouse where everything is dead quiet.

I look across at Alfie and he has this grin spreading across his face—the grin of someone in the grip of certainty—and it's awesome! I know then, at that precise moment, that—no matter what happens with this boat, or with Jasper, or even with me—Alfie will succeed. Despite my terror of everything that's happening about me, I reach across Alfie and flick the switch that I'd seen Jasper flick that day he took me and Dad out.

Instantly the air is filled with unearthly music: the centuries-old Gregorian chants. For a few seconds—maybe as long as half a minute—we sail in glorious peace, abandoning ourselves to the wind, to the sea, to our fate.

Then I see it, coming through the crack in the doorway: a small knife, sawing at the rope that's holding the door shut. In a matter of seconds, it will have cut through.

At the same time, bouncing across the waves toward us at a heck of a speed is the Coast Guard rescue inflatable, the yellow-clad figures inside getting bigger by the second.

As is the island.

We're heading straight for it. The sea is so wild by now that the rocks aren't always visible, but when the swell drops, there they are: huge black stones like whale backs curving out of the surface, and in seconds we'll be smashed up on them.

CHAPTER EIGHTY-NINE

"Release the mainsail! That one there!" shrieks Alfie, his voice shot through with fear, and I unwrap the rope from the hooks as quickly as I can. Immediately the boom swings round, the sail flaps loose, and I can feel a lessening of the boat's speed, but it's still hurtling toward the rocks under its own momentum. The rocks shield a little bay and at any second we'll be thumping down onto them like the waves, which are throwing up huge plumes of white spray.

Alfie turns the boat's wheel clockwise as fast as he can; his hands are a blur, and the boat lurches to the right. Meanwhile, in the doorway, another strand of the rope pings apart as Jasper continues his frantic sawing.

"You thieving rats!" he growls. "Wait till I get my hands on you!"

"Take the wheel!" shouts Alfie, and as soon as I do, he's pulling off his sweater and kicking off his shoes.

"What the . . . ?"

Everything is happening so fast. At exactly the moment that

Alfie dives over the side into the churning sea, disappearing beneath the surface, the final strand of rope succumbs to the pressure of Jasper's knife and the door bursts open.

I start to yell, "Alfie!" but I don't get past the first syllable and end up just screaming.

The *Jolly Roger* is still continuing its terrifying progress toward the land when a huge swell from a wave lifts us up and away from a massive black rock. Water cascades over the side of the boat, and if I wasn't clinging on to the wheel, I'd be cast overboard.

Seconds later, the yacht has righted itself, but with no wind in the sails we're at the mercy of the ocean, which will surely take us back to the looming rocks.

Jasper, who has not even said anything yet, grabs the rope attached to the sail. It's like an instinct to save himself and his boat, tightening the rope enough to give the sail some wind to work with, and as he secures it to the metal hook again, the *Jolly Roger* begins an agonizing, slow curve away from the rocks. The wind is still howling and the rain is hammering so hard into my face that I can hardly see.

All the while, from the boat's speakers comes the monks' slow, harmonious chanting.

There's so much going through my head that I can't even think straight.

The main thing, though, is Alfie. *Where is he? Is he OK?*

Wiping the sea spray and rain from my face, I try to focus on where he might be in the water, but I can't even make out where *we* are. In the last few seconds, the boat has moved many yards away from where he dived in.

Fifty yards. That's about how far we are from land.

I can swim fifty meters, I'm thinking. Most kids I know can swim at least fifty meters. That's two lengths of Tynemouth pool. Easy-peasy.

But in open water, in a North Sea storm? He doesn't stand a chance. It seems, though, that our little boat is out of immediate danger. The rocks and the island are retreating, and still the holy, haunting music is blaring.

Then Jasper's next to me, screaming in my face.

"WHAT IN GOD'S NAME ARE YOU DOING, AIDAN?"

The full answer to that is going to take much longer than I think Jasper has time for, and I'm not thinking rationally. I just say, "Alfie!"

Jasper looks at me, then at the island, then at the Coast Guard boat, which is now only a couple of hundred meters away. His mouth gapes open for a second and he blinks hard.

"Oh no. Oh no, no, no, no!"

CHAPTER NINETY

With the boat under control, we're out of immediate danger, and the surging swell of ocean subsides for a moment or two, as if the storm is taking a breather.

The rescue inflatable is alongside us now. There are three people in it, wearing yellow oilskins and bulky orange life jackets.

The man at the front throws a rope, which I catch and secure to a hook on the stern of the yacht. Pulling on the rope, he draws the inflatable close enough for him to step onto the short metal ladder that hangs from the stern and, hauling himself up, he's in the boat with us. He's huge with a grizzled gray beard and his name, WAYLAND G., is printed on his oilskin jacket.

"Are you the one that called?" he shouts to Jasper, for the wind is still noisy and the monks are still singing on the yacht's music system. "What's the problem? You said you were a prisoner! What's going on?" Then he looks at me. "No life jacket? Are you mad? Quick—go and get one on." He points to a storage locker beneath the side rail.

He obviously has no idea at all what's happened. "Alfie!" I shout. "He's in the water!"

The look on Wayland G.'s face is one of pure horror. "What? *Where?*" He spins round to look, and as he does, Jasper barges him with all his strength and Wayland G. is sent staggering backward down the steps, landing in a stunned yellow heap inside the cabin. Pushing past me, Jasper heads to the back of the boat.

What? I think.

As Wayland G. staggers to his feet, I'm still trying to pull on a life jacket. Jasper has unhooked the rope securing the rescue boat to the yacht.

Unencumbered by life jackets and oilskins, Jasper is much more agile than the two crewmen in the inflatable. With his back to the yacht, he hooks his arms over the rail and lifts up both feet to deliver a huge double kick into the chest of the first man. All the man says is, "Whoa!" and then he falls backward into the water.

By now, Wayland G. is back up the steps. He pushes me roughly aside and is one stride away from grabbing Jasper, just as Jasper lets go with his arms and lands in the rescue boat.

When he lands, the little inflatable rocks violently to one side. With a cry of "No!" the remaining man overbalances and plops into the water, popping to the surface immediately like a cork.

We're still under sail, so we're already a good distance from where the first man went in, his yellow jacket clearly visible, bobbing in the water. Jasper has taken the controls of the rescue boat and is speeding back toward the island.

What is he *doing*?

"Can you sail, son?" shouts Wayland G. to me.

I shrug noncommittally.

"Right. Release the mainsail; prepare to come about. Watch the boom!"

I think we're going to turn round and pick up Alfie and the people overboard. I can only wonder what on earth will happen when Jasper catches up with Alfie. I think of the moment when he went after the police car, claiming he wanted to comfort the lost boy. There's something else going on, clearly. He *knows* Alfie and he's after him.

The monks' chant—mournful and loud—stops suddenly as Wayland G. flicks the switch, and once again the only noise is the wind and the sea.

"Where's the OB?" shouts Wayland G. "The overboard—where did he enter the water?"

I scan the surface where Alfie was swimming, but there's no sign of him.

CHAPTER NINETY-ONE

alfie

Cold water never used to bother me. When I was little—that is, properly little, all those years ago—cold water was more or less all we had. We would wash in it, and, when we needed to wash all over, there was always the sea.

And in the winter, when the sea was too cold even to stand in and splash ourselves, Mam would warm a pot of seawater next to the fire. . . .

You see, all my thoughts go back to Mam—even now, when I am throwing my arms over my head, one after the other, trying to plow through the cold, cloudy water, and swallowing great mouthfuls of salty sea.

It is not far to the shore, but it takes me five strokes to make the progress of one in calmer water. The ocean lifts me up and swoops me down on massive waves, bringing me closer to the rocks that will split my skull. Like a wild animal, I kick my legs madly to give myself extra propulsion.

"Swim, Alve, swim!"

I hear Mam in my head, urging me on. But I cannot swim faster, or stronger, for the waves and the cold have stolen my strength; as I get weaker, they get stronger. I lift my head to take a desperate breath, and a wave top breaks in my face, making me inhale another lungful of seawater. I am choking underwater, and I become certain that that is where I will die. Like my father all those years ago, I will be taken by the ocean.

When I sink, the noise of the waves stops. The sound of the wind has gone; everything is silent, and peaceful, and dark. I feel something touch my arm: it is the sand, and I am being dragged along the bottom by the surging water, and surely it will only be a few seconds until I can feel nothing more. . . .

"Not yet, Alve," says Mam. "Not yet."

Then, strangely, Mam's imaginary voice becomes deeper and it is Rafel, my combat teacher from so long ago. His voice is in the water all around me:

"Remember, Alfie: you are at your strongest when you are at your weakest. When your enemy thinks you are beaten, that is when to strike. Find force from frailty, Alfie!"

Force from frailty.

My feet are touching the sand, my legs are bent, and I know that if I straighten them they will push against the sea bottom. From somewhere deep inside me, somewhere a thousand years ago, I find a tiny, scrappy remnant of strength, and with a final push I thrust upward to the air. Half a second more and I would have taken a fatal lungful of water, but my mouth clears the surface and I suck in a rattling, desperate breath that seems to contain my whole long life. Then a wave pushes me over again, but this time my knees hit the sand and I realize I can stand up. I suck in more air and cough up seawater, then another breath and I am on the beach, and I do not stop staggering, walking, running—anything to escape the devilish embrace of the ocean.

Breathe.

Cough.

Run.

Breathe.

Cough.

Run.

I have made it. I turn to look back at the water, the mighty foe I have defeated.

Heading toward me, out beyond the rocks, is an inflatable boat with a man at the helm.

Jasper.

CHAPTER NINETY-TWO

⚡ AIDAN ⚡

Desperately I look across the water, my eyes flicking left and right. The swell has picked up again as we bring the yacht round, tacking left and right to catch the wind, and the boat is rising and falling on the waves.

"There he is!" I yell.

I point at the little beach on the island. A small, shirtless figure is running out of the white-foam shallows up the sand. He's made it.

But Jasper is in the inflatable, with a couple of hundred yards to go. The swell is holding him back, but he'll land soon as well.

Wayland G. shakes his head in disbelief. "Crazy," he says. "Just crazy."

The yacht is getting close to one of the floating crewmen, and Wayland G. throws out a line.

I cannot take my eyes off Alfie, staggering and running and stumbling up the rain-soaked beach.

I saw a documentary on television once: a little antelope was being hunted by a lioness. It couldn't run fast enough, and the lioness kept getting closer and closer.

Watching Alfie scramble up the beach, I keep thinking, *Go, antelope, go!*

CHAPTER NINETY-THREE

Alfie

I turn from Jasper, closing in on his inflatable dinghy, and run up the beach toward a long, dry cave.

The cave: the one where Mam and I hid the pearl.

I barely notice another boat at the other end of the beach, pulled up onto the dry sand. There are some small tents too, quivering in the wind, and a larger green canvas tent, exactly the shape and color of the little plastic houses in a game of Monopoly.

The tents must belong to the archaeologists, although there is nobody about. I conclude they have left their tools and tents and returned to the mainland.

I stagger-run some more. The cave is getting closer. I have to stop to throw up, and I sink to my knees, bringing up a belly-load of seawater. I look back at the sea: the rescue boat with Jasper in it is very close to the shore now. I can make out his black beard.

I run some more, and I am at the mouth of the cave.

It stinks—an ancient smell of dry seaweed, salt, and dead seabirds.

It is dark too. Only a short distance into the cave it is already hard to see. I blink my eyes hard, but it does no good; I stumble forward, hitting my bare toes on jutting rocks.

Yet I know *exactly* where the clay box is. At the very back of the cave, it sort of splits into a fork—one fork is barely an arm's length deep, and ends in a slope of sandstone. The other is longer: a narrow passage almost as high as I am, and almost as long, that ends in a huge boulder.

The boulder conceals a turn, a bend in the rock that no one could find unless they knew it was there.

Old Paul knew. Mam knew. I know.

I can squeeze most of my body round the big boulder, then I stretch out my left arm, and feel a short, sandy ledge, and then . . .

Nothing. My breathing quickens as I pat my hand round the ledge, and the rock behind it. Have I knocked it off? It is not there, for sure, and a dreadful fear begins to rise in me.

Then I feel a cold, hard hand grab my other wrist, and I cry out.

I turn to face Jasper.

CHAPTER NINETY-FOUR

It is not Jasper. In the darkness, I can make out an older woman's face, with white hair, and it is familiar.

"I sought it vas you," she says, and I recognize the German accent.

It is Dr. Heinz, the archaeologist who spoke at school.

"Quickly," she says, "follow me."

CHAPTER NINETY-FIVE

"Is zis what you are looking for?"

We are standing in the largest tent. Outside, the wind is still rattling the canvas, but inside it is calm, the tent fabric casting a greenish glow over everything. A long trestle table is covered with boxes, files, electrical leads, devices with dials on them, and trowels and brushes. And lying on a square of folded cloth is the clay box, its coating of tallow, pine resin, and beeswax darkened and cracked with age.

I nod dumbly. "It is my mam's. Mine, I mean. Ours." I cannot take my eyes off it. I reach out my hand, but Dr. Heinz steps between me and the table, staring hard at me.

"It is incredible," she says. "But is it true?" She is tipping her head from side to side, looking at me from every angle. "The vay you spoke that day, in the school. Somesing made me . . . wonder."

I say nothing but shiver all over. My teeth are chattering.

"*Ach*, poor boy, you are cold! Here!" She gives me a blanket from a pile, which I wrap tightly round me.

"Your teachers told me about you, and the *dreadful* sing zat happened to you. And so . . . I do a little research, yes? The fire, you know? I am so, so sorry. I looked in vebsites, official records, yes? I discovered you and your mother, God rest her soul, are living in zat house for many, many years, yes?"

I nod, and sink into a nylon camping chair next to the table. I am exhausted. I cannot lie anymore.

"The legend of ze Neverdeads: it has almost been forgotten, no? But there was zat clue, hidden in ze writings of an old Durham bishop."

I sigh. "Walter."

"You knew him?"

I shrug, and think back to Old Paul. "Not personally. But I think I know who told him."

From quite a distance away, outside, comes a shout.

"Alfie! Alfie!"

Dr. Heinz gasps. "There is another person?"

"Shhh!" We fall silent.

"Alfie! I don't want to harm you! Come out!"

Peering out of the tent through the laced-up entrance, I see Jasper, soaked through, pacing up and down the mouth of the cave and shouting into it. A faint echo comes back from within.

"Alfie! Where are you?"

You . . . you . . .

He stops for a moment and looks about, his gaze finally settling on the tents. I pull back from the entrance and turn to Dr. Heinz.

"He's coming! Hide the pot!"

She moves quietly and confidently, placing the pot beneath a blanket in the corner of the tent, and standing upright at the moment the lace ties on the front flaps are pulled apart and Jasper's dripping, bearded face thrusts through, his wild eyes glinting in the greenish gloom and his long, too-white teeth bared in a grin as if ready to bite.

"Hello, Alfie!" he says.

CHAPTER NINETY-SIX
AIDAN

It seems to be only minutes before we're sailing back toward the twin piers at Amble harbor. By "we," I mean me, Wayland G., and the two other guys that Jasper sent for a swim. The inflatable rescue boat is towed behind us.

At the wheel of our boat, Wayland G. gives the command to lower the sails, and he starts up the engine for an easy steer back to the marina. He is not being friendly. "Get down there, son, and stay there till I tell you," he growls, pointing to the inside quarters of the yacht. The storm seems to be blowing out. At any rate, it's stopped raining.

I overhear him talking with the other two.

"Scramble the helicopter from Bamburgh . . . Boy in immediate danger . . . Theft of HM Coast Guard vessel . . ."

He comes down the steps and glares at me. "Does this thing work?" he says, pointing at the boat's radio.

"I . . . I don't know."

He flicks a switch. The same music blares out.

"Alleluia!"

He swears under his breath and switches it off. "No point in radioing," he says. "We're two minutes from the harbor anyway." He turns to me and says through clenched teeth, "I hope for your sake, lad, you've got a good explanation for all this."

I swallow hard.

I have an explanation, but whether it matches anyone's idea of a "good" one is doubtful.

There's a police car waiting at the harbor when we dock. A small crowd has gathered. As I get off the boat, a policewoman comes forward and takes my arm gently.

"Come on, young man. Into the car with you."

CHAPTER NINETY-SEVEN

The drive to the police station in Amble is only about a quarter of a mile. It's a new, low building the same color as the sand on the beach. Inside it smells of fresh paint.

I can hear Roxy's voice on the phone.

"I don't know, Mum. . . . I know that, Mum, it's just that . . . Yes, Mum . . . I think he's here now. . . . Bye, Mum, love you."

I'm shown into a plain room with a desk, a low beige sofa, and cream walls. Roxy leaps up from the sofa. There's a lady, not in uniform, sitting with her, holding a notebook.

"Aidan!"

Roxy dashes forward and throws her arms round me, which I wasn't expecting, and I sort of stand there awkwardly, being squeezed by this tiny girl. "I was so worried! I thought you'd sunk and drowned!"

There's something a bit odd about Roxy's behavior, and I can't quite put my finger on it.

"I told you to be careful, didn't I?" says Roxy.

And then I do: *She's acting.* Again. I have to bend down a bit to return her hug, and when I do she whispers in my ear.

"You were just messing about on your uncle's boat. All an accident."

That's all there's time for, otherwise the lady on the sofa might have got suspicious. She stands up.

"Aidan." She sounds serious. "I'm Detective Sergeant Simm, and *you* have got some explaining to do."

I go sit in a room with a uniformed officer and Detective Sergeant Simm. I am not, apparently, "under arrest." I'm just "answering questions."

Perhaps now is when I have to learn to be better at lying. Can I just say, at this point, that if you want to learn how to lie convincingly, don't practice with a police officer? For a start, they are very good at spotting liars—and besides, you should always tell the truth anyway.

That said, here is the big fat lie I tell to the police.

We wanted an adventure, I say.

We caught a bus to Amble.

While Roxy went for a swim, Alfie and I checked out Uncle Jasper's boat.

We unmoored it, and only meant to take it out into the harbor, but the wind pushed us in the wrong direction.

We hadn't known that Uncle Jasper was passed out, drunk, in the cabin.

No, it does *not* sound convincing.

Wayland G. and the rest of his crew would be telling a very different story. The true story of a boy diving off a boat into a stormy sea, and a bearded madman assaulting Coast Guard volunteers and stealing an inflatable rescue boat . . .

Then there's Mum and Dad to deal with. They're on their way with Precious Minto. It's all going to be very difficult. I do not feel well.

"May I have a glass of water, please?" I say. DS Simm gets up and leaves the room, and I am left alone with the policeman in uniform.

Neither of us says anything, and in the silence I hear a helicopter overhead.

"It's come from Bamburgh, that has," says the policeman. "They'll be pickin' up your mate."

CHAPTER NINETY-EIGHT

Alfie

The rain has eased to a drizzle. Dr. Heinz has opened the tent flaps to let the light in, and she, Jasper, and I sit in camping chairs round the trestle table. We have no choice. I mean, what else are we going to do? Fight him?

No one says anything for ages. Finally Jasper takes a deep breath and says: "It's been a while, Alve."

"You could say that." I am trying to be "cool," but inside me there is a storm just as violent as the real one that has just passed.

Jasper is sitting opposite me at a wooden table in a tent on a tiny, windswept island.

He clasps his hands, as if in prayer, and speaks slowly. "A long while to find what is rightfully mine."

"Yours?"

He nods. "Indeed mine. Until your father stole it from me."

This is an unexpected development. "He won it in battle," I say with some force.

Jasper shrugs. "Same thing. He and his . . . his *gang* attacked me and my men. I survived, but he took the biggest prize. I call that theft."

Is this the story that Mam told me?

"You and your men were raiding an undefended village, and my valiant father fought you off. If you survived, then that means my father showed you mercy. You should be thankful."

Dr. Heinz interrupts. "Vait! Vait! When was zis happening?" We both turn to her. I think we had almost forgotten she was there.

"About eleven hundred years ago," replies Jasper calmly, and she gasps. "A bit more, actually. I have suspected the life-pearl was here, on Cockett Island, for many years. But I never knew where exactly. Believe me, I have looked. I would return every few decades. I lost track of you and your mother and I thought maybe it was lost forever. Maybe you had taken it. Maybe you were both dead."

"And then you found me."

"I found a wife. She had a nephew. Who had a friend. Who was you."

There is another long pause, and then we all turn to look outside the tent at the same time. There is a faint *thap-thap-thap* sound coming from the sky. Dr. Heinz says, "A helicopter."

Soon it will land. Police will get out and after that . . . who knows?

This is my only chance, and my eyes flick to where the clay box is.

Big mistake.

"Over there, is it?" asks Jasper, almost whispering. "That lump under the blanket?" He stands up and, in one swift movement, whips the blanket away, revealing the box, which he seizes in both hands.

"Stop!" cries Dr. Heinz, getting to her feet.

"Or what, old lady?" He does not look at her; his eyes are greedily feasting on the object in his hands.

"Jasper, please!" I say. "Think about it. You are a man. I have never had the chance to grow up." I am pleading.

"When your father stole this from me, there were five *livperler* left—is that what you call them, still? Your father used one, your mother too, and you. That *should* mean that there are two remaining, should it not? That would have been one each."

My throat tightens.

"But you wasted one, did you not? You wasted one *on a cat!*"

I gasp. "It was an accident!" I am close to tears now. "I was young, I was . . . I was stupid."

"Indeed you were, Alve. Indeed you were."

"How did you know? About the cat?"

Jasper grins. "I did not. You just admitted it. It was a hunch: there were plenty of stories about a woman and her son and their cat. I just put two and two together, and you have just given me the answer." He pauses and spits out the word again. "A *cat*? Anyone so stupid deserves everything they get." His eyes burn with demented fury.

Then, without warning, he smashes the clay box onto the wooden table and it cracks apart, the hardened resin shattering. Dr. Heinz gives a little shriek.

There, nestled in a tight bundle of sheep's wool, is a small glass ball. The last remaining life-pearl in the world.

"Can you imagine what this is worth?" says Jasper, teasing the wool apart with his long, bony fingers. "The fortune I shall be able to make?"

My jaw drops open. "Y-you mean you do not want it for yourself?"

Jasper grins his sickly grin. "I am certainly *not* going to use it. What on earth did you think? Are you quite mad, little man? Modern science should have little difficulty analyzing the liquid inside. Right here is a secret that has been lost for a thousand years. Death overcome, do you see? The power to live forever." His eyes widen manically.

Dr. Heinz shakes her head and says softly, "We are not meant to live forever. It is against . . . against *everysing*."

Jasper turns his head and says with faked surprise, "Oh! Are you still here? Why?"

In the split second that his attention is distracted from the pearl of glass before us, I grab it. Jasper's hand is too slow, and

I instantly toss the glass ball into my mouth. His eyes widen in horror. I am trying to swallow it, but I just cannot: the salt water, the retching and coughing—my throat is swollen and dry.

"NO! You little devil!"

He reaches out and grabs me by the throat with both hands. "Spit it out, you son of a coward! Sick it up now! God help me, I'll kill you, you little fiend, just like I killed your father!"

This is terrifying and painful, and his strong hands squeeze my neck harder. Did he just say *"like I killed your father"*?

I am struggling to breathe, and my head is swimming and his words are bouncing around in my head, when out of the corner of my eye I see Dr. Heinz lifting up a spade, and with an almighty whack she brings it down on the back of Jasper's skull.

Now, when that sort of thing happens in films, the noise is usually a crack, or a clang if the weapon is metal. In real life, I can tell you it is not like that. It is just a very loud thud.

Also in films, the recipient of such a blow will instantly be rendered unconscious. He will slump to the floor, job done.

He will *not* do what Jasper does, which is to cry out, "*OOOWW!* You filthy old witch!"

He spins round in anger, but Dr. Heinz is holding him at bay, the spade pointing forward like a spear. I use the distraction to dash out of the tent and up the beach. A steep path leads from the sand up to a large area of dry grass at the top of the cliff, and I scramble up this to get away from him, but he follows me, bellowing curses in a language I have never even heard before.

It *was* him. On the boat. The man with the beard who shouted at me. And who pushed Da overboard. My breath is rasping in my throat but I have to keep going.

"I'll cut your face open if I need to, you hell-dog!"

Something glints in the light—a large knife in his hand—and I have no doubt at that moment that he means what he says.

Above us, the helicopter is circling. I need to keep away from Jasper just long enough for it to land on the grass. How much time will that take? Another minute?

The stones of the path are loose and they crumble away beneath my bare feet as I scramble higher up the cliff face. But Jasper is bigger, stronger, and has not just completed a massive swim.

I am exhausted, and he is getting closer.

Three paces more, two . . .

I try to reach for a tuft of grass at the top of the cliff path, and I feel Jasper's hand grab my ankle.

I scream out, "No! Get off!" but I am being dragged back, and as I open my mouth to scream, the life-pearl pops out. I see it arc through the air and bounce off a rock. It rolls back down the path, coming to rest below me, just beyond my reach.

With a desperate lunge, I extend my free arm, but I cannot stretch far enough.

Jasper has seen it but he cannot reach it, either. Above me, my fist has found a thick root to hold on to, and I have stopped slipping back.

And there we stay for a few seconds. Me hanging on to the root, with my face pressed into the cliffside, and Jasper gripping my ankle. But we are unsteady. One of Jasper's feet has nothing to support it. One slip and we will both tumble back onto the rocks.

"Just like I killed your father . . ."

Do I care if he dies?

I can feel the root giving way above me, and we both slip down the cliff face, bringing Jasper nearer to the life-pearl, but still not close enough for him to grab it.

"Just like I killed your father . . ."

The words echo back at me as though from inside a cave.

Do I care if *I* die with him?

When I dare to look down, he has the blade of the knife gripped in his teeth, freeing up his other hand to grip my ankle. The weight is pulling me down, down, and I know that the end is seconds away.

Desperately my fingers dig into the loose earth next to the root, scrabbling for a new hold, but it's no use. As I slide back, I'm screaming, "No!" when I feel something grip my thumb, and then the wrist of my bandaged arm. The agony is searing, but I cannot even scream in pain, I am so terrified.

"I've got him!" I hear from above. "Come on, son. I've got you!" I look up into the face of a man—police officer, coast guard, soldier? I do not know, but I am being pulled apart: Jasper at my ankle and this man who now has both of my wrists.

The weight of me and Jasper is pulling him over the edge as well.

With a frantic kick, my foot comes free. Jasper is hanging on with one hand, his feet frantically trying to gain a grip on the steep, pebbly path.

If I wriggle too hard, the coast guard will be pulled over the lip of the cliff and all three of us will fall, so instead I kick my foot toward the cliff face again and again, crushing Jasper's hand, until I hear a curse and feel his grip loosen.

But he does not fall. Spread-eagled against the cliff face, his toes resting on a grassy tuft, Jasper is panting hoarsely and he looks up with panic in his eyes as I'm pulled to safety.

"Help me!" he gasps.

There is no time for the man who pulled me up to do anything but check that I am safe, then turn his attention back to Jasper, hanging on to the cliffside. Another man is running from the helicopter, but it will take him several seconds to get here and Jasper does not have that long.

I lean down over the cliff edge, the stones and sharp grasses making new scratches on my bare chest, and I stretch my arm out to Jasper. I cannot let him fall. Murderer or not, I am not about to let someone die.

"No! Get back!" yells my rescuer, but Jasper is reaching for me. . . .

Reaching . . . stretching . . .

Then suddenly his eyes are no longer on mine and I follow

his gaze to the life-pearl, nestled in a crack. It is too far for me to stretch, but Jasper's eyes are crazed with greed and determination.

"No, Jasper—you can't reach," I shout. "Take my hand instead!"

I really think for a moment that he is going to. But he cannot stop himself. With a small grunt of exertion, he grabs the knife from his mouth and extends it toward the life-pearl, dislodging it from the crack. In one movement, he drops the knife and grabs the pearl in his fist. But Jasper's greed has overbalanced him. He sways backward, croaking, "Ah . . . no . . . ah . . . no . . ."

Both my rescuer and I are now leaning over the cliff edge, trying to reach him. Jasper stretches out his hand—manages to touch mine. I feel the life-pearl between our palms. Is he giving it to me? It is hard to tell. Our eyes meet, but I can't get a proper grip on his hand, and his weight is toppling him backward.

I cannot watch. I know I cannot hold him, and I screw my eyes shut as he slips away. He does not even scream.

I cannot look down.

Then I hear a sickening, dull thump on the rocks below.

There are two men above me now, and they haul me to the safety of the level grass.

I am trembling, shivering, shaking and sobbing, sucking in great lungfuls of air while the man hugs me and rocks me like Mam used to.

My fists are clenched tight and in one hand I can feel the glass ball pressing into my palm.

I am held strongly by my rescuer, who keeps saying, "Shhh, OK, son, shhh, you're OK, son."

And, for the first time since Mam died, I think I might be.

CHAPTER NINETY-NINE

The helicopter has taken Jasper to the big hospital in Cramlington. They will come back in about an hour, they said. I am left with Dr. Heinz, who has made hot tinned soup on her little camping stove, replaced the dressing on my arm, cleaned up the scratches on my chest with stuff from her first-aid kit, and wrapped me up in a blanket again. All the while, I am clutching the life-pearl tightly. I am not sure if she has noticed.

Dr. Heinz and I sit in the canvas chairs, drinking our soup and saying nothing. I do not really feel like talking, and I suppose she understands that.

I am startled when her telephone rings. Dr. Heinz steps outside the tent, but I can hear everything she says.

"Ah! Prudence, my dear. . . . Vell, I can't really talk, I have a visitor here on ze island, and I shall tell you all about it soon, but it has been a werry *dramatic* morning. . . ."

I guess that this is Pru, the lady she lives with. There is a pause while Dr. Heinz listens, and then:

"Oh, really? Vere? . . . *Ach,* the poor pussycat . . . Vill she eat anysing? . . . *Nein?* Half her *teeth? Ach schade!* That iss a pity. . . . Then yes, I agree, my dear, perhaps that is the kindest sing. . . ."

I have leaped to my feet, discarding the blanket and spilling hot soup on the sandy floor of the tent as I rush out. It's the teeth: how many cats have half their teeth missing?

"That must be Biffa!" I shout. "Give me the telephone!" I grab it without waiting and almost yell down the phone, "Is she black with patches of white on her neck?"

On the other end of the line, I hear Pru's rather startled voice. "Er . . . yes, she is. Who is this, please?"

"I am sorry. My name is Alfie Monk and I think you have found my cat. Is she alive?"

"Well, yes . . . but she is *very* weak. I'm sorry to say that I really don't think she will survive. The kindest thing is to—"

"No! Don't let her die! She is a thousand years old." Quite what Pru makes of that last statement, I do not know, but she speaks gently.

"Alfie, love, she won't eat anything. It's hopeless."

"Crab!" I say. "Anything with crab in it. That is her favorite. Tinned crab, fresh crab, crab paste . . . anything!"

"I . . . I'll try, Alfie, love, but I really don't think . . ."

Her last words are drowned out by the *thwap-thwap-thwap* of the helicopter returning to take us back to the mainland.

As we get into the helicopter, Dr. Heinz puts her mouth close to my ear and shouts above the noise: "Your secret is safe vith me, Alfie," and she squeezes my shoulder. She smiles to herself for the whole of the short helicopter journey, loving the adventure.

I look out the window at the puffins swooping below us, then catch sight of my reflection in the helicopter window, and I am surprised to see that I am smiling too.

CHAPTER ONE HUNDRED

Questions.

People.

People and questions. Everyone wants to know just what on earth has been going on.

You cannot blame them, only the truth would not work, would it?

Aidan's parents and Libby and Precious Minto have arrived in Precious's old Ford Fiesta. Sangeeta is there too, and Dr. Heinz: all of us in the little police station at Amble.

Nobody, it seems, can work out what to do.

Aidan has stuck to the line that Jasper went a bit loopy when he found us on his boat. His call to the Coast Guard about being trapped in the cabin must have been "a joke." Jasper is in a coma in the hospital and cannot contribute to the argument.

Nobody—so far—has connected Roxy to the fake call regarding her dad on a windsurfer.

My story is, in a fury that we had boarded his boat, Jasper

chased me onto the island and pursued me up the cliff path, where he stumbled and fell thirty feet onto the rocks below.

Does it make sense?

Well, it is certainly easier to believe than the truth. Besides, I am finding it hard to concentrate on anything except Biffa.

Dr. Heinz adopts an air of bewilderment and—I am certain—exaggerates her German accent to sound even more puzzled. I think she is trying to protect me from more questions.

"Vot iss zis all about?" she keeps saying. "I vos peacefully in *mein* tent sitting, und zen zere vos all zis *kerfufflen, mit* helicopters *und* everysing. *Ach, mein Gott* . . . ," and so on. I trust her.

We are all in and out of interview rooms with police officers. I have been given some spare clothes to wear, and the lifepearl is safe in my pocket. I am staring out the window during a lull, worrying about Biffa, when Sangeeta comes over and sits down on the hard sofa next to me.

She murmurs, "You know I don't believe a word of this, don't you, Alfie? I have no idea what's really going on, but I know—in my heart, I just know—that you are not telling me the full truth. Or even part of the truth, for that matter."

I look at her, really look at her, and I feel sorry. Sangeeta has not been unkind. I nod. "I understand."

She laughs softly. "You understand! I think you understand a *lot*, Alfie."

"Can we go soon, Sangeeta? I need to see my cat."

CHAPTER ONE HUNDRED AND ONE

About an hour later, the police chief arrives. It is her day off and she is not in uniform. She decides that no arrests will be made today, and we are all to be released "pending further investigations."

Turns out Jasper Hooke was known to the local police, although I do not know what for. Known enough, though, for Officer MacAllan to at least be inclined to believe us.

By seven p.m., we are on our way back.

Apparently cellular telephones are not very water-resistant, which I think is odd given that you all use them so much. Anyhow, mine was in my shorts when I dived off the *Jolly Roger* and it is now ruined.

I turn to Sangeeta, who is driving and who has been very quiet.

"May I borrow your telephone, Sangeeta? I should like to send a text message."

"Who are you texting?"

"Oh, just Roxy."

Sangeeta presses a button to unlock her telephone and hands it to me. It is different from mine, but eventually I manage to compose a text:

> Dear Roxy,
>   Please come to Dr. Heinz's house at 8 p.m.
> tonight with Aidan.
>   Yours sincerely,
>   Alfie

When I have pressed the button marked "Send," I put my hand back into my pocket to check for the reassuring presence of the small, smooth life-pearl.

CHAPTER ONE HUNDRED AND TWO

I am expecting the house to smell of cats, but it does not. Not at all. The three of us are greeted at the door by Dr. Heinz.

"I sink . . . ," she says, "I sink it should be Alfie on his own who comes to see his cat. I do not vant to disturb her."

I shake my head. "They are part of this as well, Dr. Heinz."

"*Ach*, call me Sue. Everyone else does!"

And so we go in, and in the back room is a cat basket, and lying on it is a cat. My cat. Me and Mam's cat. Skinny, with some patches of fur missing, and a crooked tail . . . but it is definitely Biffa.

And she is alive, found near-starving by Prudence in the alleyway between two houses. Next to her is an empty food bowl. Straightaway I sink to my knees and bury my face in her neck. She responds by twitching her tail and making her strange, vocal mewling.

"You were right about the crab," says Pru, who is standing above me with a soppy smile. "She ate it all."

I want to say thank you. I want to say *something*, but I cannot, for if I do I will start to cry. With sadness for everything that has happened, with sorrow for Biffa's suffering, with happiness that I have her back, with relief, with . . .

Everything.

I look up and smile broadly to stop myself from crying, and then lower my head again into Biffa's fur, which smells of woodsmoke, and caves, and ship's tar, and sea spray, and centuries and centuries of Mam. I scratch her ears and tell her again and again in our old language how much I have missed her.

I do not know how long I stay there, but when I look up again, Dr. Heinz, Prudence, Roxy, and Aidan have all gone; it is just me and Biffa: the thousand-year-old boy and his thousand-year-old cat; and I know now how I will do the one remaining thing that I need to do.

CHAPTER ONE HUNDRED AND THREE

The people on the Metro do not even look up when I get on, carrying a rucksack with wood in it and a pet carrier with a cat in it.

They all keep on staring at their cellular telephones, which seems to be the modern way. A little while ago, I would have been glad that nobody noticed me; now I am not so sure. Either way, after a couple of stops, I take out my phone as well. (Sangeeta bought me a new one, and it plays videos!)

I think about how amazed Mam would be at everyone traveling so fast to places that—not so long ago—might have taken a whole day or more to walk to.

She is with me all the time, is Mam. Not just in my head, and in my heart, but in my celluar telephone. Roxy has given me a "digital copy" of a video she was taking (secretly) the day we first met. It has Mam's voice, her face, her hands, our old house. It made me sad the first time I saw it, but now it makes me smile.

The Metro trundles on. South Gosforth, Ilford Road, West Jesmond . . . I keep looking up at the diagram on the side of the train, counting off the stations. Sixteen to go. Lots of people get off and on at Newcastle, then there is a long section when we go under the River Tyne.

The Teen, I think.

Not long now, I think as I look at the picture of Mam on my phone. A young man opposite gives me a funny look. Did I say it out loud? Oh well.

Pelaw, Hebburn, Jarrow. I smile and remember Johannes, and Old Paul. We are heading back along the south side of the river now, toward the sea. There is a station called Bede, named after the old historian. I knew an old monk once who told me his great-great-grandfather had met Bede. The thought makes me chuckle, and the man opposite looks up again, now convinced I am mad.

Finally the end of the line: South Shields, where this whole thing began.

It was not called that then, of course. I do not think it even had a name a thousand years ago.

I come out of the station with Biffa in her carrier, and look around me. It is odd to realize that, in a thousand years, I have never once been back here. I think, *Gosh, it has changed,* and then start laughing at myself. Really laughing, out loud. The man from the train walks past me, shaking his head. But I do not care.

It is all houses and shops; everything is these days.

The beach does not change, though, or the cliffs. I know that, when I see it, I will remember the little cave where my whole adventure began, so I start walking south, along the wide clifftop, and when I gaze out over the flat, iron-gray sea, I try to imagine that I am back there with my mam, and eleven years old. High above me seagulls hover, and kittiwakes swoop in and out of their cliffside roosts. I am brought back to the twenty-first century by the sound of a motor car swishing past on the distant road.

My rucksack has begun to dig into my shoulders, and Biffa is getting heavy, but I do not mind. On I walk, until I come to a little semicircular bay, like a giant has taken a bite out of the earth. There is a concrete stairway leading to the beach now; Mam and I had to carry our belongings down a rocky path.

Even though it is summer, the bay is deserted. The cave is unchanged, although there are signs that people have been here: empty beer cans, mainly.

I let Biffa out of the pet carrier. Normally she would go and explore; instead she sniffs the air and plods over to the rocky shelf where she made herself comfortable all those years ago. She cannot remember, surely? On the other hand, if *I* can remember, maybe she does too. She mewls loudly and settles down to watch.

From my bag, I take the wood, a big wax firelighter, and some matches. I thought about doing it the old way. The lenses of my spectacles would have worked to create a flame in the same way as Da's fire-glass, but today the sun is behind a sky-wide white sheet of cloud.

In a moment, the fire is flickering to life.

In the top section of my rucksack is a small square box: a tiny, battery-operated projector—another find from Roxy's dumpster diving. The surface has a deep scratch, and the audio does not work, which is perhaps why it was thrown out, but it is otherwise fine. I push my telephone into the slot and press Play.

And there she is, life-size, on the ridged and rocky cave wall. My mam. Biffa yawns and gives a little growl of approval.

By now, my hands are sweating as I pull the last item from my bag: Da's little steel knife. From my pocket, I take the last remaining life-pearl in the world: warm and smooth.

I know the film of Mam second by second, and I look up at the projected image. There is a bit coming up when Mam looks at the camera and gives a little nod. That is the bit I am waiting for as I hold the knife to the flame.

When it comes, I do not hesitate. With two swift slashes, I cut into the scars on my arm and crack open the life-pearl between my teeth. My heart is racing, which is probably a good thing: it will propel the droplets through my body all the quicker. A drop oozes out, which I pour into the bloody wound on my arm. Another one, and another.

It stings, as it should, like fresh nettles as I wrap a bandage round my arm.

Here she looks at the paper in her hand and pauses as she peers through her glasses. It is as if she is doing it deliberately, to build suspense, but I do not think she is.

". . . between four thousand . . ."

Wait. What?

". . . and four thousand two hundred . . ."

What is she saying?

". . . days. Which is roughly between eleven years, and eleven years and three months. Completely consistent with your stated age, Alfie."

I start back at school tomorrow.

CHAPTER ONE HUNDRED AND FIVE

SIX MONTHS LATER

AIDAN

Jasper died in the hospital "without regaining consciousness."

It turns out he was rather rich and it all went to Aunty Alice: he had no other relatives.

She has been "very generous," Mum said, which means, I think, that our money worries are over, for the time being at any rate. Mum has been promoted at the call center and Dad has had loads of job interviews. I expect we'll be moving house again, just as the redecorating has been completed. ("No thanks to you, matey!" said Dad, but he was joking. Sort of.)

It has to be a house that's big enough to have a room for Alfie. Mum and Dad are starting the process that will enable us to adopt him. Sangeeta has been over to our house a lot, and other people too from social services. It's all looking good.

Alfie will be my older brother. (My *much* older brother!) And there'll be a huge bookshelf to house a very special collection of Charles Dickens books.

Libby is pleased too, but maybe she's just happy that we'll get Biffa.

Inigo Delombra, by the way, has moved school. Only to Monkseaton High, but it's far enough away for me. On his last day, he came up to me and Alfie and said, "Linklater, Monk, what *is* it with you two? There's something you're hiding, and it's gonna bug me forever."

"Forever, eh?" said Alfie. "That's a long time, Delombra. Just so long as you're OK with that," and we walked off, leaving Inigo to stew. We high-fived when we were out of his sight.

And Roxy? Roxy's just . . . Roxy. She's taken to calling Alfie "old chap," as in "Good to see you, Alfie, *old chap*!" It's kind of funny, but only we understand the joke.

Alfie's had his teeth done, and he's OK-looking. He's joined Roxy's drama group, and she says he's very good at playing old men. Funny that.

Thanks to Sangeeta (who said she "called in some favors"), Precious Minto has had a stair lift installed. She's stopped walking with a cane, and every few days her loud, warbling voice penetrates the thin walls, singing hymns.

> *"Thine be tha gloree, risen conquerin' son!*
> *Endless is tha vict'ry thou o'er deat' hast won!"*

It is not at all tuneful, but Roxy says it's the best thing she's ever heard.

Speaking of singing . . . We were in the car, singing along to a song on the radio (Alfie still calls it the wireless, which is hilarious), and he hit this really deep note. A proper man's bass note that went, "Oh *yeahhhh!*"

Mum heard us.

"Listen to you, Alfie!" she said. "Your voice is breaking! You're growing up!"

I looked over at Alfie, and he gave a shy smile, and then blinked really hard as if he was crying. But it's hard to tell with Alfie, even though he's such an old friend.

AUTHOR'S NOTE

This is not a "historical novel." Nor is it a geography lesson, or a linguistics guide. In other words: I made most of it up. References to historical dates, places, and words in old languages are accurate only in the sense of being "not very."

As always, I owe a huge debt to a lot of people who do not get to have their names on the front cover, especially Nick Lake, my ever-patient editor; Samantha Stewart; Jane Tait; Mary O'Riordan; and everyone else whose job is to make me appear to be a better writer than I really am.

To them all: thank you.

ABOUT THE AUTHOR

ROSS WELFORD worked as a business journalist before becoming a freelance writer and television producer. His debut novel, *Time Traveling with a Hamster*, was called "smart, engaging, and heartwarming" in a starred review by *Booklist* and was named both a New York Public Library and Bank Street College of Education Best Children's Book of the year. He is also the author of *What Not to Do If You Turn Invisible*. Ross lives in London.